## WHO'S WHO AT SHALIMAR

*BILL PERCEVAL* is a good looking, dynamic politician who already has an eye on the White House. But there's a skeleton in the Mayor's closet that even his wife Jane knows nothing about.

*EMILY PEABODY* was brought up on the best Boston traditions. Her Caribbean love life would have raised a lot of eyebrows back on Beacon Hill.

*DAVID SAMPSON'S* rugged masculine image and bestselling novels have fascinated millions of women readers, but his pretty young wife is one of the unhappiest women on the island.

*DENISE WILCOX*, the bored and voluptuous wife of Shalimar's ambitious manager, has found her own way to keep her husband's guests happy—and herself as well.

They're just a few of the wealthy, uninhibited pleasure seekers who come together for a weekend in paradise.

AVON
PUBLISHERS OF BARD, CAMELOT, DISCUS, EQUINOX AND FLARE BOOKS.

ISLAND PARADISE is an original publication of Avon Books.
This work has never before appeared in any form.

AVON BOOKS
A division of
The Hearst Corporation
959 Eighth Avenue
New York, New York 10019


Published by arrangement with the authors.
Library of Congress Catalog Card Number: 73-82717.



First Avon Printing, August, 1973.



Printed in the U.S.A.

CONTENTS

# *Prologue: St. Phillipe*

IN THE *sixteenth century when England challenged Spain for the supremacy of the seas, their dog fights took them into the pelucid waters of the Caribbean Sea. On board some of the royal barques were adventurous French who found the Caribbean climate far more appealing than the cold dampness of Northern France.*

*These gallant pioneers jumped ship and remained on the islands.*

*St. Phillipe was one. Its name was not St. Phillipe then, but a mysterious sounding Indian one, since the inhabitants of the island were of mixed Caribe and Arawak blood.*

*The original French settlers brought with them strong currents of violence and just enough imagination to devise unique methods of torture.*

*So it came to pass that the original French settlers with their mail order wives, spawned New World French progeny in whom the appetite for violence was now coupled with even more refined methods of punishment.*

*Gradually most of the Indian population were massacred and in their place, thanks to a lively slave trade, came new blood from Africa. Strong, handsome males and sensuous child-bearing females spawned like salmon and the new sugar plantations had their labor force.*

*They intermarried with a few of the remaining Indians, creating an attractive people. They in turn captured the fancy of the French plantation owners and another hybrid was born, still handsome and strong, now considerably lighter.*

*Deeply rooted in the island's and the black's heritage was a powerful belief in voodoo. And try as it might, the Catholic Church, which had arrived with the French, was unable to stamp out its rituals.*

*The island lay sleepily out of the mainstream of the motherland and Caribbean politics until the coming of the big planes and the restless moneyed class in search of unspoiled new playgrounds.*

*The first non-islander to see St. Phillipe was an ordinary seaman of Her Majesty's Navy. More recently a rich man's spoiled son, while flying his own plane, noted the natural deep-water harbor, incomparable miles of deserted sandy beaches, barrier reef, headland and a rain forest. Upon landing he discovered the beautiful, apparently happy and docile natives.*

*The above-mentioned gentleman had already received a fair amount of notoriety by (1) stealing his best friend's wife (2) building an exclusive club—now defunct—on the North Shore of Long Island with money not his own (3) producing the first all-nude musical in the Western World (4) giving a million dollars of his father's money to the Black Panthers.*

*His eyes had lighted up at the sight of St. Phillipe and the first thought that flashed across his brain was RESORT. In his search for a name that would embody the exotic design he visualized, he thought back to a romantic houseboat weekend in Kashmir. The misty land had intrigued him and the song "Pale Hands I Love . . ." played over and over in his mind. And so Shalimar from the song of the same name was born on the unspoiled beetle-shaped island of St. Phillipe. And to celebrate its birth, there was to be a party. It was fated to be no ordinary party.*

*The plans for it had begun auspiciously in the locker room of the Racquet Club. Shalimar, if successful, would be the first in a planned series of private, posh clubs to be opened in the better watering spots around the world. While plans were being finalized in the subdued atmosphere of the Racquet Club for one hundred carefully chosen guests, other plans were being discussed in an unusual storeroom in St. Phillipe. A surprise party which would coincide with Shalimar's gilttering opening. These plans, outlined by a bearded black militant, were enthusiastically received by his equally militant followers.*

*None of the careful investigations which had preceded the choice of St. Phillipe as the site for Shalimar had indicated any threat to the peace and tranquility of the island. In fact, the waves of change sweeping through many of the neighboring islands seemed nonexistent here. Its newly formed government seemed to have given St. Phillipe the stability lacking elsewhere in the Caribbean.*

*The black rebels who were planning their little surprise had been as careful to keep their plans secret as the backers in New York had been determined to publicize theirs.*

# *Thursday*

ALL THE advance publicity, the flossy brochures, the speculation had not prepared anyone for Shalimar; newest jewel in the necklace of playthings designed for the amusement of people with huge amounts of discretionary income. No existing pleasure palace could compare with the splendor of this gleaming collection of curves and squares of white stone and marble.

Only the genius of an Italian architect, an English gardener, a French decorator and unlimited quantities of American dollars could have put it together. Shalimar would definitely be this year's status resort.

Not the luxurious plane trip down; not the publicity party with groaning tables of food and drink catered by one of New York's best restaurants and languid beguines played by a name orchestra could have prepared any of them for the out-and-out luxury, the total fantasy of Shalimar.

No sooner had they debarked, than their luggage was stowed in the baggage racks of a small armada of waiting cabs.

Certainly the trip through the small town of Port Royale had not prepared them for Shalimar. It was like a dozen other small Caribbean towns. Quaint, seedy, a little ragged around the edges, white gingerbread houses with sun-bleached pastel shutters and the usual contingent of brightly plummaged natives, darkly handsome, leisurely paced. Despite the busy clusters of people, the town seemed deceptively quiet.

David Sampson felt uneasy in the unnatural calm. He had been in too many, too-quiet capitals just before the shattering storm of upheaval. Berlin, befor the wall divided the city with the sureness of a surgeon's knife; Haifa before the blockade turned the resort city into an armed camp; Warsaw, happily disbelieving even as the dangerous rumbles of hobnailed boots reached the outskirts of the city.

David Sampson, one of the most successful writers in the world, did not look like a successful writer. With an insouciance born of fame, David affected a Norman Mailer casualness in his dress and personal habits. And like Mailer had an animal magnetism that attracted men and women alike. Stocky with massive shoulders and slim hips, he wore his faded sandy hair in a leonine ruff. When he talked many a steel-hearted publisher quailed under the onslaught of his glacial blue eyes. But those same eyes could be meltingly soft when he set on conquering a desirable female fortress.

Karen Sampson, born Sarah Sue Butler, had been an easy fortress to take. Beautiful Karen with the endless legs and the sinuous walk, the cornsilk hair and cornflower eyes, had become the third Mrs. Sampson at twenty-four. David was a ferocious fifty. They had met at Squaw Valley while David was still married to the second Mrs. Sampson. Karen had caught his eye and he pursued her with the same passion with which he pursued the Fabergé eggs he collected. Every man who had ever seen her on two continents had wanted her, too. David, knowing it full well, had stormed, courted and cried until he won her. Now she occupied the same place as the rest of the things he had always wanted so badly and won. Once possessed—immediately forgotten—until someone else coveted.

David Sampson was feeling itchy. The cab driver who had brought them to Shalimar displayed—not an open rudeness—but rather a surely secretiveness, avoiding David as he tried to engage him in conversation. That over-concentration on a narrow road he could have driven blindfolded. That quick sweep of hot black eyes, more animal than admiring, when he looked too long at Karen. David had smouldered at that, wondering if Karen had noticed. Probably not. It wasn't her style.

Karen Sampson had been completely aware of the cab driver's eyes. She was always conscious of men's stares. Every pore of her body was a small receiving station. Even as a child, she had had this sixth sense. Her parents, plain Ohio farmers, had had Karen late in life, long after they had ever hoped to have children. Karen, a beautiful baby, had grown into an even more beautiful little girl and then into a fabulously beautiful woman. The rough farm boys at home had repelled her and when her gym teacher had suggested modelling, she had cajoled her parents to send her to New York. They had resisted half-heartedly, but could deny her nothing and finally had given her a thousand hard-earned dollars to tide her over until she got going.

Karen arrived in New York in time to capitalize on the sudden vogue for natural beauties. She was one of the first of the fresh-faced outdoor models and she made it to the top quickly. The glamorous life she had expected turned out to be far less. Without enough sleep, she photographed badly and eating too much put weight on her. No wonderful man fell in love with her, but she had lost her virginity to the most depraved photographer in New York, a virgin collector who took better pictures of women than any photographer in the world. Karen was easy to con, because all her life she had believed what she saw in the movies and read in the magazines.

When the photographer dumped her, she took an overdose of barbiturates, but was discovered by her roommate and pumped out before anything could happen. She went home to Ohio and in a few months felt well enough to embark again. This time it was California to visit an old school chum. There she bloomed in the sun and when the friend suggested a ski weekend in Squaw Valley, Karen felt excitement for the first time in months.

It was in Squaw Valley that she had run into David Sampson. Literally ran into him on the ski slope. He had been furious, she had done a complete flip.

From that point on, Karen loved David with a desperate single-mindedness.

Even with a choked datebook, invitations to country estates, plush ski lodges and the constant reassurance of her hairdresser, her masseur and her dressmaker, Karen was unconvinced of her desirability. David Sampson ignored her. Karen's insecurity grew. Her reflection was a constant source of concern and she checked it in a compact, a plate-glass window or a man's eye at every opportunity. If she walked down a street and a single male eye refused a second glance, she dove into her handbag for the omnipresent mirror to check for a flaw; an infinitesimal smear of lipstick, a hair out of place, a wrinkle. Not that she wanted the man, only his approval and a sign of his desire.

She looked for it now. The slim, elegant man who shared their cab was paying more attention to David than to her—at least when he wasn't watching the cab driver.

David, who wondered if the other man had noticed the cab driver's covert perusal of Karen, realized with a wry smile that he was far more interested in the driver's supple muscles. What a pansy. That lavender skirt and sand-colored worsted suit with the vents up to the armpits. Yecchk.

David Sampson suffered from the short man's syndrome. Everytime he saw a tall, slim-hipped, overdressed peacock, he branded him homosexual until proven otherwise. He'd never admit to himself it was pure envy.

Duke Dexter had recognized the expression in David's eyes. He had seen it so many times in straight men. He would have turned red with anger, but it would have clashed with his shirt.

As the movie reviewer and critic-at-large for a plush male magazine, Duke was in a position to take advantage of the revolution in male dress. In fact, he was one of the first to break out of gray flannel conformity.

He had recognized David from his photographs, even felt that there might be a bond between them. After all,they were both writers.

But when David chose not to acknowledge him, he was damned if he would make any further overtures. He smouldered silently in the cab, wishing now he had made a move towards that English photographer.

Although he loathed the word, he had to admit the man had a certain amount of *class*. His boots must have cost a small fortune. Only an Englishman would have attempted that blazer and ruffled shirt and only an Englishman could have carried it off. He only knew Simon by reputation, but his credentials were untainted even though the reputation was not.

Even today when longish hair was de rigeur with

anyone under forty, Simon Chadwick-Smith attracted attention when he appeared. His coal black hair hung in soft waves well below his ears, reaching to the top of his custom-made collar. His eyes were a deep blue, even more startling when contrasted with his carefully nurtured tan. Had he not been so obviously British, he could have been mistaken for Black Irish.

Duke Dexter was familiar with Simon's work—as was most of the civilized world. Simon had first attracted attention in London with his sensitive photographic essay on life in the East End slums. From there his rise had been meteoric. He had become the pet of the swinging London scene. Now his work was divided between covering the comings and goings of the beautiful people and serious reports aimed at revealing the pitiful poverty existing around the world.

Duke had also heard—through the international underground—many stories about Simon and his wildly successful pursuit of pleasure. He was sorry now that he had not attempted to share Simon's cab for the ride to Shalimar.

In the second cab the accents of Locust Valley and London intertwined.

Simon Chadwick-Smith, in his best Cockney put-on voice inquired, "'ow did you two birds get 'ere?"

Pammy couldn't resist the pun, "We flew." And the two girls erupted into giggles.

"Now, seriously," he resumed in impeccable diction, "Aren't you two a bit underage for one of these junkets?"

Pammy and Buffy had not been underage for any activity since they graduated from Miss Porter's Classes. In the three years since, they had lost much of their Locust Valley attitude if not the accent.

"I should have expected your parents to be invited," Simon continued.

"Can you picture Mummy in her Liberty lawns down here?" Buffy asked Pammy. Pammy lifted her silken eyebrows in mock horror. "Perish the thought!"

"I still think you might be a bit young for this sort of thing," Simon reiterated.

"You didn't think we were so young last year at your party," Pammy said smugly.

"My party? Which party?" Simon looked puzzled.

"The one in your studio," Buffy reminded him.

"Ohhh!" he drew the word out as if the memory pained him. "That one."

"That one." The girls answered in unison and with knowing looks.

"That one," he repeated and the three smiled in complete complicity.

"We must have one of those again sometime soon," said Buffy.

"It can't be too wild this weekend. The Percevals are here," Pam said.

In a third cab the Percevals were as relaxed as they ever were. Jane Perceval worried about leaving the children unchaperoned for this long weekend. Bill Perceval worried about leaving the City Council unchaperoned for even an hour.

Next to them, Margaret Bradley was preoccupied with the litany of worries that seemed to grow with every new indiscretion of her family. She had surprised herself by accepting this invitation. It was something her former husband would have been more likely to do or her daughters now included in that detestable phrase "jet set."

The sensible presence of the Percevals had mollified her and reassured her that the weekend would not be give up completely to the excessive banalities so much the life style of this society.

Margaret, after trading a few words with the Percevals, had settled back to watch the island landscape unfold. Now the taxi had turned into a private drive of crushed coral. Giant palm trees arched gracefully on each side, their crowns forming an umbrella of green over the drive. Beyond them great clumps of bouganvillea, hibiscus and frangi-pani mingled in a riot of red and purple, slashing the dense green undergrowth with an obscenity of color. Margaret turned her eyes away, intimidated by the overt sensuality of the island. The perfumes of the rich, damp earth and tropical flowers embarrassed her. She felt raped by the landscape.

The coolness of the driveway gave way to warmth as the cabs swept under the bright blue canvas canopy stretched over the circular entrance to the club.

Shalimar sat proudly on a high piece of ground, a dazzling sweep of lace-fretted concrete, glass and marble. Giant pots of cultivated tropical foliage stood on every step of the broad marble stairs.

Standing on the steps, waiting to welcome these very special invited guests, were Grosvenor Wilcox and his wife Denise.

Grov was even better-looking than his photographs. And time had been very gentle to him. He still looked like the powerful young man who had shone in every amateur tennis tournament on three continents. The power and grace of his hardened body was still apparent, despite his slightly thickening middle, now concealed by a voile shirt and immaculately tailored white linen slacks. His hair, once blonde, now bleached white by the tropic sun, was still thick and full, startling above the rich bronze of his skin. Tennis was still his first love, the second was his wife Denise.

A look at Denise and one knew she was tan all over. She had chosen a conservative costume to welcome her guests: white jersey trousers with floppy legs and a matching midriff halter that displayed an expanse of ripely mature, honey-colored skin. Her hair, streaky blonde (whether by design or accident), hung almost to her waist. She was full-bosomed and long-legged for a Frenchwoman.

Simon appraised Denise with a professional eye. Through a mental camera lens he saw her nude, ripe and inviting, poised against the white and blue of this setting, a spectacular jungle animal. He felt confident she wouldn't mind posing for him.

Denise watched the guests get out of the taxis. Her coffee-colored eyes identified each in turn, judging them quickly with no change of expression on her face.

She had learned to keep her face veiled, but her French mind worked with the speed of a computer.

Denise was looking for the one person who might be amusing enough to shatter the monotony of five days of forced conviviality with this carefully hand-picked crowd.

From long experience she knew that the famous, the rich and the socially prominent, despite their little vices, could easily be the most boring collection of people. She had bitterly resented coming to St. Phillipe so far in advance of Shalimar's actual opening. The only thing she had to show for it was a tan.

Grov, preoccupied with the myriad details of the opening, had given Denise precious little of his time. By evening, he was too exhausted to do anything but fall into bed and sleep. Denise, on the other hand, felt sleep was an unnecessary evil. How many nights had she lain awake by his side waiting for him to become aware of her non-sleeping body. Waiting for him to wake and sleepily take her. It used to be their best time.

Denise enjoyed her sex like her meals—when she was hungry. And she much preferred nibbling at odd hours.

The entrance was now swirling with dozens of

people, baggage and thin black boys trying to move all into the main lobby. As the bellboys matched luggage to cottages, Denise was busily attaching names to faces.

She saw David and tagged him. The long-legged girl by his side was obviously the new young wife. Nothing to be gained here. A young wife left little for anyone else.

But why was she so nervous? That unbelievably beautiful young thing had checked her appearance half-a-dozen times already, flicking a puff over her flawless satiny skin and tucking ends of hair that were already perfectly arranged. American girls, thought Denise, no matter how beautiful, they still behaved like awkward colts.

The slender young man with the lock of hair falling into his lavender-tinted glasses, Duke Dexter, was checked and dismissed instantly. Her eyes lingered a moment on Simon Chadwick-Smith's English tailoring. She had a weakness for Englishmen. They looked cold but they were amazingly inventive in bed. She remembered with amusement a young English boy she had met on her last trip to France. He was untraditional about everything but his tea time. But even that had changed one day. She remembered how he had insisted on spreading her with jam instead of his scones. Yes, that had been quite a novelty. Simon's mouth intrigued her and she liked the elegance of his body. Was he or wasn't he? One couldn't be sure.

Ah, that's a fish-face, she thought, looking at Jane Perceval's tight face. Why did men like those angular women? Those bones must be painful in bed. And then she saw Bill Perceval unfold his lanky frame, saw the professional smile, the quickly outthrust hand of the politician and knew this was the young mayor and his wife. He was very attractive in that American way. Grov was looking forward to playing tennis with him. Perhaps she might keep it in the family, occupying some part of his evening.

Grov welcomed each person with his usual suavity. He was a perfect host, everywhere at once, with a word, a smile, a suggestion. He had thoughtfully arranged for a bar to be set up in welcome. There was nothing worse than that moment of arrival, the checking in, the waiting for bags, the unpacking, the general impatience of settling in. Grov wanted to make the transition from one world to the other as pleasant as possible. The open bar, the cool drinks, the comfort of the white linen ottomans were working perfectly. There was a relaxed ease about the travellers. And instead of waiting in line to check in, the desk came to them in the guise of several white-jacketed aides who checked them in and assigned boys to take them to their waiting cottages.

Even David Sampson had to admit Shalimar promised to be the ultimate in smooth, silent, efficient service. He, of all the guests, was one of the most well-travelled. Wherever he went, his name brought the best accommodations. Yet he had never received such careful treatment at the Ritz or the Palace. He saw his wife Karen's eyes shining like a child's at Christmas, but he couldn't be sure whether it came from excitement or booze.

Many of the guests had been shown to their respective cottages. Grov was talking in a corner to Margaret Bradley. He felt kindly toward her, not because of what he knew of her, but rather because she had arrived alone and appeared so ill at ease.

He saw Denise out of the corner of his eye. She was standing too close to Simon. He must remind her to be a little more discreet. Not that he cared what Denise did, only how she did it and where. She was an undeniable asset to him in his role of host of a chic new resort. He still found her more attractive than any other woman he knew. Long ago he had accepted the fact that Denise had insatiable appetites that he could not handle by himself. They had come to an understanding and the only thing he asked of her was to maintain a certain façade.

Denise, in conversation with Simon, a conversation of trivialities, had already found several excuses to touch him. She was now employing one of her favorite get-closer techniques. The one which, accompanied by earnest conversation, required that you put your hand on another person for emphasis. Simon had known many Denises in his short life and was familiar with their little ploys. He, too, had developed ways to avoid these meaningful little touches without giving away his innate feeling of distaste.

He was just about to make his own counter-movement. Denise felt him move away from her slightly and smiled as he reached for a handkerchief.

"You've been most charming, Mrs. Wilcox." It sounded like a dismissal, but Denise wasn't quite ready to be dismissed.

"Denise," she corrected.

"Denise," he smiled. "I simply must get out of these things and into something more comfortable."

"Of course, you must," Denise agreed.

"I think I'd like a swim before getting dressed. If you'll excuse me . . ."

"Yes, you must have a swim. The pool is divine. Then, do hurry back. We will have drinks and supper later around the pool. You know we've a marvelous French chef."

"That's super. Island food is generally so . . . so . . . you know?" he wiped his mouth delicately with the handkerchief.

She tossed her heavy blonde mane of hair in reply.

"So, then, ciao," he saluted her.

"À tout à l'heure!" Denise replied in her most promising voice.

David and Karen Sampson were following the skinny black boy through a series of marble breeze-ways to their cottage. It nestled in a tangle of brilliant flowers and vines, separated from the cottage next to it by a stone lattice wall.

"It's like having your own little house," Karen exclaimed. "Aren't they darling, the way the vines and flowers make it all so private?"

David agreed that they had done a nice job, but there was no great enthusiasm in his voice.

"Don't you like it?" Karen asked. She felt her temples pound. The heat and the rum drink together with a lack of sleep were giving her a migraine.

"Sure, it's fine. What makes you think I don't like it?"

"You're not saying anything."

"I'm thinking."

*"Oh,"* she said, as if those two words explained everything away.

The boy showed them how to work the air-conditioning and also pushed a button to show them one of Shalimar's small marvels. With a whirring sound, one entire glass wall swung up and slid under the roof, opening the cottage completely to the outdoors.

Karen was entranced, David, who loved mechanical things, looked impressed for the first time. He looked out on the scene. Beneath him lay the cruciform pool. A fountain in the center sent a fine arc of spray into a reflecting pond. Palms and flower beds made attractive touches of color against the white wrought iron tables, and hanging flower baskets seemed everywhere.

The Sampson cottage stood on a high slope, the other cottages could be seen below, descending to Lafitte Cove, a sheltered private swimming beach for those who preferred the ocean to the pool. On the other side of Lafitte Cove was the Shalimar Marina, a semi-circle of anchorage dredged deep enough for the largest yachts. Around the far curve, four immaculately groomed tennis courts waited for devotees. In the distance, the towering cone of Mt. Eustace, an extinct volcano, disappeared in a necklace of clouds. The island was a mélange of white sand, tropical jungle and soaring mountains—truly a picture postcard.

Karen sat on the edge of the bed and leaned back with a sigh.

"What's the matter now?" asked David.

"I'm getting a migraine."

David, unpacking his bag said, "I'll get you some aspirin."

He looked through his kit. "Jesus, Karen, can't you do anything right? There isn't a goddamn aspirin in here."

"Maybe there's some in mine?" It was more a hopeful question than a statement of fact. He looked through her cosmetic bag, a jumble of jars and bottles and finally dumped the contents on the bed.

"Look for it yourself. Who the hell can find anything in this mess?"

She fished around and then whispered, "I guess I forgot them." She was ready to cry.

David looked at her face and felt guilty, hating himself for being so rough. She was really a good kid. She'd do anything for him. Why was he always kicking her in the teeth?

"OK, baby, it's all right. Don't sweat it. I'm sure there's some kind of shop here that sells junk like that. I'll run down and get some."

Karen wiped her eyes and hugged him with gratitude. As David left, she reached into a small satchel and pulled out a silver flask. The Scotch burned her throat.

As the bell boy turned to leave the Percevals, he asked with supercilious servility if there was anything else he could do for them.

"Just disconnect the phone and everything will be perfect," Jane said, sinking into one of the deep chairs and kicking off her shoes. The boy shot an inquiring look at Bill.

"That's just a little joke, there's nothing else," Bill interrupted, handing him an oversize tip to make up for Jane's teasing.

"Now, why did you say a thing like that?" he asked after the boy had silently closed the door behind him.

"He asked me if there was anything else I wanted and that's what I want right now more than anything else," she said, beginning to make them drinks. The management had thoughtfully supplied every cottage with recent American and European magazines as well as a tray holding the ingredients any cocktail a civilized palate could crave.

"Does it really bother you that much?"

"Yes, it really does. Not so much the phone calls, but the way you react to them. You're like Pavlov's dog, the phone rings and you're on. Before some crisis breaks, what would you like to drink? The usual?"

"The management seems determined to keep us sloshed for the entire weekend," he said, nodding and indicating the lavish supply on the tray.

"Don't worry," she said handing him his martini straight up, "There isn't a constituent within thousands of miles, thank heaven. Cheers!"

"You're right. We should try to get away more often. Maybe take the kids, too. I forget how unfair it is to all of you when I get involved."

"Don't tell me I've actually gotten through to you? And it's only taken two campaigns and two terms in that office to do it."

He smiled the boyish grin that the voters had found as irresistible as she had all those years ago. Those lazy summer afternoons sailing in bright sun, both of them home from college and filled with dreams of the future. How could she then have imagined he would be bitten by that most virulent of ambitions, political power. Neither of them had come from families with political aspirations. Neither had a deep concern or commitment to any cause. And they were about as far from the liberal party which now supported Bill as any two families could be. Their families did their good works through the proper charities and thought no more of it.

But Bill had hardly settled into that Wall Street law firm, had hardly made the first programmed steps up the ladder to a name on the door, when he decided to run for Congress. At the time, she'd been as enthusiastic as he, with visions of him writing important legislation, of becoming one of the leading young liberals of his far-from-liberal party. He had been encouraged by party big-wigs who knew how badly the party image needed reshaping. God, they would never even have won an election if they hadn't nominated a war hero for president. But after two terms in Congress and a growing family, she would have been glad to see him back on Wall Street with regular hours and a life he could call his own.

Instead he had chosen to run for Mayor—an impossible job at any time—now made even more so by the tides of change sweeping the country's urban centers. He was so committed, she wondered if she'd ever have him to herself again.

She'd often thought of leaving him. But she knew he would fight it. And she could never know if the fight would be made out of love for her or the necessity of protecting his precious public image. Instead, she had stood by him, fighting her own war of attrition. It hadn't been fair to either of them.

But she had finally won this one little battle. Though he despised these kinds of things and really worried about being away from the city so long, they'd accepted this invitation to the opening of Shalimar. She wondered if he would ever feel sure enough of himself to give a little less of himself to his public and a little more to his family.

Thinking of the family brought little worry lines to her forehead.

"Now what crossed your mind to bring on that look of concern in this pleasure dome?" he asked teasingly.

"It's nothing, really. I was just wondering how the kids were doing without us."

"If you're concerned, give them a call—before they disconnect the phone," he said handing it to her.

"I don't want them to think we're spying on them"

"You'll find a way to say it so they won't. Tell them you just wanted to let them know we arrived safely. Describe some of the wonders of Shalimar. Kathy'll eat it up. You make another round and I'll put the call through."

She watched him and wondered how, feeling as deeply as she did about him, the quarrels they'd been having lately could be so bitter.

Duke Dexter followed his houseboy like a chick a mother hen. The boy was bending under the weight of the two Gucci cases that contained several dozen changes of clothes. Duke carried his matching fitted toiletries bag, attaché case and typewriter.

The boy kicked open the door of the cottage and dropped the two bags heavily to the floor.

"Be careful, you clumsy idiot," Duke hissed. "Those two bags are worth more money than you'll ever see in your life."

The boy looked at him blandly, then smiled with an arrogance that chilled Duke. He felt threatened by the boy's attitude. When you grow up in Louisiana, you knew what to expect. You never let them forget their place. Even though he was more liberal than most Southerners and always rode in the front seat with the colored chauffeur just to make everyone else furious, he knew you had to keep the upper hand. And it wasn't hard after all. The advantages of breeding and education in the Southern tradition taught a man how to behave with the help. To his advantage the Negro houseboy had been born and brought up in the islands and knew nothing of Louisiana and its traditions.

The boy hovered in the doorway and Duke sensing his presence turned and looked at him. "Yes, is there something?"

The boy shuffled a bit and then stared at him cooly, straight on. They stood for a moment, locking stares until the boy broke the connection and left, aware finally he would not be tipped.

The nerve, thought Duke, doesn't he think I know gratuities are taken care of by the management.

Duke peeled off his lavender shirt. It was soaked through with perspiration. He sniffed delicately at himself. The new deodorant was effective in this climate. Now he wanted a refreshing shower, a fresh change and a nice, tall drink.

He quickly stepped out of the rest of his clothes and looked at his nude body in the full length mirror, appraising it as cooly and objectively as any model. How lucky he was not to have that unsightly mat of hair covering his chest. His skin shone like satin, smoothly muscled from four days a week at the gym lifting weights and swimming. His hips were narrow and flat, his legs were better shaped than most women's. He stroked himself appreciatively and watched himself respond to his own gentle touch.

"Down boy," he said. "Don't be impatient. Everything in its own time."

He turned on the shower and twiddled with the faucets until he had the water at the exact temperature he preferred, then slipped into its needle spray, careful not to wet his hair.

He soaked himself thoroughly, then remembered he'd forgotten his soap. He stepped out of the shower and went to his kit, finding his Caswell-Massey whale sperm soap exactly where he had packed it and hopped back into the shower. He rewet himself, then stirred up a lather in his hands and soaped himself carefully. His touch with the slippery soap had the lulling effect of a massage. He stroked the soap over his arms and chest and closed his eyes.

A momentary pang seized him; a flash of memory cast its chill fingers through the warm water. The lulling pleasantness had been the same he had felt when, at twelve, he had been introduced to himself by an older boy and had discovered the forbidden joys of mutual masturbation. An only child with a doting, fretful mother, he was lonely most of the time. Masturbation brought him a world of undreamed fantasy until, one day, his father caught him and beat him. The next scene still brought revulsion to Duke. His father had then viciously opened his own fly and taken out an engorged red penis and put Duke's hands on it. "That, boy, is a cock. It goes in a woman and don't you forget it. You ever touch your thing again, I'll break your fingers. And don't you forget that, either!" Duke had been petrified. And from that brutal moment on had hated and feared his father. Yet felt a sick fascination and pride at the same time. Under his armpits, over his chest, around his narrow waist, the soap went. As he reached his groin, the feel of the soap and his own hand caused an instant reaction.

He stroked himself with a sure, deliberate touch, soaping his thighs and backside, returning with a teasing touch to the front and finally dispensing with the soap, he rubbed the slippery froth on his body, around and around, over and over again on his shivering, erect cock. He moved in a rhythm with his hand, loving his touch with the forbidden fear and delight of his youth. He shifted his position, planting his legs slightly apart, like a runner primed for the starting gun. His hand was now working steadily and with a shudder, he felt a sluice-way open deep in the pit of his insides, gather force and break through. His breathing became more shallow and he uttered sharp little "Oh's" as his pleasure burst forth and mingled with soap and the steady downpour of the shower.

He let out a deep sigh and slumped against the wall of the shower, his knees suddenly weak. Dizzy from the steam, the activity and the power of his own release, he steadied himself against the faucets, then turned them off.

It took a moment to recover his poise and find the terry bathrobe. In spite of all his care, his hair was damp. How annoying! Now he'd have to waste time fussing with it.

No time was being wasted in the cottage assigned to Pam, Buffy and Tiger, their poodle. Settling in to a resort for a fun weekend came as naturally to them as breathing. Bikinis and body stockings were tossed into drawers, minis and caftans were hung away in closets.

Tiger busied himself with a thorough investigation of floors and woodwork. Since the three of them were the first residents of the cottage there was nothing of interest to his highly sophisticated and jaded nose. That was the trouble with new places. He sniffed dejectedly, no chance to catch up on the comings and goings of friends. His exquisitely tuned nose turned now to the coffee table where little plates of exotic snacks waited tantalizingly above his head. He began to beg, whimpering in that pathetic way he had trained himself to do so well.

"You know all that sort of thing is bad for you,"

Pammy told him firmly, reaching into the bottom of one of her cases and bringing out his own little snacks: People Crackers and Doggy Donuts.

"Here, this should hold you till we've time to scout the kitchen," she said throwing him a handful.

"Half an hour till the cocktail thing," Buffy said, reading the neatly printed card on the dressing table.

"That's really all the time I need to take a quick dip. How 'bout you?"

"Last one in's a big bore!"

The speed with which the two girls changed from their travelling clothes into their infinitesimal bathing suits would have done a quick-change artist proud. It was a shame that only Tiger was a witness as the nymphs threw themselves into the ripple-free aquamarine pool. Their suits, which had been priced by the amount of material omitted, showed off their beautifully kept bodies to full advantage.

Long-legged, without appearing coltish; well-developed but not overripe, they represented the best of the so-called all-American girl.

Their suits, which had been startling enough when dry, were spectacular wet. When they pulled themselves out of the pool and headed for their cottage, they passed David Sampson in the breezeway.

Torn between annoyance with Karen and relief for an excuse to get away from her for a few minutes, David headed for the lobby.

Damn—nobody around when you needed them. He'd have to look for himself. He walked through the breezeway lobby, the pool a tempting blue on one side, the curving coral drive on the other.

A tiny shop with native crafts in the window appeared to be the only sign of commercialism in the cool white atmosphere which said "private club" more subtly than any sign.

He went in and looked casually around. The proprietress, for she must have been that, was bent low, arranging some colorful lengths of handwoven fabrics in a display case.

He cleared his throat, "Uh, pardon me?"

She looked up quickly, not expecting anyone at this hour.

David was speechless for an instant. "Jesus Christ," he finally breathed.

"No," the voice replied cooly, "Emily Guilford."

"What in god's name are you doing here?"

"I live here."

"You're a long way from home for a proper Bostonian." The word "proper" brought a fleeting smile. "I've tried so often to get in touch. What the hell happened to you?" he insisted.

She wondered how to answer his question under the circumstances. Her New England pride would not allow her to tell him everything. She was torn between her own secret hurt and an overwhelming desire to hurt back.

"What would you expect to happen to me after what happened to us?"

He flushed. "I was afraid you had forgotten what happened to us."

"That's something one doesn't forget so easily."

"Well, where do we go from here?"

The question irritated her. The man's nerve brought an angry flush to her face, "I notice by the register that you brought Karen along with you."

"What's that supposed to mean? She is my wife after all," he said with annoyance.

"You remembered. Did you bring her for protection or amusement?"

"Knock it off, Em. You know I hate it when you're brittle."

"I wish I'd been brittle two summers ago."

"It's not like you to be hostile."

"What makes you think you know what I'm really like?"

"Well, we did get close that summer."

"Beig in bed with someone doesn't necessarily mean you're close."

"Aren't we overplaying the ravaged virgin?"

He thought back to that moment of shock when he realized, in fact, that she was a virgin. He couldn't believe it. He, David Sampson, fifty years old, had found the one remaining, practicing virgin among the liberal, love-in activists on the East Coast. It was one of the few things that had happened to him he'd never use in a novel. Who would believe it in this day and age?

It had all started when he had accepted, for the first time, an invitation to one of those summer culture festivals of writing, painting, music and drama.

As writer-in-residence, he had to give one lecture a day to a group of middle-aged housewives looking for new fulfillment, preferably in an art easy to clean up after. It was a boring chore until he noticed the fresh, young face of Emily Guilford one day. She clung to every word he said, heady flattery to a man who had never gotten enough flattery in his life. In her he had found those qualities he had always hoped to find: a sweet innocence coupled with a sharp, probing mind. He liked the questions she asked. And for the first time in years, he had found himself unable to be glib. She would not accept a pat evaluation. She challenged him and he found himself rising to those challenges and meeting them. She made him feel an excitement he hadn't felt in twenty years.

After one particularly disturbing exchange, she had stayed after everyone else had gone to clarify a particular point. It seemed natural to invite her to share a cup of coffee with him.

Coffee had led to dinner and dinner to a nightcap. David was not a time-waster. At his age, flowery phrases and setups were a bore. Either you did or you didn't. At first, Emily was no exception. But when he found he was extending the evening just to talk to her, rather than for the usual reasons, it was inevitable that they would end up in bed. Her virginity was a shock to him at first. Then, as many men his age, he found it a touching and tender gift.

"Emily, you still haven't told me what happened to you."

Emily was remembering, too. She had come to the conference to get away from Boston and the conflicts there and to try to give her life some new direction. Though she, along with her classmates, was rebelling against the value judgments of the establishment, they still held a strong hold on her.

Emily had chosen this conference rather than a trip abroad that summer, hoping to find bodily relaxation and mental stimulation from the author whose books she admired so. Those first few days in the soft, green countryside of New Hampshire had been doubly disappointing.

She had resented David and his slick, superficial explanations. She found him patronizing, treating the women as though they hadn't brains enough to fill a thimble.

Yet, despite his apparent boredom, beyond his arrogance, occasional flashes of wit and profundity held her.

She was curious about that part of him and why he took such pains to avoid showing more of it. The invitation to coffee, accepted as a challenge, turned into a pleasure. Dinner had been an opportunity to get even closer. It was the first time she had ever dined with a famous writer.

To her still unsophisticated mind, writers were special people with special gifts. She was surprised to find him almost ordinary. That had been comforting and reassuring. So it was natural and easy to accept the invitation for the nightcap. She was even more surprised to find in this grizzled, established writer a still-young, revolutionary spirit.

He understood the youth movement, recognized the validity of revitalizing decaying institutions. He knew the power of change was in the hands of the young, but warned about tearing down old structures before they had replacements.

She did not protest when he sought deeper intimacy. She had felt frightened for the moment, strange with the new feeling and remembered whispering to him, "Please, be careful." It was their first misunderstanding.

By the time the seminar ended, she had learned more than had been promised in the catalogue and by the end of the second month, she had gotten more than she had bargained for. Her college doctor had reaffirmed what she had suspected.

David, by that time, was in Europe researching another book. His promised letter had never arrived and she knew she had to do something within the next month.

Now she was months and miles away from the ravaged virgin, a new kind of life beckoned and she had no wish to share any of it with David.

"David, you came here for something more than memory lane."

"Oh, Christ, I almost forgot. Karen's got a headache and no aspirin." He looked around at the colorful wares and said, "I don't suppose I'll find anything as simple as aspirin here."

"The island is well advanced medically. We haven't had to call the witch doctor for months." She handed him a bottle of aspirin, then turned and left him standing in the middle of the floor with a bundle of unanswered questions.

Another famous Caribbean sunset was in the making over Shalimar. Deep purples, corals and scarlets bruised the sky, turning the white marble of Shalimar into a shimmer of pinks. The breeze blew in from the ocean, fresh, salty, with a touch of coolness. Palm leaves danced against palm leaves and the cicadas warmed up for an evening of noisy lovemaking.

Even in this relaxed atmosphere, Margaret Bradley could not overcome her habit of punctuality. So, she was first to arrive poolside.

Denise, in an exotically printed silk jersy culotte, eyed Margaret's simple white linen dress, put the price at $500, knew it came from that snob American designer who was the favorite of so many society women.

Margaret envied Denise her freedom. A freedom to wear a clinging jersey without underwear, a freedom that let her exhibit long tan legs and gypsy jewelry and unconfined tawny hair. Bedroom hair, Hal would have called it. She smiled ironically. She understood, for the first time in all these years since Hal had left her, why he could break up his home for a woman like this.

Margaret nervously fingered her pearls and Grov, ever-sensitive, came to her side. "Mrs. Bradley, you look charming."

Margaret smiled tightly, unaccustomed to the flattery of a strange man and thanked him.

"May I offer you a drink?"

Denise interrupted, "Darling, why not give Mrs. Bradley one of our famous concoctions?"

Margaret drew back imperceptibly.

Grov, with a look at Denise, reassured her, "Denise is only suggesting one of our marvelous rum and fruit drinks. Most refreshing and not in the least lethal."

Simon Chadwick-Smith, who had taken less time to settle in than the rest, arrived in immaculate white flannels and a dark blue voile shirt, with a silk bandana around his neck. He approached the group, inquiring what the drink of the club was, but opted for Scotch on one rock instead of the rum drink. There were just so many compromises one should make, even in the colonies.

He took his drink and walked to the steps, studying the setting with a professional eye, backing into the Percevals coming through the archway. He apologized as they walked past him and stared after them. Again he wondered why so many attractive public men always chose such dreary-looking wives. Was it planned or accidental? He knew how it worked in his own country. Now it seemed to be an international standard.

Bill and Jane accepted rum swizzles from Grov and walked over to join Margaret. She welcomed their presence with unfeigned pleasure.

Simon cast an appraising glance at Denise but before he had a chance to reach her side, David and Karen Sampson arrived.

The poolside had started to hum with the sound of voices when the sharp yaps of Tiger announced the arrival of Pam and Buffy. The decibel rate increased even more as the Locust Valley threesome descended. Pam and Buffy, nubile nymphs in swimsuits, were even more suggestive in their hand-crocheted mini dresses, underlined by sheer body stockings.

Simon hailed them and they bounced to his side with dozens of questions and comments and squeals of delight. Simon basked in their attention, but found himself talking to the back of Pammy's head as Rod Brigham arrived.

"Oh, he's divine," said Pammy.

"Super," breathed Buffy.

The brief characterizations, while trite, were not far off the mark. He was indeed divine and super. Close to six feet tall, he had a tawny tan and a shock of tousled, sun-streaked blonde hair that had made women far more sophisticated than Pammy and Buffy lose their heads.

This was his first winter away from the slopes. Since he had dropped out of college his sophomore year, he had divided his time between riding the waves as a Malibu Beach boy and schussing on the slopes as ski instructor/stud at the posher American and European resorts.

But last year he had seen one too many aging ski instructors cowtowing to one too many old harridans. And he had made up his mind that it wouldn't happen to him—not if he could help it. Not as long as he still had the body to attract someone closer to his own age. When he had heard of Shalimar and the kind of members it was attracting, he had decided it was the perfect place for him to make what he thought of as "the final contact." Whether it would be a lifetime arrangement, or not, he neither cared nor thought about. But it would be sufficiently long-standing and legally recognized to set him up in the kind of life he was now convinced he wanted.

He had looked over the guest list for this opening weekend party and had realized he would probably not find what he was after among those invited. But there was always a chance, and so he had prepared carefully his entrance.

He wore crisp white ducks, skin tight to show off his lean hips, his taut thighs. Following the curve of his muscular chest was a sheer jade green cotton body shirt, open almost to the waist, which was the exact color of his eyes.

Realizing that he was no match for such a splendid specimen, Simon teased the girls, "You cut me to the quick, ladies, with your fickleness."

"You're divine, too," said Buffy. And having exhausted her vocabulary, whispered to Tiger, "Go fetch."

Tiger looked adoringly at Buffy and trotted over to Rod's side, then began his small act, famous from Kitzbuhel to Cannes. He tugged at Rod's bell bottoms for attention and getting it, proceeded to sit on his back legs and paw the air frantically.

"What's the matter, didn't anyone give you a drink?" asked Rod.

Tiger replied with more frantic pawing as Pammy and Buffy answered in chorus, "Oh, he doesn't drink."

Rod looked at the two girls appreciatively and noticed with relief that the crowd was, for the most part, youngish and attractive. No rich bitches over fifty to contend with.

"We didn't notice you on the plane," Pammy remarked.

"I'm a native," Rod teased.

"Funny you don't look native."

Buffy giggled.

"You two sisters?" he inquired.

"Yes," they chorused again.

"Funny, you don't look like sisters."

The girls peeled off into a squadron of giggles again.

He took them by the arm and escorted them to the bar, "C'mon, I'll let you buy me a drink."

Duke Dexter, with his infallible sense of timing, arrived as the cocktail party moved into high gear. David, the first to see him, said loudly enough to be heard over the hum of conversation, "Here it comes, the Mauve Decadent."

The description was as accurate as it was unkind.

Duke was indeed splendidly mauve. From his cut velvet hip-huggers to his French ribbon-striped voile shirt and knotted parma violet scarf. Simon smiled as he noticed the almost imperceptible trace of mauve eye shadow, grudgingly admiring any man who had the audacity to be so obvious.

Pammy, whose attention span was brief at best, left Rod's side and bubbled up to Duke, "Where did you ever find such a smashing shirt? Really divine." She touched his arm.

Torn between her hip language and the flattery, Duke decided to smile condescendingly and replied, "My shirtmaker made it for me."

Rod watched the scene with some amazement. A girl leaving him for *that!* And then, the amazement grew into incredulity as the mauve shirt was obscured by a cluster of admiring females. He found it reassuring that none of the men even gave Duke so much as a glance.

The sound of a bull horn turned the entire crowd's eyes toward the cove and Duke found himself taking second place to a sleek white sailboat slipping into the protection of the deep-water marina, white sails fluttering as they were lowered and swiftly furled by the professional crew aboard.

Rod was impressed. He'd seen plenty of luxury yachts in his short, young life, but this was something else. He tried to make out the name and home port of the boat but it had dropped anchor too far out.

Grov, too noticed the boat. "That'll be the Gramsons," he explained.

"Oh, so that's the famous *Cassandra?*" Rod exclaimed.

"The makeup mogul," Buffy recognized.

Duke added, "I understand the appointments are beyond belief."

"Oh?" Denise was immediately interested.

"Yes," said Duke as if he had been aboard dozens of times. "Porthault sheets and Baccarat crystal and marble bathrooms, not to mention a small art museum."

"They say Billy did the decor," added another, first-naming a well-known society decorator.

Everyone's eyes were now turned to the tender knifing through the water to pick up the owners, the invited guests who'd elected to arrive in their own boat rather than the plane which had brought everyone else.

On board, the cosmetic king, born poor and become Midas-rich, paced the deck. His white ducks and Commodore blue blazer were magnificently tailored, but the Saville Row tailoring could not hide the background he revealed with his first words.

"You've had four lousy, stinking days to get ready for this crumby party. Now what the hell is keeping you." The voice was as abrasive as a fingernail on the blackboard.

"I'm not sure what you want me to wear," a soft voice close to tears answered.

"What's the matter? You never been to a cocktail party before?"

Sandy Gramson looked at her husband. "You're always so critical. And I'd rather have your opinion now instead of later in front of an audience."

He was about to defend himself but thought better of it. Sandy stood in front of him in white crepe halter-neck culotte. She was smoothly tanned from the days on the boat, her make-up skillfully nonexistent. Marty looked at her and thought how spectacular she looked, but he couldn't, wouldn't allow himself the pleasure of saying it aloud. She turned for his inspection and he noticed the unbroken, clean line of her bare back, the way the crepe outlined the sweet roundness of her body. He couldn't stand skinny women. His mind scrambled for something to say, but the only thing he could come up with was, "Why do you have to wear that schmatah around your hair? Can't you just let it hang? And how come you're not wearing any jewelry? God knows, I've given you enough."

"I didn't think it was appropriate." Then, seeing

his face gather black clouds she asked patiently, "Which piece would you like me to wear?"

"What about the emeralds."

Sandy would have preferred to wear only her wedding band, but rather than incur any more anger, she obediently went to the safe in the master cabin and arrived back on deck with a long rope of cabochon emeralds from which dangled a large tear-drop diamond. I'm going to look like a Christmas tree, she thought to herself. How many times had she smarted from the women's page editors' snide remarks. "Mrs. Gramson again opened the family safe and appeared with the usual amount of jewels—too much." Marty got furious, but his fury only served to make him more insistent. Each public appearance seemed to find her with one more jewel than the last.

"Okay, get your ass out of its sling and let's get going."

The crowd watched the arrival of the *Cassandra*, conjecture and questions made the air vibrate with sound.

The tender, clinging to the side of the boat, waited for the crew to drop the steps.

The Wilcoxes by this time, playing solicitous hosts, stood on the dock waiting to welcome the couple to Shalimar.

Denise's practised eye caught by the gleam around Sandy's neck, recognized the value, if not the inappropriateness of Sandy's jewel and mentally tagged it. Marty would have been amazed to find that her guess came within a few hundred dollars of what he had paid.

Denise was well-versed in the Gramson jewels. Now she turned her attention to the bestower of the largesse. He was not unattractive. Not nearly as handsome as Grov, but then on the other hand, Grov was no Gramson in the jewel department.

Gramson was slightly taller than Denise and as Denise took him in with a swift glance of her tawny eyes, she suspected that under the immaculate cut of his jacket was a man fighting to keep in shape. Oh, well, a little bulge here and there was no great tragedy. Beautiful young men with great figures were easy to come by, money was not. Besides Marty's dark looks had a dangerous excitement about them.

"We're delighted you came," Grov extended his hand. "Everyone is on the pool terrace. You're just in time for the second round."

Marty turned on the charm and Sandy watched the public Gramson return Grov's welcome with equal urbanity.

"Mrs. Gramson, may I escort you?" Grov offered his arm to Sandy, leaving Denise to slip her arm knowingly through Gramson's. She gave a small wiggle and he responded to the pressure of her body with a returning pressure of his own.

Marty thought to himself, open house really means open house here and he said, loudly enough for Sandy to hear, "Mrs. Wilcox, that's a great outfit you're almost wearing."

"Call me Denise," the lady purred.

Marty smiled expansively, "I will if you'll call me Martin."

Duke was the first of the crowd to approach the Gramson's. Marty watched the mauve apparition flutter toward them and raised an eyebrow as Duke introduced himself and went into exaggerated raptures over the boat.

A waiter appeared at Marty's elbow with a tray of rum swizzles, and Marty waved him away with annoyance. "I had my fruit this morning," he said, watching Duke flush. "I want a Tanqueray martini, on the rocks, *very* dry."

Sandy stopped the waiter with her hand. "I'll

have one, please. They look delicious." She turned her back on Marty to show her disapproval, leaving him to cope with Duke, thinking to herself maliciously, "He deserves it."

Simon Chadwick-Smith recognized Sandy and the famous Gramson emeralds immediately. He had seen the two of them photographed several times in a number of magazines. He had, indeed wanted to photograph her himself and now seemed the perfect time to approach her. Sandy was pleased by his attention and in a moment they were deep in conversation, so deep, Marty's intrusion was a real jolt.

"Thanks a lot for leaving me with that faggot," he growled.

Simon looked at Marty with distaste, then smiled tightly, "Oh, he's not a bad chap, once one gets to know him."

Marty looked at him suspiciously. English accents bothered him.

Sandy tried to overcome Marty's bad manners by introducing the two men.

Out of deference to Sandy, Simon turned to Marty, "I've been trying to encourage your charming wife to let me take some pictures of her."

Marty looked up at Simon's lanky face, "You have good taste. What do you want? Nudes or fashion?"

Sandy flushed, "He's not a nude photographer, Marty."

"So that doesn't mean he don't take nudes."

Simon winced at the bad grammar. His English accent became ever crisper, "Mr. Gramson, there are nudes and there are nudes. But I happen to find clothes more revealing, therefore more suggestive."

"Yeah, I bet."

"And your wife is very lovely," Simon continued, ignoring the remark. "She wears clothes beautifully."

Marty laughed, "And how she does. But would

you believe she didn't know a Gucci from a Pucci before I married her?"

Sandy flushed with embarrassment.

David, overhearing the remark, bristled. It confirmed his immediate first impression of dislike. "What a bastard he is."

"How can he be so cruel to her?" Karen Sampson asked. "She seems like such a nice person. Why is he so unkind?" She might be asking the same question of David.

He tried to cover with a flip remark, "You always hurt the one you love."

"Must you?" asked Karen. David gave her a long look, then patted her arm.

Torches and the fire of the huge barbecue pit sent tongues of flame dancing into the night air. The smell of suckling pig, the bountiful trays of tropical fruit, the warmth of the day brought a moment of silence to the group. And in the flickering flames, faces reflected their thoughts.

The revealing light caught the sad, lost look on Margaret Bradley's face, brought into sharp relief the lines under Duke's careful make-up. Karen felt David's remoteness. Jane felt closer to Bill than she had in years and later that night they would consummate this new feeling in the privacy of their cottage.

Pammy, Buffy and Tiger were starved.

# *Friday*

Though it was barely ten o'clock, the morning sun had the intensity of high noon. It turned the white marble tiles surrounding the pool into blazing griddles of heat. The pool shimmered in the light with the dazzle of crushed aquamarines. Under a brightly colored awning, a long buffet table awaited guests with an awesome breakfast: great frosty silver pitchers of fresh orange and papaya juice, silver urns of fragrant coffee, native fruits nestling in beds of crushed ice, warmers of freshly baked brioche and sweet buns.

An impassive chef, the color of good coffee, clad in snow white Bermuda shorts and shirt, stood ready to make anything from a soufflé to eggs benedict.

Circling the pool, under the welcome shelter of blue and yellow umbrellas, clusters of small white tables were set for breakfast.

On a blue mat, the bronze body of Denise Wilcox lay in the sizzle of the sun. She was practially nude; her body gleamed with oil. Tiny blue eye cups shielded her eyes; two small seashells concealed the nipples of her breasts. The brief top of her bikini lay over a chair within easy reach of her hand while the bottoms covered as little of her as possible. She had been lying in this comatose state for almost an hour. Now, sensing she was not alone, but too indolent to look, she murmured, "Someone here?"

Duke, no mean sunworshipper himself, had hurried through an eye-opening cup of coffee in his cottage to rush down for serious sun-bathing before the noise of the crowd would make it tiresome. Now in brief lavender-checked trunks, a lavender towel around his shoulders, he viewed Denise with a mixture of annoyance and pleasure.

"Duke Dexter," he drawled, "at your service."

Denise smiled at him. She was sure he didn't quite mean what he said. The only service he could render was . . .

"Well," he purred, "I see you're a sun lover, too. I expected to be the first down."

"You must rise early in the morning to beat me to the sun." Neither Denise nor Duke had changed position.

He was amused by Denise's bathing costume, or rather, lack of costume. No question she was hands-off winner in the "can you untop this" sweepstakes. Well, at least, he didn't have to wear seashells.

"Aren't you having any breakfast?" Denise asked, not budging from her prone position.

A voice interrupted, "Who needs breakfast when they can feast their eyes on you?"

The strange voice finally roused Denise. She propped herself up on her arms and removed her blue eye shields to see its owner.

Marty Gramson and Duke Dexter watched in fascination, waiting for the shells to fall away from Denise's breasts, but they remained in place through some secret gravity-defying force of their own. She saw their astonished faces, looked around, then noticed the shells on her nipples and laughed. One fell off from her movement and she calmly replaced it as Marty felt his mouth go dry.

"You have to hand it to those French broads," Marty said to Duke, "they sure know what to do with a body."

"Oh, I don't know," sniffed Duke. "If you ask me . . ."

"I didn't," Marty snapped. And turned to the buffet table.

"Scrambled eggs." He proceeded to describe in careful detail exactly how he wanted his eggs. The chef's face remained bland through the recital, but the eyes smouldered with dislike. "And send a waiter over with black coffee right now." He called over his shoulder. He took the chair near Denise, picked up her bra top and stroked it unconsciously.

Denise smiled at the stroking, then resumed her recumbent position, turning onto her stomach so she could watch Marty.

"I'm so glad you're here," she teased.

"So am I," he smiled.

"Yes, now you can rub some oil on my back."

"Pleasure," he replied. She handed him the bottle.

He looked at it, "Why aren't you using my Tropic Tanning Creme?" He poured the oil on her back and started to rub it in with slow, deliberate strokes.

"Ummmm," she crooned, "that feels good. I use our native concoction. But I'll be happy to try yours, if you give it to me."

Every little phrase of Denise's was loaded with double entendre. Marty continued to rub the oil in, enjoying the opportunity to touch her skin, moving under her arms toward her bosom and down her long back, pausing for an instant to decide where to go next.

"I'll have one of the boys bring you some off the boat. It's damn good stuff."

"You should know, you make it. Some on my legs, please?"

Marty poured more oil in the palm of his hand and stroked it down her long legs. He let his hand cup her thigh and move to its inside and was pleased when he felt her squeeze her legs against his hand.

"Good morning, everyone."

At Sandy's arrival, Duke, emerging from the pool, saw Marty's hand withdraw swiftly from Denise's thigh.

"Mrs. Gramson, you look utterly divine, like a young Diana." Duke no doubt referred to Sandy's brief white jersey sun cover. He threw a look at Denise to see if she was reacting.

Denise fielded the remark, understanding its purpose, turned to Sandy and agreed, "Yes, he's quite right."

The little jersey showed the smooth olive freshness of Sandy's skin. She untied it and slipped out of its voluminous folds. The tawny body emerging had the look of dark lustrous satin and her little white jersey bikini set it off with breathtaking effectiveness. She turned and plunged smoothly into the pool, swam across and returned to the table, water streaming off her.

"If your wife is any endorsement, your sun tan cream works wonders." Denise admitted.

Sandy smiled and protested mildly, "I'm just lucky. I get this without too much effort. I really don't have the patience to just lie in the sun."

From another woman, Sandy's statement would have seemed a jibe. But she was so guileless, Denise just made a face, excusing herself with "I have to work so hard at it."

"Some of us do," Duke said pointedly.

Sandy felt the little tensions vibrating through the air and felt weary.

Why had they come? She was so tired of being on

the receiving end of envious women. And Marty's unpredictible moods sapped her. She was tired of the Denise's and the Duke's, tired of trading herself for a mess of pottage even if the pottage was a queen's ransom of jewels and furs. She thought of her two boys from her first marriage living with their nanny in a separate apartment because Martin couldn't stand them underfoot. She thought of the countless indignities suffered and the countless presents paid out to compensate for them. All she wanted was peace now, to paint, to enjoy the feeling of sun and water, to be with the children, to be a real wife. Where had this awful need for self-punishment come from? Where the guilt? Why had she allowed Marty to dazzle her with his success and money? How could she have mistaken possession for love? And yet, Marty did love her, she was sure of that. That he loved her, yet hated himself for being weak. More importantly, did she love him? Was he even lovable? How strange. If only . . . if, it was the copout word in the dictionary. If's never became certainties.

"Would you like something from the buffet?" Duke asked.

Sandy was about to ask for coffee when Marty was at her side, "I can take care of my wife."

There. There was another amazing side of Marty. His jealousy. Even a man like Duke made Marty jealous. Don't touch my possession, was that it? She accepted fruit and coffee from Marty.

"What's on your agenda today?" Marty asked.

"I'd like to try some scuba diving," she ventured.

"Why not?" Marty encouraged her. "You might like it."

Sandy stared at Marty. Did he really want her to enjoy herself? Marty was thinking ahead. Get Sandy into the water for sports and maybe he could get Denise into bed for some indoor sport. She seemed willing. Why not? She knew who he was. She had nothing to lose. Besides paradise can be a bore. Every little change helped. Denise was not the kind of woman who allowed herself emotional involvements. Denise's attachment was to Denise.

"Did I hear someone say something about scuba diving?" Rod, dressed in a pair of faded blue jeans arrived, tossing an orange in the air. He bit off the top and sucked noisily at the juice.

Duke's eyes watched him covetously. Rod was a delicious sight. Tight jeans, golden body, sun-streaked hair. He had the cheerful look of a tousled lion. Sandy smiled at him. How engaging he was. He probably had the morals of an alley cat, but he was pleasant about it, she was sure.

Sandy replied, "I thought I might give it a try."

"Always looking for eager students," he said with a lopsided smile. Thank God, he thought, his first pupil was to be Sandy instead of old Dukey-doodles, the poolside pansy. Sandy was definitely his style. Good-looking. And rich.

"Are you really the instructor?" she teased. He made a low bow in reply. Sandy was delighted. It would be a lot more fun with him than that hulking ape of a body/life guard Marty kept on board.

"When can we begin?" she asked eagerly.

"Soon as I have my milk and a roll. Can I fill your cup?"

"Hi. Dar-ling," chirped Pammy materializing at his elbow, "I'd adore a cup."

Rod turned and saw the three of them looking like a full color page in one of the flossy magazines. Terry beach coats just long enough to cover their bikinis—and holy cow—the dog, too, had on his terry coat.

"Tiger, been in for your morning dip?" He inquired directly of the small animated piece of fluff.

"Just on his way," Buffy answered for him.

"But we can't do our beach thing without a little

something to sustain us," Pammy said, eyeing the well-stocked table enthusiastically. "C'mon, Tiger, there must be something in all those yummies with your name on it."

Delighted as the girls were with Rod, they were well-versed in the ways of resorts like this, knowing attractive men were always around, but food was served only at certain hours. They descended upon the chef like a pair of pretty scavengers.

The chef behind the chafing dish, who had merely condescended to the others' orders, couldn't help liking the two girls and their amusing pet. He fixed a plate of tidbits for Tiger as the girls helped themselves to one of everything.

By the time Pammy and Buffy set their plates on Rod's table, Rod had finished his milk and Sandy her coffee. He stood up and moved to Sandy's chair to help her up.

"You're not leaving?" Pammy asked with a pout.

"Duty calls," Rod answered, taking Sandy by the elbow.

The girls looked puzzled, Sandy smiled in explanation, "He's going to teach me how to scuba dive."

Pammy looked quickly at Buffy. Buffy's return look agreed that before the weekend was over, they too, would know all about scuba diving. They giggled conspiratorily.

"That giggle bodes no good for some hapless male, I'm sure," Simon said teasingly as he joined their table.

"Would you like company with your victuals?" Without waiting for the affirmative answer he was certain to get, he slid into the chair between them, placing his small continental breakfast on the table. It looked like an appetizer compared to the plates in front of the girls.

"I like to see young girls eating so well," he said.

"How do you keep your superb figures with all that?"

"We're terribly active," Pammy answered.

"Yes, we're having scuba diving lessons. Would you like to join us?"

"I'm afraid not. I know all I care to about diving. And I'm really here on assignment, you know. Local color and all that."

"You mean you're saving your strength for the London birds?" Buffy teased.

"Something like that," Simon said, hiding his smile in his coffee cup.

Over the edge of his cup he saw the Percevals approaching. They looked years younger than they had the night before. He knew the young mayor by reputation and now looking at him, he wondered what the driving power was behind him. American men had this ambition, a zealous dedication that left little time for anything else. Europeans managed to mix ambition and amusement much better and for the most part seemed far more interesting human beings into the bargain.

They nodded to Simon and passed quickly to the buffet, picking and choosing as they went. The silence between them was a cozy one, a natural one following last night's rediscovery. They hadn't felt this close in years. And each seemed loathe to break the silence for fear the fragile spell might disintegrate with it.

"The sun feels wonderful, doesn't it, Bill?"

He agreed, comfortably munching a flaky biscuit. "I think I'll challenge Grov to a couple of sets of tennis. What would you like to do?"

"I may just loll around the pool and be very lazy. Then maybe if you have any strength left, you'll play a few sets with your wife."

"I'd love to play with you." Margaret Bradley, arriving poolside, overheard Jane's remark and couldn't resist volunteering.

"Margaret," Bill jumped up to pull out a chair. "You look mighty attractive. Join us. May I get you something?"

Margaret accepted the proffered chair and said, "Just some juice and coffee for the moment, thank you." Then turning to Jane, she reiterated, "I'd be delighted to play tennis with you, if you'd like."

"I hope you're good. My wife is a tiger on the courts."

"I know. I saw her play at the club before you resigned." The club Margaret referred to was one of those proper clubs whose rigid membership requirements were creating such hostility in liberal circles. Bill and Jane had given up their membership with much highly favorable publicity.

But Jane had missed the club—missed the easy contact with the people she had grown up with. It had seemed like no sacrifice at all for Bill, but it had been different for Jane. The club and its members were an important part of her life. No amount of entertaining of pols and minority groups could ever make up to her for that loss. With the easy grace that had been instilled in her from childhood she had done a remarkably good job of playing the role of the Mayor's hostess. She had smiled at and talked with people she would never have dreamed existed, let alone met, had he not been the mayor. And she had not complained.

Yet she did resent having to drop the ones she considered "their real friends" in order to pacify those who were shaping Bill into even more of a liberal than he actually was. After so many years, she was now so out of it as far as that tight little circle of club members was concerned, she wasn't even sure she could carry on a simple conversation with Margaret. In that circle, if a summer's pregnancy kept you off the tennis courts for one season, you fell an entire year behind in the social gossip and just never caught up.

You found yourself becoming chummier and chummier with women whose children were the exact age as your own. It was no coincidence. Yet even in those carefree years before they had dropped out of the club, Jane hardly ever remembered seeing Margaret there.

"Of course, I'd forgotten you were a member. We hardly ever saw you." Jane observed.

Margaret avoided an explanation for her absence, replying instead, "I think I can give you a good game. I certainly won't win, but I used to be quite good when I was at Manhattanville and Hal," a bitter smile shadowed her face for an instant, "and I played quite a bit."

"Wonderful, dear," Jane turned to Bill, "You're off the hook."

Bill replied, "Now, Jane, you know I enjoy playing with you."

"Very gallant, dear," Jane patted his hand, "but not necessary. You go ahead and have a wonderful time with Grov Wilcox. Just remember he was top ten."

"Yes, but I'm younger and faster."

The two women smiled at him. A bell-chime interrupted their conversation and to their surprise, they discovered it came from a telephone. The sweet sing-song accents of the colored boy called out for Mee-sus Brad-lee.

"That's me," Margaret said with some surprise.

Bill waved at the boy and called him over. "This is Mrs. Bradley."

"A call for you from Palm Beach. Will you take it here?"

"Please," said Margaret. "I wonder who it can be?"

The boy plugged the phone into a mysterious socket and handed the receiver to Margaret.

"Hello?" she answered tentatively. "Yes? Phillip? What a surprise! Yes." She looked at the Percevals with some embarrassment. As they made a motion to get up and give her privacy, Margaret covered the mouthpiece with her hand, "*no*, no, please don't go. There's no need for you to leave."

And she turned back to the phone. "Phillip, you're dear to call, but I don't think we need discuss this over the phone. What? Well, of course, if you want to, sail down but—but it's not necessary. As you wish. Yes. I'm fine. Really, quite well. Yes, goodbye." There was a pause as the man on the other end said something. Jane saw Margaret's face turn pink. She tried to make idle chatter with Bill, but with a woman's ability to keep her attention on several things at once, had divined much of the conversation.

She knew quite a bit about Margaret Bradley—as who didn't. In their set, gossip was the second most important activity after charitable balls. She remembered the attendant publicity when Hal Bradley had left his wife of twenty years for a glamorous French divorcée he had met in Sardinia. There was much talk about frigidity on her part, adultery and drinking on his. Stories about the two daughters occupied much time at the expensive salons—both beauty and dressmaking—and between fittings, pedicures, facials and make-ups, the stories had achieved an almost legendary fame.

When her older daughter's brief affair with a ski instructor had resulted in pregnancy, Margaret's husband Hal had "bought" a husband to give the child a suitable name. After a considerable exchange of money, one year of marriage and fights that made newspaper headlines, the couple was divorced without ever having consummated the marriage. The penniless Italian count came out a rich count and the rich *enfant* now carried one of Europe's most auspicious titles.

Now, there was much conjecture about Phillip Reed, the wealthy industrialist who had been Margaret's faithful suitor for several years. It was common knowledge that Phillip wanted very much to marry Margaret although many could not understand his attraction to her.

Jane, looking at Margaret now, thought she understood why. Margaret's soft vulnerability was a powerful magnet to a man with Phillip's inclinations.

He was an aristocrat of American society, great-grandson of a man who had accumulated his wealth through human exploitation. In a society of ruthless robber barons, his great grandfather was the Grand Duke. Phillip had grown up with the outer security of great wealth and an overwhelming inner guilt for the manner in which the family money had been accumulated. The back-room gossip of years had served to give him an erratic temper, a pair of ready fists and a life-long dedication to using his share of the estate in a meaningful way. No matter how many museums and cultural centers he endowed, no matter how many scholarships he sponsored, he could not wipe away the guilt he carried in his gut. His early peccadilloes—part willfullness, part desperate search for approval—had been covered up by his father. They had finally been brought under control after Phillip came back from the service with a determination to master himself for his own good.

Margaret, though not underprivileged, was a woman easily brutalized by a world she was not equipped to handle. Brought up in the rigid discipline of her church, she had never learned how to relax and enjoy the pure pleasure of being an attractive female.

As Jane watched Margaret's face reflect the confusion of her mind, the phone chimed again.

She held her breath as the boy answered.

"Mis-tah Mayor, the phone is for you. It is your

office." The lilting sing-song voice took the edge off the ominous words.

The Mayor took the phone and Jane looked at him anxiously. She heard his clipped monosyllabic answers and watched his cheerful face cloud over. It was his "mayor's face" and it boded trouble. Jane waited patiently for Bill to finish. When he hung up abruptly, he looked off, averting his eyes from Jane. Margaret, sensing the possibility that Bill and Jane might want to talk, got up, "If you'll excuse me, I just remembered something I left in my room."

Jane and Bill murmured something about not leaving on their account but were relieved to have the table to themselves.

"What was that all about?" Jane asked with concern.

"I'm not really sure." Bill replied.

"Not sure, or don't want to tell me?"

"There's no reason why your rest should be upset."

"But it will be if there's something wrong and you're upset. What is it, Bill?" she insisted.

"That was Bill O'Hara." Bill O'Hara was the Mayor's press secretary.

"Oh?"

"There's something about Arleo, the press has—the press has gotten hold of something. Bill's afraid it might blow open the administration."

"What about Arleo?" she asked.

"He's getting more facts for me," Bill said. "But the papers are intimating that Arleo is mixed up in bribe-taking."

"I knew it. I never trusted him."

"Hold on, Jane. There's no reason to believe that any of this is true. He was my appointee and I've known him a long time. He's absolutely above that sort of thing."

"No man is above that sort of thing." she pronounced.

"No man? I suppose that includes me by definition."

"I didn't mean it that way Bill. You're different. You've always been."

"That's not what you said. Look Jane, just because a man's in politics doesn't automatically turn him into a corrupt devil."

"There are all kinds of corruption," she said meaningfully, "Money is just one."

"Jane, I hate to say this to you. But your background is showing. You're a big liberal when it's expedient and doesn't cost you anything. Just because the man's name is Arleo, you see Mafia and big-time crime and murder in the streets. You're a victim of your own stereotypes."

"Don't you dare say that to me. That's not true."

"Look, Jane," Bill said wearily, "let's not argue. I'm more concerned about whether I should go back and start some fact-finding on my own."

"Can't Bill do it? You said yourself that you wanted to find out more about it."

"Yesss," he said, unconvinced. "All right, but I better make a couple of calls to some people. But Jane," he turned to her, "don't be too upset if I have to leave before the weekend is over."

Jane reached for his hand, "I'm sorry for what I said before. I'm sure that there's nothing to the Arleo rumor."

She said it but she was not convinced. She had been a political wife too long. She knew the old saw: where there was smoke, there was fire. And when the press sniffed the smoke, they looked for the arsonist. Nothing was accidental with the press.

Nothing was accidental for the guests at Shalimar, either. Although everything appeared totally relaxed and casually organized, Grov had spent days planning activities. There was no fun and games leader, no perpetually smiling, insistently friendly staff member pushing guests from one forced entertainment to another. But every possible amusement had been made available.

Parasailing, scuba diving, Yoga, gymnastics, water skiing caught up many of the guests. Duke, though, chose to immobilize himself poolside, turning himself slowly to catch every bronzing ray of sun. David and Karen Sampson took a long leisurely walk along the beach, poking into coves for the prize shells of the island. The tennis courts accepted matches of mixed doubles, while white jacketed waiters were kept busy supplying thirsty guests with cooling drinks. But they were no busier than Marty Gramson with Denise. At the club's pure white beach, Pammy and Buffy, two splendid water sprites, buzzed around Rod, while Simon moved inconspicuously around the club catching all with his camera.

Grov was well satisfied with the way Shalimar's first full day was turning out.

Now Grov was allowing himself the luxury of a quiet pipe before the formal dinner of the evening. He stood on a high point overlooking the sea, watching the dying rays of the sun flicker out at the horizon level. Beethoven's Emperor Concerto soared over the stillness, hidden speakers mixing the sound with concert hall clarity. The night fell with tropic suddeness.

Behind him, the well-oiled machinery of his team hummed smoothly. Chefs, cooks and bakers behind the scenes prepared sumptuous morsels. Waiters set flowers on tables, bartenders polished their glasses and filled ice tubs. The waves lapped softly and the air was sweet with the smell of flowers. Off in the distance, a fired sugar cane field sent a corona of orange flame into the deep purple sky.

He sighed and pulled on his pipe. It was the best time of the evening. He enjoyed the peace, the moments away from the querulous demands of guests, the complaints and problems of his staff. He hoped the weekend would continue smoothly. The guests, for the most part, seemed relaxed. Even Denise was better than she had been in weeks. It had been too long since she had had the company of off-island people. And this special group of guests had much to offer: bankers, writers, minor royalty, French society, international stars, business entrepreneurs. The combine that put the club together knew what they were doing. Invite enough of the right people and the rest of the right people would flock to get in.

He thought of his day. How he had looked forward to playing with Bill Perceval, an amateur with a fine reputation. It was disappointing. He was surprised by Perceval's poor showing. Grov had beaten him easily. He suspected that Perceval played better; but this morning Perceval seemed to have something other than tennis on his mind. On the other hand, he had been more than impressed with the play of Jane Perceval and Margaret Bradley. They were neatly matched and played with strength and grace.

As he turned to go back in, his glance caught the pinpoints of light in the various cottages. Denise was probably still in theirs, doing her marathon dressing job. He showered and dressed in half-an-hour, but Denise took hours. Considering how little she wore, he still wondered what took so long.

Duke's cottage, next on the line, showed a light in the bathroom. No doubt, Grov thought, he would put most of the women to shame tonight with his costume.

The next cottage was totally dark. The Samson's. Grov wondered if they were napping or making love.

In the cottage, David lay on the bed smoking. Karen nestled into his shoulder. David, feeling guilty about Emily and his abrupt treatment of Karen, had made amends in the only way she understood. Karen was basically simple. If her husband made love to her, it meant he loved her. And David knew when he needed forgiveness, sex was the most direct avenue. Karen had no way of knowing that David could make love at any time to anyone with ease. Now, making love to Karen served a double purpose. It reassured her and prevented her from drinking. David realized Karen had a drinking problem, but refused to believe it might have reached serious proportions. Poor Karen. If she were a little more articulate, perhaps she wouldn't find herself turning to alcohol to escape. Instead of finding outlets for herself, she devoted herself to him. Good and sweet and undemanding when he was writing and that's why he married her, wasn't it?

The light was subdued in the cottage shared by those two darling but loony children and their poodle. Grov wondered what they were up to, wondered, too, if it was coincidence that Simon's cottage was dark.

In Pammy and Buffy's cottage, no one had started dressing yet. Rod and Simon, who had been invited for drinks by the two girls, were still in swim trunks, while the girls padded around in bare feet and shifts.

Rod fished around in the small canvas bag he carried and pulled out a pack of cigarettes. He took one out and lit it. At the first smell of the smoke, Simon looked at Rod.

"Is it good stuff?"

"Tiajuana gold, the best. I have a few well-placed friends who bring it in for me."

"Bring what?" Pammy asked, sniffing the unusual sweetness in the air.

"Oh, Pammy," Buffy squealed, "can't you guess? I bet it's pot."

"You've got to be kidding," said Pammy disdainfully. "How square."

"Oh," Rod sniffed airily, "you kids old hands at the stuff?"

"We're mainliners," Pammy said.

Simon and Rod did a double take in unison, "You're what?"

Pammy laughed. "It's a pun, you silly. Besides pot is terribly non-u."

"It's non-us, too." Buffy giggled.

"How do you know until you've tried it?" Rod teased.

"What makes you so sure we haven't?"

"My non-u instincts tell me."

Simon interrupted, "Oh, a little pot never hurt a girl."

"Depends on where she has it." Pammy bluffed, patting her flat stomach.

Rod had passed the joint to Simon as the girls stalled and he sucked in a deep breath, then let out a sigh. The girls stared with open fascination, watching the ritual, waiting for Simon to do a Dr. Jekyll—Mr. Hyde in front of them.

But he smiled with no apparent change and handed the cigarette to Buffy. She looked at his outstretched hand, half-expecting it to do some unexpected mad thing. When he urged, "Go ahead, take it, you're among friends," Buffy thought for a moment, well, it's now or never, and reached out a tentative hand. She stared at the joint, trying to remember how Simon had puffed it. Then she carefully put it in the middle of her mouth and held it.

"Hurry up," Rod prompted. "Puff it, don't waste it. It burns fast."

Buffy took a deep drag and swallowed it. The smoke was strangely flat as it went down. She coughed daintily and was surprised to feel nothing. Relaxation followed her relief.

Pammy stared at her nervously. Buffy passed the cigarette and stared cooly. Her glance said, if you don't do it, I'll disown you. Pammy got the message, took the cigarette and duplicated the maneuver, experiencing the same result. Both girls were relieved to find they had not suddenly gone to pieces. Somehow they had expected to turn into raving addicts at the first puff. Everything they had learned at Miss Porter's had prepared them for the opposite of what they were feeling.

The cigarette was passed to Rod.

"Frankly, Pammy, I think the whole thing is a put-on." Buffy said airily.

"One puff does not a pothead make," explained Ron. He had a feeling the girls were having their first experience with the joint and pretending to be old-hands at it.

Simon smiled as Rod handed back the cigarette. convinced the whole big thing with grass was nothing but a tempest in a teapot.

Pammy giggled. But Pammy giggled at everything. Buffy had no way of knowing the qualitative difference between the giggles. The cigarette was having an effect. Pammy slumped into the cushions comfortably saying, "I feel nice."

Rod patted her bare thigh, "You certainly do."

Simon settled back contentedly, watching, smoking, without speaking.

Suddenly Pammy bolted upright, startling the men, "I'm ravenous."

Buffy looked up in surprise, "Me, too."

Rod smiled, "That's a sure sign it got to you. Ok, Simon, whatta you say we leave our addicts to get dressed and meet them later?"

"Righto," agreed Simon, "good idea. Let's all put on the rags and go forth to dazzle one and all."

Simon and Rod left the girls buzzing and giggling.

"You know," Rod turned to Simon, "they never had any of the stuff before."

Simon smiled, "I know that, but they were quite adorable about it and good sports."

Rod nodded his agreement. "You know I bet those two kids would try anything if it didn't get back to Piping Rock."

"Ah, youth," moralized Simon, "what shall become of them?"

"I'll let you know."

As they passed the Gramson cottage, Rod nudged Simon, "What do you suppose the *Cassandra's* lord and master is up to? Did you get a look at that hunk of boat?"

"Yes," said Simon, "quite nice."

"Quite nice," Rod exclaimed, "Is that supposed to be British understatement?"

"Rod," Simon reminded airily, "you must remember we are a seafaring nation and have seen boats come and go for centuries. Part of being British is to remain under-impressed at all times. It's called English reserve or some such thing like that."

"You're putting me on." Rod said. "Or down."

The real put-down was happening inside the Gramson cottage.

Sandy Gramson, wet hair streaming down her back, was humming. Her husband stared at her with disbelief.

"What the hell do you have to hum about?"

"They passed a law against humming?" Sandy asked innocently.

"Don't get smart-ass with me."

"Oh, Marty," she moved toward him, "I've had a lovely day; please don't spoil it."

"I guess you did. You were gone most of it. What did you do?"

"I learned how to scuba. Then I went out to the reef and I found all these." She spread her shells out for him to see.

A glowing pink and white conch, all mysterious

hollows and curves, a shiny amber speckled spiral, a delicate fan of cobweb coral were tenderly taken out of the plastic bag.

"Look. You'd be amazed what it looks like under the water."

"Spare me the eloquence. A bunch of fish and a heap of stones. Shells." He spat the word out as if it were dirt in his mouth. "That's for kids."

She turned on him, her cheeks flaming. "You're a spoiler. Nothing beautiful comes in and touches you unless it comes out of your laboratories and you can take credit for it. All you know how to do is make me feel less than human."

Marty looked at his wife with amazement. How beautiful she seemed, angry, flushed, glowing, giving off sparks. He was strangely excited by her and seized her arm, but she pushed him away with revulsion, "Don't touch me."

Her anger was a strange, strong aphrodisiac to him. Her usual docile self turning him off, but when she threatened him, he felt excitement rise in his groin.

"I'm going to call the children," she said, pulling the phone to her.

Marty's back stiffened. Sandy saw it and said more gently, "I want to call them. Bad enough you force me to maintain separate quarters for them. Don't try to cut me off completely. I love them—even if you don't. And I feel guilty enough being here without them."

One of the conditions of their marriage which Sandy bitterly regretted now, was that Sandy's children by a previous marriage would not live with them. Sandy, desperate to marry Marty and have the security and status she had always needed, agreed.

Marty watched her dial. He wanted to strike out at her and looked for something to use against her. Her hair streaming down her back, damp and disheveled, gave him his opening.

"What are you going to do about your hair?" he asked gruffly.

"Oh," she ran her fingers through the lank strands, "I'll think of something. Don't worry, I won't embarrass you." She turned her attention to the phone and listened to the call being put through. She turned her back to him, "I don't need a hairdresser. I know that upsets you."

To stay and listen to the happy intimate talk that went on between his wife and her children would have upset Marty even more. Slipping into his silk shantung dinner jacket, he called over his shoulder before he left the room, "I'll be in the bar," then added with all the petulance of a small child, "in case you care."

It was that deep dusk time of the day that makes everything tropical seem so much more romantic and promising. It did for the landscape what a veil does for a woman, suggesting rather than stating. Marty hoped he'd run into Denise in the bar.

There were only a few other guests at the bar, but Marty's disappointment was short-lived. As he sat at the bar with a vodka and tonic and looked around, he was aware of a startling shift of scenery and mood. When he had walked into the bar, he'd been surrounded by a cool underwater scene. In a minute the scene had shifted and he was suddenly in a jungle surrounded by lions. As he watched in utter fascination, he counted three more shifts of scene in as many minutes. From the jungle, he was plunged into an acid head's dream of light and texture, then switched to a romantic field of daisies, then startled by a dramatic black and white night scene of New York.

He turned to the bartender, "You've either got the

fastest working vodka in the world, or the best lighting director in town."

The bartender stared back at him and smiled widely. His voice gave his origin away. He was pure cockney. "Some do, I'd say!"

"Is it all done with mirrors?"

"No—some bloke photographer worked it out an' sold the whole bloomin' idea to the boss. I thought the bloody idea was awful. I mean, a bloke 'as too much to drink, say, the poor bloody fool don't know what 'it 'im."

"But how does it work?"

"It works kinda like one of them eight track stereo jobs." He pointed behind the bar to four miniscule openings. "See, it all works outta there. Only 'stead of music pourin' forth, it's them bloody pictures. On some kind of time doodad, linked up somehow to the music."

Marty's eyes gleamed. Like a kid with a new toy, he had a flash of genius. Wait till Joy hears about this idea. He asked the bartender for a phone. Why not call her now. But on checking his watch, realized it was too late to call New York.

He looked around the bar once more, allowing himself to be caught up in the changing scene that enveloped him. He noticed now for the first time that all the chairs, and even the little cocktail tables scattered at discreetly separated distances about the room were of clear plastic or glass. This not only made the room seem more open and airier, but it also permitted the pictures to pass right through the transparent furniture on their way to the opposite walls.

As his eyes became more accustomed to the shifting light, he realized he was not alone in the bar. Seated at a small table in one of the far corners were Duke and Simon. Marty had wondered about Simon when he'd first seen him dancing around taking his pictures, but now he was sure. He turned his back on them and ordered another drink. They hadn't waited long to find each other, he thought to himself.

Actually it was Duke who hadn't waited. He had seen Simon pass his cabana, and go into the bar alone. It was just the opportunity he'd been waiting for. He thought he'd never find him without that gaggle of silly girls around him. By then Duke had spent the obligatory hour on his dressing and grooming, and was merely waiting for the most auspicious moment to show himself. The waiting was over. He had eyed the guests carefully yesterday when they'd arrived, and if he was wrong about Simon, it looked like it would be a lost weekend as far as he was concerned. His usual languid amble switched to swift mincing steps as he made his way quickly to the bar.

He saw Simon standing at the bar. That wouldn't do. He moved to his side silently, then, "Say, you know I think we have some mutual friends."

Simon, slightly startled by the sibilance at his elbow, turned and pulled back in one move. "Oh!" He raised one eyebrow imperceptibly and smoothed a long sideburn with the flat of his hand.

"Yes, I'm sure now," Duke said enjoying his own private innuendo. "But let's move over to a table where we can be more comfortable and talk."

Simon didn't really want to go to a table, but he saw no graceful way out. He couldn't afford to offend this one so early in the game. After all, he'd be a marvelous source of those little quips and bits of gossip that so delighted Simon's editors. Duke was notorious for the acidity of his wit and the accuracy of his material. He wielded his rapier tongue with all the sureness of a surgeon's scalpel. Starring in one of Duke's epithets could make or break you in the high flying, fast moving, easily distracted society in which they both moved and Simon knew it. Simon could see he was going to be an expensive friend to make, but he'd be an even more expensive enemy.

Simon decided he'd have to play along according to Duke's rules—at least for a little while. Half reluctantly he followed Duke to the corner table. As he eased himself into one of the wraparound chairs he asked, "Now, who are those mutual friends?"

Duke leaned forward conspiratorially. "Palmer and Honor Fitzroy." He dropped the names and watched carefully for a reaction the way a dog might drop a treasured find on the floor before his master. Seeking approval, or at the very least recognition.

Simon gave Duke a hard look. This game wasn't going to be as easy to play as he had hoped. Palmer and Honor were one of the most notoriously amoral couples in England. Palmer with his penchant for young boys and Honor who would bed down with anything regardless of race, color, creed or sex, used each other as procurors. They were young leaders in Britain's underground society of thrill seeking, drug-oriented young peers and peeresses, photographers, artists, writers and theater people. They made La Dolce Vita look like Andy Hardy.

"Well, of course, everyone in London knows the Fitzroys," Simon hedged playing for time. Duke was willing to change the subject. He'd wait until Simon loosened up a bit. The English, no matter how depraved, always insisted on keeping up certain appearances. That suited him fine. He was not in that much of a hurry, and he did enjoy this verbal foreplay. "And what do you think of our little band of well-heeled gypsies here this weekend?"

"Quite a pleasant bunch, actually. With perhaps one or two exceptions." Simon realized he'd have to go carefully with this one, but he wasn't going to let Duke control the play completely.

"Now let me guess," Duke said waspishly. "Certainly one of those exceptions couldn't possibly be the proper Mrs. Bradley."

"Why, of course not," Simon bristled. "How could anyone dislike her? She seems rather sad to me."

"That's just a put-on, of course. It's standard operating procedure for all those psycho-nymphomaniacs," Duke giggled.

"What under the sun is that?"

"Dear boy, someone who does it in her head instead of in a bed." Duke broke into gales of laughter.

"I still feel rather sorry for her. She's not had the happiest of all lives. Certainly not the sort of life someone with her expectations might have seen coming. All that unattractive business about that French lovely after all those years and then the open secret of her daughter's marriage."

"Poor darling, of course, but it's not been without its rewards either. Twenty years as the reigning queen of car city, then one of the fattest settlements of all time. Oh, it's had its rewards. Dear heart, we should all be as well paid for our time. And I gather she gave him little else but time." Duke snickered again and went on, "And now I understand, there's another man on the scene. With the necessary money, and this time with even better credentials."

"I'm sure you'd know a lot more about that than I would. Off on my little hallowed spot, we hear everything second and third hand. We've none of your sources, nor half your ability to sniff stories."

Duke chose to take this as open flattery. "You give me too much credit," he almost whispered, leaning embarrassingly close now. "My life's an open book, and I'm afraid it's got too many well-thumbed pages. But let's talk about you." He reached under the table and rested his hand on Simon's thigh.

Crossing his legs to avoid the gesture, then realizing he was trapped in this obscene little corner, he rose. There was a limit on how far he'd go along with this little flit, even for a chance to pick his cesspool of a brain. "There's nothing very interesting to report about me, except that right now, I'm in need of another drink." He held up his empty glass and started for the bar. Duke almost upset the little table in his haste to follow him. If this one got away, he thought to himself, it was going to be one helluva dull weekend.

At the bar, Simon came to an abrupt halt, and Duke who had been trailing him just inches away, used the opportunity to stumble against him. As Simon turned to murmur an automatic "I-beg-your-pardon", Duke made his move. His carefully manicured hand shot forward and squeezed him.

Simon felt a hot flash of anger seize him. This was further than he'd go for any pimping editor. "Why you dirty little scum," Simon hissed under his breath. He didn't want to be overheard by Gramson who was now staring openly at the two of them across the bar. "What the hell do you think you're doing?"

Duke had now gone too far to retreat, even if he'd wanted to. And he didn't. "Come, come," he coaxed, "don't play the sweet young virgin with me. I know all about you and that one you're married to."

"Leave my wife out of this. She's got nothing to do with it."

Duke could see that he had found a weakness and he pressed his advantage. "Oh, I know all about her little romances. Some of her girl friends aren't so discreet. And if you're married to a girl fancier, what must you fancy?"

Simon had no intention of making a scene here. By now Gramson was making a point of not noticing them. One sudden move would change all that. And so with a superhuman effort, he restrained himself. "I'll let that remark go with the explanation that you've had too much to drink."

"Don't make excuses for me," Duke said angrily. But it was apparent that he had indeed had too much to drink and was not in full control of himself.

"Besides, I don't know why you're being so bitchy with me. You should be flattered."

"Your attentions are not only *not* flattering, your innuendoes are too vile to even answer. If we were alone, I'd splatter your made-up face all over these walls."

Even as he spoke, the walls were dissolving from a night scene on the Grand Canal to a riot of blue and white paisley. Dinner chimes rang out and could be heard over the soft background music in the bar.

The club's band was setting up, musicians tuning their instruments and fumbling with speakers. Groups of guests arriving in the dining room were ushered to small tables by a white jacketed maitre d'.

The glass walls of the room had been opened to let in the softly scented balm of night air. The candles flickered in the undulating breeze. The atmosphere was tingling with expectancy. From an arch overlooking the room, Grov and Denise surveyed the scene.

"Now," said Grov with a sweep of his hand, "wasn't it all worth the struggle? Look!"

Denise followed his outstretched hand and admitted the room looked romantic as well as beautiful. "Thank heaven, it doesn't look like the usual hotel dining room."

The dining pavillon, as befitting a resort named Shalimar, resembled an emir's tent, matching exactly the pattern which had enveloped Marty as he left the bar. Bright blue and white paisley formed a tented ceiling and alternated with lacquered blue bamboo mouldings on the walls. White marble tables on burnished steel pedestals held individual bouquets of flowers clustered around scented Rigaud candles. Comfortable matching paisley cushioned chairs around each table; banquettes in the corners of the room were ready to receive weary dancers into the comfortable coziness of masses of jewel-colored pillows.

Instead of the usual formal table with guests jockeying for position, Grov had opted for a large number of small tables. He and Denise would be seated with Sebastian Lalange, the prime minister of the island and Emily Guilford, who not only ran the boutique but was Sebastian's good and close friend. Sebastian had been prevailed upon to make a small welcoming speech to the club's invited guests. Grov hoped this gesture would be the beginning of an amity between the islanders and the many guests who, with proper treatment, could make the club a financial and social success.

"Oh, there're the Gramsons," Grov pointed. "Let's say hello and get them seated. She looks lovely, doesn't she?"

"Why not, she's wearing a queen's ranson in sapphires." Denise's eyes glittered with a fire as bright as the jewels. "And that simple little white crept costume must have cost him at least a thousand dollars. It's a Norell."

"Who's Norell?"

"Money, my sweet, money."

"My love, do I detect a touch of envy?"

"Not a touch, a full blown crop, my sweet."

He chided her. "That's what you get for marrying a ne'er-do-well tennis player. Your French mother warned you."

"Yes, I know. But who listens to mothers? Besides you were so handsome."

"Were?"

She squeezed his elbow.

"Well, shall we?"

"If we must, we must. I feel so tacky."

"You look smashing, love." Grov reassured her.

They met the Gramsons half-way and Grov extended his hand.

Sandy took it and complimented him on the room's decor and then turned to Denise to admire her dress. But Marty interrupted, "Denise, you look spectacular."

Grov bristled and gallantly turned to Sandy, "I must say, your wife is extremely attractive tonight."

"If I spent that kind of money, I'd look good, too." A smooth smiled covered the barb of Marty's remark.

Grov fought back his desire to slap the man's face.

Sandy flushed at her husband's gratuitous remark and graciously accepted the compliment as she gave Marty a hurt look.

Grov noticed the Percevals and Margaret came in and breathed with relief. Anything to get away from this repellent man. "If you'll excuse me?" He turned to Denise, "Love, would you please take care of the Gramsons while I see to the others?"

"Of course," purred Denise, slipping her arm through Marty's and resting her other lightly on Sandy's shoulder. She squeezed Marty's and he returned the signal.

As Grov reached the Percevals, Pammy, Buffy, Simon, Karen and David were arriving. The room filled rapidly. Murmurs of conversation increased. Waiters moved noiselessly about the tables with trays of rum cocos, a potent drink of rum, fresh coconut and coconut milk steeped in cane.

With the consumption of drinks peaking, conversational noise crescendoed. It emphasized the sudden silence when Sebastian Lalange walked into the room with Emily.

Her silky blonde hair was pulled into an Edwardian twist, emphasizing her fine bones and clear grey-blue eyes. The severe hair was in striking contrast with her gown. A brilliant native print, one of the new designs conceived by Emily, had been cleverly wrapped and tied over one shoulder with no other apparent fastenings. As she walked the side opened to show a flash of tan calf and shell sandals. They would have brought conversation to a halt anywhere for they were a handsome couple. But here, they were outstanding for Emily's pale patrician beauty was in sharp contrast to the rich mahogany color of Sebastian.

David Sampson fell into a fit of coughing while swallowing a drink. Karen turned to him in surprise and tried to pound his back. He shoved her hand away hard and choked out, "Jesus, the guy's a black."

The gentleman sharing the table with them, said with a heavy French accent, "That is not so surprising. He was born on this Island. And he happens to be its prime minister."

Karen stared with unabashed admiration, "Black or white, he's the most beautiful man I've ever seen."

Sebastian was over six feet tall and the body beneath the immaculate white dinner jacket was graceful and lean. His steel gray hair clung close to his well-shaped head. In profile, his acquiline nose and narrow lips seemed to be carved from a piece of stone. When he turned, there was a light gasp. His eyes were a brilliant blue.

David stared with disbelief. "He's no pure-blooded black. Not with those eyes."

The gentleman again spoke, explaining the mixture of Spanish and French blood.

David's anger rose as he watched Sebastian put his arm easily through Emily's. The couple walked across the floor, seemingly unconscious of the stir.

Even Margaret was amazed to feel a rising excitement and had the grace to blush at her own suddenly unleased thoughts.

"Who is that divine man with the little shopkeeper?" Pammy asked of no one in particular.

Simon smiled. "I'm sure they'd both expire if they could hear you. That, luv, is the Prime Minister."

"I thought prime ministers were old and fat."

"Only Winston Churchill."

"Well, this one looks like a movie star. What's he see in that tacky little thing? And did you notice what she's wearing. I didn't know this was to be a costume party.

"She's obviously trying to pass as a native," Buffy sniffed.

Grov rose to meet the couple and escort them to his table, not unaware of the excited buzz of conversation which followed their entrance. He took advantage of a sudden lull in the talk to introduce them.

"Ladies and gentlemen, I would like to present to you, the honorable Sebastian Lalange, Prime Minister of our island. And I'm sure you all know Miss Emily Guilford by now."

Beneath his white dinner jacket, Sebastian was wringing wet with perspiration. He had waited all his life for this moment. In front of him was the wealth, power and prestige he had always dreamed of. What lay behind those curious, expectant eyes? What did they want of him? A soft shoe routine? The story of a black man's rise to fame through hard work and application? The truth? Or a palatable fiction? Were they wondering about the aristocratic Emily Guilford's relationship with him?

He knew this first impression was immensely important. (Hadn't his father burned that into him at an early age?) The success of Shalimar would be his success, too. He had not spent all those years diligently learning how to get along with the power structure for nothing.

Tonight they would know that a black leader was not only possible but proper. He swept the crowd with his magnetic blue eyes, saw the envious stares of some of the men, saw one bejewelled woman look at him with unconcealed sexuality. Those looks were not unfamiliar to him. From the moment he walked into the Sorbonne as a fearful, unsure, insecure young man, it had only been a question of time before he realized his exceptional good fortune. His blue eyes, his powerful lean body, his lazy Creole French attracted women immediately. From the female students who shared the crowded classrooms to the sophisticated older woman, wife of one of his professors who had taught him more during their brief affair than he had learned in his four years at the Sorbonne. He thought of her now—with her mocking eyes, the long slender fingers with the blood red nails that could hurt and soothe, the attentuated body so intensely passionate yet curiously unsexy. After her, had he ever looked at a plump woman with pleasure again? That in itself made him different from his brothers in St. Phillipe. He remembered, too, the carefully held back tears when he announced the affair was over.

And so he had grown into manhood, learning to use and expand the early boyish charm that had ingratiated him with the French governor of the island.

He was a good student, observing the ways and manners of the confident, sophisticated French. And in England he had perfected the art, though there he was not as easily accepted as he had been in France. There he had had to work hard to earn the respect of the caste-conscious, generally black aristocracy. But he had learned—and well.

In France love had come first. In England, love came last, long after duty and enlightened self-interest.

Now after years of knuckling under and playing up to the whites, it was finally paying off. It had been a personal triumph. The island and his position in it would make it all worthwhile.

He cleared his throat lightly. Then in that devasting half-English, half-French accent he had so carefully cultivated, he delivered a brief but eloquent welcoming speech to Shalimar and his island. The speech had the right proportion of pride, humility and deference. Its careful planning paid off handsomely. The group rose to its feet and applauded him.

He bowed lightly in acceptance, his heart pounding. The ingratiating smile froze to his lips as he accepted their acceptance. For an instant he felt like a headwaiter conning for a big tip. But only for an instant.

"He sounds like de Lawd in that play," a voice stage whispered. "What was it? Oh, yes, *Green Pastures.*"

David noticed the open adulation in Emily's eyes as she listened to Sebastian speak.

"Goddamn hero worshipper," he thought. "It didn't take her long to find another god to worship." He was feeling violent.

Jane Perceval turned to Bill and winked. "How'd you like to run against him in the next election?"

Bill rolled his eyes, "No thank you. Not in today's climate."

"I must say he's an exceptionally attractive man," said Margaret. "I wonder where he went to school?"

"Certainly not here," said Bill. "I smell Oxford and maybe the Sorbonne."

Bill's guess had been close, actually it had been Cambridge and the Sorbonne.

After Sebastian's welcoming speech, Grov signalled the waiters to start bringing in the food. The lights in the room dimmed dramatically, a hushed silence fell over the guests and a parade, a part-Barnum/part-Beard, moved among the tables.

It was a ritual to bring tears to the eyes of the most dedicated gourmet. On the first trolley were appetizers fresh from the seas: crayfish vinaigrette, langoustina in green mayonnaise, clumps of crabmeat piled high on shiny green avocado halves and tossed with a spicy sauce surrounding a magnificent salmon en gelée.

Following this extravaganza were three more trolleys. On one was a suckling pig with a roasted apple forcing its face into a foolish grin. On the second, were plump little partridge hens glazed in fruit syrup and barbecued a deep gold and a deep-rimmed pan of paella, fragrant with native seafood, rice and spices.

The third ushered in platters of delicate snapper en papillote.

Each trolley vied for supremacy in the art of garni. Loving and clever hands had fashioned tiny flowers and imaginative little animals from aspics, fruits, vegetables and palm fronds. The waiters, lavish in their service, piled delicacy upon delicacy, enough to please a gourmand yet not bring shudders to the heart of a gourmet.

"Have you ever seen anything like it?" Karen gasped to David. "It looks too good to eat." But eat they did.

David, not realizing Karen spoke of the food, grunted in agreement, still with the memory of Sebastian and Emily burned into his thoughts.

"I don't know what Miss Craig will say when she discovers all these goodies lodged on my hips and waist." Margaret, strangely animated, had almost giggled.

"What Miss Craig and Elizabeth Arden can't dispose of, I'm sure Mainbocher can disguise—and beautifully, too." Duke replied knowledgeably.

Pammy and Buffy were quiet for the first time in days. They shared a devotion to good food that overshadowed their interest in small talk. Perhaps one day they would turn into those pillar-shaped matrons that were a continuing challenge to the Bermuda Shop; but in the meantime, they were adoring every delicious calorie.

Simon, enjoying good food with the same zeal, took delight in watching the girls. Miss Porter's classes had taught them not to wolf down their food, but if there was a skillful way to delicately devour everything in sight, they had mastered it. Rod, too, ate with the same seriousness and singlemindedness that he approached any necessary effort designed to keep his body in shape.

At the Gramson table, the presence of an unknown couple had kept Marty's behavior starchly civil. Sandy softly thanked God no soup had been served. Soup was not something Marty did well. He took twisted pleasure in making as much noise as possible with it. Sandy was never sure when he would decide to perform his amusing little act. Never one for light conversation or social chitchat, he had stopped all forms of communication when the first plate had been put before him. In a way it had been a relief to Sandy that the food had been served swiftly and in such quantity. Marty was unpredictable and would lapse into basic and usually private vulgarities in front of others without warning. Lately, he seemed more discreet, saving his nasties for the privacy of their boudoir. Still, Sandy felt she couldn't rely on him in public.

As she savored the delicious crabmeat, she wondered why his misbehavior upset her the way it did. Why she didn't speak out or walk out when he got too much to take? Rich people were allowed eccentricities, Marty explained, it was her middle class upbringing that made her over-zealous about manners.

Marty flashed Sandy a winning smile, cutting through her doubts, including their tablemates in its dazzle, "I think they've stolen the chef from Caravelle, if this sauce is any clue." He savored the taste with the airs of a French count.

"Say," he included the unsmiling English couple in

his largesse, "why don't I order a little wine for us?"

Without waiting for their compliance, he gestured discreetly to the hovering waiter and asked for the wine list.

The waiter summoned the sommelier who presented a vast red leather folio to Marty. He disappeared behind it and studied it carefully, waiting for a familiar name to catch his eye. The Haut Brion '55 leaped at him. It was a safe, although expensive choice. At least he had learned that much from Joy. She'd have laughed to see him here, he knew, and some of the show-off little boy in him wished he could share the whole experience with her.

Grov felt an undeniable surge of satisfaction as the sumptuous trays and trollies were brought in and served. It hadn't been easy dealing with the native help. Especially of late, he had noticed an almost militant surliness about them, but they had certainly rallied round this evening. Even if he had sent to England for a staff, they could not have been better than the young men who worked for him tonight. Yet, the militancy still nagged at him. Grov, who had neither knowledge nor interest in island politics, was puzzled by the intransigence.

When he'd first come down with the backers of Shalimar, they had been welcomed warmly. Shalimar promised jobs to many and a new vitality in the island economy, so long dependent on sugar cane.

But as building progressed, relations with the islanders rapidly deteriorated. At first it was nothing specific, more a question of attitude. When the pressure to complete the work had mounted, he'd noticed several incidents of open hostility. Just before the opening it had reached dangerous proportions and Grov was worried that some of the most observant guests might notice trouble in paradise.

Grov had even called the staff together Thursday morning for a pep talk, promising generous bonuses if the weekend went smoothly. He'd have to find a way to excuse himself to his management, but it was essential that nothing go wrong this opening week. The bonuses had obviously worked wonders. Grov sighed with contented relief; the service could not have been smoother. He relaxed even more as the waiters supervised the removal of used dishes and prepared for the entrance of the desserts.

Again the lights were dimmed; the musicians struck up a gay carnival tune and the parade of desserts commenced. Flaming fruits led the way, followed by crystal bowls of zuppa inglese under crowns of whipped cream, then meringue glacés, rich ice creams topped with fruits soaked in liqueurs and colorful sherbets. Then, almost as an after thought, the final trolley entered, groaning under its load of silver trays, each one with a breathtaking assortment of miniature French pastries and tarts. While the desserts were served with rich black coffee and espresso, the music switched to a smooth and languid beguine.

Sebastian and Emily, along with the Wilcoxes, led the dancing. The glazed eyes of sated guests turned to the floor and watched the couples. But their eyes stayed on Sebastian and Emily, who danced together as one, matching movement to movement. There was an undulating grace, a naturalness with the music which brought envious feelings to the men and sheer jealousy to the women. To move that unconsciously!

After a while, Grov cut in on Sebastian and they exchanged partners. Sebastian swept Denise into a showy display of dips and swirls as she laughed with delight, Denise adored dancing.

David, whose eyes had followed the couple's every move, seized the opportunity and danced Karen close to Grov and Emily.

"Grov," he smiled, "how about changing partners?"

Emily flashed a warning glance at Grov, who felt

her arm stiffen on his neck, then let go. She knew she couldn't avoid dancing with David without causing a scene.

The exchange was made neatly but David felt a tremor of guilt as he saw the surprised and questioning look on Karen's face.

"Well, Emily?"

"Well, David?"

The questions burned unasked on his lips. Emily seemed in no mood to help him. They danced stiffly apart. Each time David tried to bring her closer, her back stiffened and resisted his hand.

"I didn't realize escorts were so hard to come by on the island. What would the good Boston people think about all this?"

"There was a time when it might have mattered."

"But now it doesn't. We're big white liberal stuff now."

"I've learned a lot in the last year and a half."

"You seem to have found an excellent teacher."

"How can you be so disgraceful? You of all people. He's a fine man; he's done much for the island. What difference does it make what his color is?"

"Spare me the violins and the social conscience. What I don't get is what you're doing with him."

"Why do you automatically assume a connection?"

"Don't tell me you just happened to bump into him in the lobby?" He wore the skeptical, closed look Emily remembered.

She flushed. "We've been good friends for a long time."

"How good and how long?"

Emily fought with her rising anger. "What right have you to ask all these questions?"

They danced in stony silence. Then Emily spoke flatly as if she were answering an interviewer's questions from a memorized script, "We've been working together."

"At what?" David pressed.

Emily sighed. "At developing a native craft industry. I'm taking their traditional weaving methods and introducing new designs and colors. Then I develop outlets. Like they do for Mexico. We have a growing little business . . ."

David interrupted. "So, little Emily Guilford from Beacon Hill is down here teaching basket-weaving to the natives. You never got over being a Girl Scout."

"David, if you insist on being insufferable, I'm going to walk away from you this instant."

"Cool it, Emily, I'm just trying to find out what the hell is going on here with you."

"Why is it your business?"

"I'm making it mine."

"You're a little late."

The ping pong match of words grew more acerbic.

She continued, "Your concern might have been more appreciated a year ago."

"Stop talking in oblique sentences and get to the point. You keep alluding to some horrible thing I did but you won't tell me what it was."

Anger flooded into Emily's brain, she felt dizzy. Her voice was cold with fury, "You spend an idyllic six weeks with me, you run off to Europe and I don't hear a word from you. The next thing I know you're married and I'm left with a," she paused almost imperceptibly, "fond memory."

"Why are you making such a big deal about this? We had a wonderful time together, but we made no commitments"

"I made you the strongest commitment I ever made in my life."

"Emily," he poohed, "let's not overdramatize. I came back from Europe and tried to get in touch with you dozens of times but no one knew where you were and if they did, they weren't talking. You disappeared like a thief in the night."

Her cold anger flamed into heat now. It came out, under her breath, burning and freezing, "More like a murderer."

"What does that mean?" The puzzlement was real. He couldn't follow her allusions.

Her voice continued, murderously calm and soft, but each word delivered with the sting of a whip, "You, the sensitive writer, the experienced man of the world, the great lover, you still haven't been able to piece together the picture."

David stopped. They stood in the middle of the floor, staring at each other. Emily's eyes were full of tears and David suddenly felt understanding flow to his brain, "You mean . . . ?"

"I mean," the tears overcame her. She dashed at them with annoyance.

"Why didn't you let me know?"

"Where was I to find you?"

"You could have called my publisher?"

"You could have written to me and told me where you were."

"I was on the move a lot," he said evasively. "But that's beside the point. You knew I would be back."

"I couldn't afford to wait."

"Where did you go?"

"It was done in Puerto Rico."

"Through the painful conversation, the words "pregnant" and "abortion" had been carefully avoided.

"And then what?"

"And then, then I started running away from myself. But I couldn't. We never can. I ended up here somehow. I met Sebastian somehow. And I started to do things. The rest you know."

He had resumed dancing with her, but she

stopped. "I'd like to sit down now. Besides Karen is beginning to wonder what we're up to."

A tap on the shoulder sent David whirling around angrily. Sebastian's mellow voice interrupted, "May I have Emily back for a dance, please?" His eyes moved between Emily and David, trying to guess the content of their conversation.

"I was just telling Mr. Sampson about our work, Sebastian." Emily said in an attempt to lessen the tension.

"'Indeed?" Sebastian commented drily. Then turning to David, "It's all Emily's doing, you know. She's an amazing woman."

David locked eyes with Sebastian, trying to read more into the word amazing, but Sebastian said no more. Instinctively he felt that David was his enemy, waiting to pierce his carefully constructed social armor to reach the real Sebastian. Was it because of Emily or a natural distrust of anything black? He smiled at David, then swept Emily off in his arms. David fumed as he saw Emily's back relax; noticed, too, the confident way she moved with him, as if she belonged.

He watched a moment, a sardonic smile on his face, then returned to his table, self-consciously avoiding Karen's questioning look, knowing he would have to make some feeble excuse sooner or later, preferably later.

Enough food and drink had been served to have put everyone into a politely stupefied condition; that natural follow-up of any formal dinner, whether at Shalimar or the Sheraton. The Percevals yawned politely behind napkins as they made desultory conversation with Margaret, anxious not to appear to be breaking up the evening.

David, nerves on edge and growing edgier since the confrontation with Emily, had had all he could take of conversation, music and dancing. He had stayed on just to please Karen and allay her suspicions, but his patience was as thin as an overstretched elastic. Finally, he could stand no more. He took Karen firmly by the elbow and steered her toward the door after grunting an unintelligible excuse to the couple sharing their table.

At the table shared by Simon, Rod, Pammy and Buffy, the night's activities were just beginning. They all enjoyed dancing but complained bitterly of the slow pace maintained by the club's group. As the evening wore on, the tempo of the music had worn down until the activity was a slow-motion film.

"If these people have all the rhythm they're credited with, this group's doing them a great disservice," noted Simon. "There must be better sounds on this island somewhere."

"Must be," Pammy agreed, "I remembers mah deah ole Mammy rockin' me to sleep with jungle rock."

"Wrong continent," said Rod, "but I know a place where they really groove. Let's go." He got up from the table and motioned his charges to follow.

"Can we get a cab?" asked Simon.

"Don't need one," Rod replied, "With a little squeezing we can all go in my car."

"A little squeezing never hurt a girl," Buffy smiled, "let's do it."

Linking arms, they marched directly to the parking lot reserved for staff, singing Le Marseillaise happily. The cars were big, old American models—much the worse for wear—which had put in years of service as island cabs before being retired into the used car market. Tucked in between a Buick and a Studebaker was Rod's shiny red Porsche. He'd spent too much on it, he knew, but it had been an investment that had paid off. Most women adjusted their opinion of him upward when he pulled up in it.

With some effort, Simon and Buffy doubled up into the rear half-seat built more to the measurements of dolls than people while Pammy slipped into the low bucket seat next to Rod. Rod kicked the car in gear and with a low gurgle of power from the finely tuned engine, it leaped forward.

The car raced through the darkness of the thick foliage like a jungle cat. In minutes they were at the dusty outskirts of one of the tiny villages which dotted the island. Rod downshifted to maneuver the twisted narrow alleys that led down a hill to one of the native clubs. He had been on the island long enough to sniff out the authentic ones, eschewing the pseudo bôites invented to lure the tourists from the big hotels at the far end of the island.

The Trianon was authentic, no frills, hardly any whites and the best music on the island. Rod parked the car close to the entrance; preferring not to walk the girls any distance through the dark lot. Perception was not his long suit, but even he was aware of the "situation" on the island.

He hoped there would be no trouble tonight, but figured he and Simon could handle any if it should crop up. Just to make sure, he reached into the glove compartment and slipped a switch blade into his pocket as he helped Buffy out.

A sudden burst of music sent Pammy into raptures and she urged them to hurry. Inside it was dark as pitch, the only illumination coming from candles in rum bottles and a feeble blue spot on the bandstand. The air was heavy with smoke, the musky smell of many bodies, sweating freely from generous tots of rum and endless bottles of the local beer.

Buffy sniffed delicately, "I'm not sure I can take much of this."

"You'll get used to it. You wanted authenticity."

When she winced, Simon gallantly offered, "Well, then, let's take this table by the door. You'll get an occasional whiff of fresh air. And besides, this looks like the kind of place we might want to leave in a hurry."

Even in the murky room, Simon could see the sullen looks aimed at their little party by natives at the other tables. But most of the mesmerized dancers hadn't even noticed their arrival.

The waiter who also owned the establishment walked that fine line between civility and surliness that characterized his calling throughout the world. They ordered a round of drinks impatient to join the other dancers, hesitating to leave the safe harbor of their table. But the music was so insistent they were soon caught up and moving to the beat with the same frenzy as the others.

The music suddenly slowed down, then stopped mid-phrase. The grumbling couples, annoyed by this silent interruption, looked around restlessly for a reason. They found it in the doorway in the persons of Sebastian Lalange and Emily Guilford. Lalange nodded a brief greeting to several couples close by, but made no move to enter further into the room, waiting for the owner to come to him. He did and with some embarrassment and a sweep of his hand indicated that all the tables were occupied.

Simon, standing close enough to hear Sebastian say, "But surely, Florant, you can put another small table somewhere near the far end of the room, it's just us. And we don't require that much room." He put his arm around Emily's waist.

When the owner continued to resist, Simon walked over to them and said, "Good evening, perhaps you'd like to join us at our table. It's just over there and we can make room for you if our genial host will supply chairs."

Simon smiled innocently at the owner, daring him to refuse. Emily seemed uncertain but Sebastian accepted, thanking Simon graciously.

"We seem to have caused quite a stir," Sebastian

explained as he joined Simon's table. The music still had not started, voices still hummed with a nasty excitement. There was a brief moment of awkwardness as the two girls stared at Sebastian. Sebastian inquired as to their drinks and smoothly ordered. His control of the situation showed an experienced hand. But Simon sensed him seething beneath the surface.

"I'm surprised to find people from Shalimar have discovered Trianon so quickly." Sebastian commented.

"But we have this most marvelous native guide," Pammy said, putting her arm around Rod and her foot in her mouth simultaneously.

"Rod's our leader," Simon said quickly in an attempt to cover everyone's embarrassment. "And thank heaven, for we were all about to be ossified by the music at the club."

"Yes, but they have really marvy music here," Buffy added. Pammy felt quite rightly that she had said more than enough.

"It is the best on the island, I think." Sebastian agreed. Our people here love to dance and do it extremely well." They all agreed, pointing out several fine exponents on the dance floor.

"Have you been here long?" Sebastian inquired. "I didn't notice you leave."

"Just long enough to work up a sweat and a thirst." Rod answered, looking around to see what had happened to their drinks. The music had started again. Sebastian rose and held his hand out to Emily. She hesitated at first, but then knowing how much Sebastian enjoyed dancing, moved with him to the floor. It was crowded again, so they kept to the outside edge, close to the table, away from the other dancers.

They were unaware, but Simon was not, of the hostile stares. It puzzled him. Mixed couples were not unusual; it was happening all over Europe and

America. But that was not admiration in those huge dark eyes which followed every move Sebastian and Emily made. Did Sebastian perceive the situation and chose to ignore it? Or was he missing the signals? In any case, he danced close to Emily, holding her possessively, their bodies moving in a sensuous dance of love that betrayed their true feeling for each other.

With each movement, Simon could feel something ugly in the crowd, yet hesitated to say anything or bring it to the attention of the little group. He began to feel edgy as he heard the hum of hostility grow, a new presence in an already crowded room.

He stared at them, willing with his eyes that they take notice of something other than themselves. Pammy, misreading his attention suggested, "If it looks that good to you, let's join them."

Emily moved dreamily in Sebastian's arms, thinking of the first time she had danced with him. Even then, it had been like making love. The setting was so perfect: black night with so many stars it was almost day-bright, inside the caressing low glow of lights and everywhere the steady beat of the insinuating music, the movement of hands and shoulders and hips, smiles inviting and free. And with the slow beguine beat, the cessation of movement, just swaying, the feeling of being held hard and close. She remembered the smell of him, the dampness of his sweat, the little rays of heat emanating from his body. How he pulled her away and looked at her, brushed her forehead with his lips, then closed his arms around her again. She felt the hardness of his back and stroked it, felt a lightness and a pressure in her stomach and then realized he was so close she could feel his muscular contractions leading the movement. She let herself be led by his strength, looked up at him. He bent to kiss her. And it was like the first kiss she had ever had. Before that kiss, she felt she had never kissed a man before, never made love before. It was like a rebirth.

Now that all of them were on the dance floor, Simon tried to forget the thoughts that were bothering him. Pammy had insinuated herself into the very center of the dancing mass and it took all his attention to steer her back to the edge of the floor near their table. If trouble came, he didn't want to be in its center. As soon as he could do it graciously, he suggested they sit down again. Pammy agreed without too much coaxing and immediately after, they were joined by Rod and Buffy.

"Maybe it's just me," Rod noted, "but this crowd is beginning to make me nervous."

"Precisely why we are here and not out there amongst the thundering herd," said Simon.

"Oooh, is there going to be a riot?" squeaked Pammy.

"Not if we can avoid it," Simon answered. Was this fuzzy-brained creature next to him really so irresponsible as to be looking forward to a riot? He knew the two girls lived in some private never-never land protected by their father's money, but surely they must see papers or watch news on television and know the rest of the world was not so insulated.

Sebastian and Emily continued to dance in that same oblivious way. When the music stopped, Simon sighed with relief as they headed across the floor toward the table.

"You were certainly right about the music," Buffy remarked as Sebastian held Emily's chair for her. He smiled and was about to answer when he was grabbed from behind by one of the men who had been watching him closely.

Sebastian wheeled around, straightening up, towering over the other man, who stood his ground firmly.

"Black not good enough for you Mis-tah Sebastian," the man snarled and indicated Emily with a savage nod of his head. The angry words didn't match the musical sing-song of his voice.

"I think you've had too much to drink," Sebastian said quietly as he tried to edge the man away from the table, toward the door. But the man twisted out of Sebastian's grasp and moved to the table, putting both hands on it. He thrust his face to within inches of Emily's and spat out, "You heard Mistah Sebastian talk, he say this be an all black island run by blacks for blacks. No room in that plan for you, Miss Emily do-good."

Sebastian's face was a study in fury as he put both hands on the man's shoulders and spun him around and away from the table.

Those hands cut into the other man with the force of steel bands. Sebastian took a sadistic pleasure in the pain he knew he was causing. He would make him an object to anyone with similar threats to his authority.

Now there was no mistaking the mood of the crowd. It was ugly and fissures showed steam about to erupt. Simon, quickly appraising the situation, moved swiftly. "Let's all leave quietly," he said softly, calmly, as much for Sebastian's benefit as for Rod's and the girls'.

Rod sprang to his feet instantly, shepherding the two girls ahead of him toward the door. Emily, too, face ashen, was on her feet and headed for the door. Only Sebastian did not move.

He stood with his back to the door, facing the crowd that flowed toward him in one single unit. He caught Emily's arm without looking at her, "Wait with me, Emily. I haven't worked all these years to see this island turned into a place as unfit for whites as it once was for blacks."

Emily hesitated a moment, then realizing his remark was meant more for the blacks than for her, replied, "I'll wait for you outside. I'm the one who caused the trouble." She slipped from his grasp and was away before he could retrieve her.

"If any one of you has cause for complaint, my office is the place for discussion. As to my private life, it is precisely that—private!" He turned from them and hastened to find Emily. He did not want her standing alone outside for even an instant. But she was with Rod next to his car, in the full light of the bright sign of the club.

"Why didn't you stay with me as I asked you?" he asked brusquely.

"I think I've caused enough trouble." she answered quietly.

"You needn't worry. I'm accustomed to handling trouble." His voice was cold and she shivered as it enveloped her, thinking how she had failed him. Was it shame, embarrassment or her own guilt?

Rod, standing nearby, was embarrassed to be a part of this too-private discussion. The rest of his group was already in the car. " 'Fraid I can't offer you two a lift, I've got a full load here," he said opening the door and sliding under the wheel.

Sebastian regained his composure, "Don't give it a thought. I have my car right over there," he pointed to an elderly Citroen, parked a few steps away. He took Emily by the arm and led her to the car and opened the door for her. She slid in, making herself small in the corner, wishing she were invisible.

Sebastian walked around and got in, slamming the door with unnecessary violence. She saw the granite cast of his face under the thin stream of light blend into the darkness of the night. The car skidded into gear and out of the lot on to the black-topped road. Sebastian was a massive black shadow and even as her eyes accustomed themselves to the murky night, she could barely see his profile. The car seemed to be piloted by an invisible driver.

They rode in silence for a mile or so before Sebastian spoke.

"You, of all people," he spat.

"I'm sorry. I didn't want to disappoint you like this."

"What are you talking about?"

She looked at him with confusion. "Inside. Not listening when you asked me to stay."

"I didn't mean that. I meant that attack on you."

For just an instant Emily felt suspicious. Was he angry because of the attack on her or was it the challenge to his authority? She knew that Sebastian craved respect from whites and blacks alike, but wondered if he could get it from both.

"Why not?" she asked softly.

"But you're no ordinary white woman."

"I'm white. That seems to be enough."

"It's not enough. After what you've done, how dare they? How dare they question my authority? Sometimes I wonder. Maybe we are an inferior race. Maybe we are past the stage of redemption." He had used the collective "we" but for a heartsick moment Emily wondered if he hadn't meant "they."

"Sebastian. You're being melodramatic." The white hand reached out and set itself softly on the dark one clenched about the wheel. "I am still a white woman. And you're their leader, they idolize you. They look to you to set the standards of their lives. To them you've invaded a white world and conquered it. And you of all people have let a white woman in your life. To them, you're a betrayer."

"I don't want those kinds of differences to exist here."

"I know that. But they're not ready to accept it. You can't force it. It takes time." This conversation was all reversed. Here was the white woman with empathy for the black hostility. Sebastian, the black man, pressing for an acceptance of whites that could only be possible in the unpredictable future. How much time and anger and understanding had to be expended before the two races could look at each other without seeing differences in color.

"Sebastian?"

"Yes." His fine voice softened, the anger ebbing at the truths she spoke.

"You're not taking me home?"

"Do you want to go home?"

"No."

"Then I'm not taking you home." She sensed the smile and felt the returning pressure of his hand.

Emily looked out at the night, saw the towering bulk of the palms along the road, tried to see past the dense growth of the encroaching forest, the occasional pinpoints of light, the radar of flying insects making their way through the brush.

The tiny lights became those of La Croisette, a tiny crossroads town; ghostly twinkles of swinging light turned out to be small lanterns marking the turns of the road. The car plunged through the town, now silent and deserted except for a few couples who walked, arms about each other's waists, towards the little stucco cottages that circled the outskirts.

Sebastian swerved the car off the road into a smaller one leading to the water, then screeched to a halt in front of an intricate wrought-iron gate. A sentry snapped to attention smartly and Sebastian put his head through to identify himself to the white shirted guard. The gates swung open and Sebastian proceeded down the driveway and around to the back of a low-slung white stone villa, his official residence.

The villa sat on a knoll overlooking a cove leading to the Caribbean waters. This side entrance afforded Sebastian the opportunity to come and go with a certain freedom. It was the entrance he used when

Emily accompanied him. It was not done out of shame, but out of expedience.

The guard at the rear saluted discreetly, then turned back to the door without seeming to notice Emily's presence.

Sebastian's apartments on the second floor were comfortably masculine, an attractive admixture of French, English and native Carib. In his study, he pulled back the heavy linen draperies and opened the louvered doors to let in the velvety night air.

At the small portable bar, his man had thoughtfully left a crystal bowl of ice and glasses for Sebastian's night cap. He poured a brandy and soda. Emily refused a drink, choosing to pace nervously around the room, pulling a book from the shelves, leafing through it absently and then replacing it. Sebastian watched her pick up a huge conch shell, put her ear to it and listen.

"Emily," his voice half-pleaded, half-commanded. "Come."

She walked to him and stood in front of him as an offering. He set his glass down and put his arms around her gently. She leaned against him wearily, then sank to her knees. He was embarrassed by her gesture and joined her on the floor. The long fingers stroked her smooth hair, then pulled the pins from it, letting it flow through them. Slowly he combed it away from her face and looked at her with tenderness.

She returned his look with a combination of fear, love, longing and sadness.

"Oh, Sebastian," she tightened her arms around his waist and hugged him to her. "I'm so sorry for us."

"Why," he said gently, "it's been good. We've worked hard. We've accomplished much. No woman could have done more."

"Yes," she said bitterly. "Only one problem."

"What's that?"

"Sebastian," she pulled away and looked at him. "You're the most intelligent man I know, but sometimes I think you deliberately choose not to see the obvious."

"Hush," he stroked her hair again. "You're seeing monsters where there are none." He was about to say 'niggers in the woodpile' but stopped himself, hating those phrases that had become part of a language but still demonstrated the bigotry behind them.

"No," she pulled away again, "you're refusing to see the monsters where they are. They won't let me fit in." She paused, then continued sadly, "And they're probably right. You belong with them now."

"Nonsense," he said with a certainty he didn't altogether feel. "No one is going to tell me how to run my life. I've earned the right to do what I want."

He sipped the rest of his drink, watching her stand up and continue her pacing. Then softly, almost to himself, he said, "I've played their game long enough, made all the right sacrifices. I've earned my right."

Her shoulders slumped. He went to her and stood behind her with his arms about her waist. Together they stared at the moon-struck water and thought their own private thoughts.

She saw herself leaving the island, leaving Sebastian. What irony. To have wanted so much and to have found it in a man she was not entitled to have.

If Sebastian were an ordinary man, she wouldn't give a hang for what her society might say. But he was the leader of an island republic, trying to bring his people into a modern world which included independence, self-government and economic stability. His mind and his heart were committed to this, not to some love-struck girl from a strait-laced, aristocratic New England family. Even though the Guilford liberal tradition dated back to the time of George III, there was a difference between fighting for an ideal and marrying a cynosure.

Sebastian led Emily to the bedroom. He removed his shirt, the body gleamed in the half-light of the room, the fine film of sweat turning his skin to rich brown satin. "I think I'll have a shower."

She nodded absently, undressing automatically as she heard the water sluice on. In a closet hung her light cotton robe. In the dresser drawer, she felt for a hair brush and took it out. Walking around the room, she brushed her hair with nervous strokes.

Sebastian, a huge white towel wrapped around his middle, emerged from the bathroom and stopped, watching her brush with spastic strokes.

Gently he set her in a chair and taking the brush from her hand brushed her hair slowly and soothingly. He let the towel he was wearing drop, and pulled her up to him. They kissed. Her hands moved up and down the lean curve of his back, lingering at each vertebrae.

His body stood aside and allowed the girl her pleasure as his mind boiled with other thoughts. He would play this dual role now to the bitter end.

When at last he carried her to the huge mahogany fourposter bed and drew the mosquito netting around them, he allowed himself one last tender thought. Here in this bower they would be protected from the outside and everything alien within.

He looked at her graceful body against the whiteness of the sheets, tracing the outlines of her bikini with a forefinger. She quivered under his touch and when she could bear it no longer, she reached for him and brought him to her with a deep sigh.

They made love fiercely, tearing at each other with animal hunger. Underneath it all, Emily felt the bitter sweetness of the lover who knows that each night might be the last. In the middle of their embrace, she remembered the other one. The proudly beautiful black woman. The constant companion, until she, Emily, had gradually moved into Sebastian's life.

Sebastian had never mentioned the woman. Emily had heard of her only through snatches of conversation here and there. How they had met in England. She had been from one of the British islands. A brilliant student. How Sebastian had been able to convince her to return with him and help him put into action some of the ideas he had formulated during the years of exile. Words like exploitation, using, selfish, piled on top of the other thoughts in her mind. Was she next in line for dismissal? And who would her successor be?

She forced the ugly thoughts away by seizing him in a strangling embrace, trying to convince herself through sheer physicality that everything would be all right.

She stroked him with a touch of wonderment, kissing his face, his eyes, his neck, his entire body as though she wished to commit every line of him to memory.

Sebastian returned her lovemaking stroke for stroke, thrilled by her instant responses, the fierceness of her meeting with him. Yet he knew the quality of his lovemaking was different. His mind was committed to other things.

His decision lent a new urgency to his loving. They strained toward each other. He felt himself suffocating as Emily clutched him with a strength that frightened and fascinated him.

No white woman would ever possess him again. No other woman either. At least not publicly. Not until he had achieved what he had set out to do.

She cried out in pain as he assaulted her, they fell back against the pillows, breathing with deep shallow gasps. He collapsed against her, their bodies intermingling wetnesses. With a groan of half-satisfaction, half-reluctance, he rolled away from her and lay on his back staring at the ceiling. There was no room for personal ties in his life now.

And as he thought, he absently stroked her belly. Her knees came up spasmodically.

"Again?" she asked. She stroked him.

"No." He said, but his body said otherwise.

"No?" she cried softly.

That extraordinary physical response seized him again. How amazing it was. This woman with her careful upbringing was as naturally passionate as a guileless native.

Why not, he thought. It's the least I can do under the circumstances. I owe her that much. And he moved on top of her.

He felt her frenzy, her fright and knew that she knew.

Emily, with Sebastian deep within her, strained to him one more moment, knowing in her love, he would leave her.

She cried. With every thrust of herself, she cried silently. It isn't fair. Why are you doing this to us, Sebastian? Is everything else more important? Is this how you did it to her? In bed? In a lover's embrace?

He felt the tears spill on his shoulder and held her closer.

Emily melted under him and cried his name over and over.

He held her for how long he didn't know. Her pain gave him guilt. Yet it was necessary. Someone always had to be hurt.

She finally fell asleep against him. He lay awake until the room lightened with dawn, then fell asleep, too. His dreams were hideous and ugly and he awoke with a cry that froze her. It was the cry of an animal caught in a trap. She felt the wound invade her heart.

# *Saturday*

THE TASTE of too many cigarettes, the stale smell of alcohol exhuding from pores were the first things that David noticed when he awoke Saturday morning. As he stumbled out of bed to look out on the morning, he felt the rockiness, a nagging pain flashed across his forehead. He pulled one of the blinds down to see the day. Its brilliance added another dimension of pain. He tried to focus on his watch, waiting for the black hands to form some visible pattern. It appeared to be eight. Karen lay on her back, breathing heavily, one hand thrown out over his pillow as if to reassure herself, even in sleep, that he had not disappeared in the night.

He tip-toed to the bathroom and turned the shower on cold, then stepped under its needle spray, gasping from the shock. He let the water pour over his head for a full minute, willing himself to stand the sharpness of the cold, then moved it to hot. When he felt his eyes clear and his brain unfuzz, he stepped out and into the folds of his terry robe.

The mirror sent back a steamy fun-house reflection of his face: eyes dissatisfied, hostile, puffy from too much drinking. He surveyed its lines, wondering whether to shave or not—and decided not. He didn't have to impress anyone. Besides, it felt a little raw from the too long exposure to yesterday's sun. Better to give it a few more hours rest. He scrubbed his teeth viciously, trying to wipe away the stale taste in his mouth with clouds of foaming toothpaste. His hands combed his curly sandy hair to no avail; he attacked it with a brush.

Returning to the bedroom, he carefully and quietly looked for a pair of bathing trunks and a shirt, then decided to forego the trunks for a pair of khakis. No point in getting more sun on top of his tightly stretched skin. He pulled the trousers on, gingerly feeling the stiffness in his sunburned knees as he straightened them. Goddamn. He felt awful. The best thing now was to leave the room before Karen awoke and go pour some orange juice and coffee down his throat. Now that his teeth were clean, he felt the dehydration that followed drinking too much. Would he never learn not to mix his drinks.

He slipped out the door. Karen had not stirred, thank God for that. The marble floors felt cool and pleasant to his feet. He held his rubber thongs in his hands and continued to tip-toe down the halls, then stopped with an embarrassed smile. He didn't have to worry about waking anyone out here.

As he passed through one breezeway, he found himself in front of Emily's cottage and stopped, hand outstretched. He looked at the door, deciding whether to knock. He wrestled with himself, then taking a deep breath, knocked softly. No answer. He tried again, rapping more sharply. Still no answer. His hand reached for the knob and turned it tentatively. It opened easily and with a daring that surprised him, he stepped through the door and stood cautiously looking around the room, ready to run if discovered. The room was pleasantly murky but even in that dim light, he could see the still made-up bed. He felt a wave of shock and nausea sweep over him and furiously he backed out of the room, slamming the door.

Now his step was determined. He arrived poolside and stood with his hands on his hips, belligerantly, as if expecting an immediate confrontation with her. Then he realized how foolish he looked, especially since the entire area was deserted—with two exceptions. Simon sat under an umbrella sipping coffee and reading the *Times*. At the far end of the pool, Duke lay soaking up the sun.

David's presence had obviously set up vibrations, for Simon looked up and seeing him, called, "Good morning. We seem to be early birds. Come join me if you like."

"Thanks," David replied grumpily.

"Bad night?" Simon inquired.

"No worse than usual. How was yours?"

"Rather interesting, actually. You as a writer might find it so, too."

"Oh. How so?"

"What's your impression of the island so far?"

"Typical Caribbean-island-in-the-sun stuff. Looks like paradise, but probably seething with all sorts of underground currents and pressures."

"Damn close." complimented Simon. "I have reason to think the island is in trouble. Matter of fact, I'd like to do a little nosing about today. Interested?"

"Depends. What exactly do you mean by trouble?"

"Well, I was in the middle of a little scene last night that tells me all is not well in Paradise. That Sebastian Lalange has problems on his hands."

At the mention of Sebastian's name, David's headache magically disappeared; he leaned forward. "Yes, what happened?"

"Why don't you get your breakfast and I'll tell you while you eat," Simon suggested.

David hastily grabbed some juice and coffee and

was back at the table before Simon had finished his sentence.

"I don't know whether you noticed, but the girls and Rod, that young stag, and I left early last night."

"I vaguely remember."

"We went to one of the native clubs for some good music." And Simon recounted the evening's adventure. His English sense of the dramatic encouraged him to take the long way around the evening, describing it in complete detail, painting mood and texture. David suffered with controlled impatience until Simon reached the moment of the arrival of Emily and Sebastian. Then his impatience knew no bounds and he interrupted Simon frequently with questions. When Simon described the leave-taking, it took no genius to put together the rest of the evening. David's imagination took over and he saw Emily and Sebastian, nude in the night, making love and a knife of jealousy stabbed his gut. He was surprised by the irrationality of his feelings. When he caught Simon staring at him curiously, he discovered that in his anguish and anger he had completely bent his spoon out of shape. David stared at it foolishly. Then cooly bent it back.

Simon continued. "So, I thought perhaps it might be interesting to poke around town, ask some questions. There might be a story there. At least I can get some background and pictures and have a leg up when the time comes for such a story."

His cool, objective writer's mind prevailed and David looked at him with grudging admiration. "That sounds like a goood idea. Maybe I will tag along."

"I want to load my cameras and get some stuff together, so why don't we meet out front in, say," Simon rose and looked at his watch, "about fifteen minutes."

"Good. I'll just leave word with Karen where I'm

going." David was feeling a little guilty. "Oh, by the way, have you rounded up a car?"

"Yes, Grov's lending me the Rover. Good man, Grov."

As Simon left, he almost collided with Jane Perceval and Margaret Bradley.

"You're up with the dawn," he smiled in greeting.

"Early tennis," Jane explained, "before it gets too hot. Bill's been playing almost an hour already."

"Quite a chap, your husband."

"I think so," Jane smiled back. At least sometimes I do, she reminded herself. Bill had been trying very hard to make this seem like a real vacation. But Jane, from years of analyzing the unspoken words between them, knew he was feeling edgy about the Arleo affair. For his sake, she truly hoped it amounted to nothing. He could ill-afford a scandal in his administration, especially after making corruption such an issue in his last campaign.

The two women, ensconced under an umbrella, accepted juice and coffee from one of the waiters. They had taken on a healthy glow from the day before and in their proper tennis whites, they were the epitome of two Town & Country ladies of breeding.

They chatted quietly as they enjoyed breakfast. Chatting that woman-trivia of children and colds and allowances and dating. Jane still had young children to worry about while Margaret's had left the nest to make their maiden voyage in the waters of international society.

"Well, at least one thing I've managed to escape is this young drug scene. I don't think I would have been able to cope with it." Margaret sighed.

"No one's ever able to cope with it. I dread the day when it happens in our family," shivered Jane.

"It doesn't have to happen, does it?" Margaret always felt strong family ties were enough to protect any child. "After all, the children must know they have a responsibility to their father's office."

"One would hope so, but children—even ours—aren't particularly impressed with exalted offices. The Mayor, the President and the shoemaker are all the same to them."

"What's that about the President?" said Bill Perceval, his white Lacoste shirt wringing wet, as he leaned forward to kiss his wife on the cheek.

"Nothing really, I was just telling Margaret about our cool children."

"Oh, our local chapter is quite a handful. By the way, Margaret, I was playing doubles with Harold Thompson. Have you met him yet?"

"I know who he is, but I hadn't noticed him here."

"No, he's not with this crowd. He has a house here on the island, likes to play tennis with Grov, so they invited him over for doubles. We were talking about Phillip."

"Oh." Margaret blushed, but didn't ask what they were talking about.

Bill obligingly continued. "Yes, I didn't know he was behind that huge neighborhood project."

Margaret looked at him with curiosity.

Bill was befuddled by Margaret's expression. "You mean you don't know about it either?"

"I'm not sure what you're talking about. I know Phillip's involvement with community projects, but I don't think I know which one you're talking about."

"That huge neighborhood project in Brooklyn. It was his money and his influence that put that whole thing together. I knew there was someone behind that thing but he seemed to wish to be anonymous. But Thompson and I were talking about the concept in terms of other neighborhood rehabilitations, and he suggested going to the real source. I was embarrassed to say I didn't know who the real source was. Well, Thompson told me. I don't know why I was surprised. Phillip was the logical one. His work over the past twenty years should have been clue enough."

Margaret listened with rapt attention as this glowing picture of public service and dedication was limned in by a sophisticated political figure; then wondered why one part of her felt such a glowing feeling of pride and the other part a twinge of irrational fear. Again her neurotic vulnerability, her fright at the brutality she felt lurking in all men would not permit her to place complete trust in this man. All this because of one man's betrayal? Did he give her a chance, show warmth, tenderness and understanding when she needed it? But, the nagging reminder was there, didn't she disappoint him?

"Margaret, if you'll forgive me," she turned as Bill interrupted her chaotic skein of thought, "If you'll forgive me for being presumptuous, I think you're a very fortunate woman to know a man like Phillip."

Margaret smiled with embarrassment. Jane, her woman's antenna picking vibrations, looked at Bill warningly. Don't, it said. This is a woman in trouble with herself. Don't force it.

The strained moment was shattered by the phone's ring. All three breathed a sigh at the reprieve. Bill had a premonition it would be for him and he was right.

He signalled to the waiter his whereabouts when his name was called and within a minute of answering the phone knew the dam was about to crack. Curtly, he spoke into the mouthpiece, "Let me get back to you in a minute. We need to talk this over in private."

Jane's face tightened, had it come at last? All the little prickles of warning, all the little edgy signs she knew so well said "trouble."

When Bill excused himself, she remained with

Margaret toying with her coffee cup and lighting one cigarette after another. Finally, she turned to the other woman, "Margaret, would you mind terribly if we postponed our tennis for a bit? I think Bill might need me. You understand?"

"Of course," Margaret had too much breeding to ask even the most innocent questions. She could see Jane's distress, even if Jane tried to cover it with her public calm. Margaret even found herself grateful that Jane had this little human failing. She had always felt intimidated by Jane's cool composure. She was like the Kennedy women, always in control in any situation, showing the united family front against any odds. And now Jane had cracked the image somewhat by showing concern. Didn't that make her just the least bit more like everyone else? Now that Margaret had accepted Jane's frailty, her concern for her concern rose.

Jane stood up and turned as if unsure of her direction; then aware that Margaret's eyes were watching, she pulled herself together and headed toward the cottage.

She opened the door softly. Bill was sitting on the edge of the chair with the phone in his hands, waiting impatiently for his call to go through. His fingers were making an arpeggio of taps on his knee. He looked up when she entered. A sudden look of annoyance, or was it embarrassment, crossed his face.

Jane prowled around the room as Bill continued to drum his fingers nervously on his bare knee.

"Yes, now, I can talk. What's going on? What have they found out?" Bill's face gathered into an intense frown of concentration as he listened carefully. Jane watched him with trepidation, looking for a clue to the conversation on the other end. She longed to break in and ask but knew better and leafed abstractedly through a magazine as she waited.

"I can't believe it" Jane heard Bill say. "Do they know for sure or are they just guessing?"

Jane knew what they were talking about and had her fears justified as Bill said. "I'm going to ask Arleo directly."

She averted her face at this remark.

"What do you mean I can't ask him? Oh, I see what you mean. No, of course, I won't call him from here. I'll ask him when I get back to the city." A few more cryptic remarks passed and Bill slammed the receiver on to the hook, staring at the silent instrument.

"Well," Jane asked, "what was that all about? I don't have to ask, do I?" Bill looked at her, anger still tightening his face. "O'Hara thinks the press has the evidence to pin a graft rap on Arleo."

"How could they?"

Bill replied angrily, "It seems they have a source I don't have."

"What do they say he's done?"

"You know the park that abuts the International Mart Tower?"

"Yes."

"Well, it seems that Arleo has taken $50,000 under the table to give them the rights to close off the park."

"Is that legal?"

"Yes, because when they build—and we've given them permission to build right up against it, they must close off the park. Flying rubble or falling material could mean a big damage suit."

"So what kind of problem can that cause?"

"I didn't think there could be any. But it seems that Arleo has made a separate deal whereby the city gets and he gets."

"I don't understand," said Jane.

"Ok. This is the way it works. The building people give the city x amount of dollars which will be used to restore and modernize the park after the building is finished next year. That was agreed to with Davidson. Now, when Davidson left and I appointed Arleo in his place, he obviously renegotiated on his own and requested the builder make another contribution. The builder agreed to give the city a deal which would be half cash and half work.

"So what's illegal about that?"

"Nothing, except the price on the work which probably would not be more than $10,000 turned out to be $50,000. That means that somebody got $40,000 and it wasn't the city."

"So they think Arleo pocketed it."

"They don't think, they have proof, it seems. Somebody blew the whistle on him."

"Who, for heaven's sake?"

"Would you believe the builder's brother?"

"I never heard of anything like that. What would make a brother turn on a brother?"

"Conflict of interests. One brother started to sniff around the other brother's deal, greased a few palms and loosened a few tongues and there was Arleo right in the middle."

"Why don't you phone Arleo right now and find out how much is true?"

"It would be too easy to trace a phone call from here and by the time the press got hold of it, it would look like collusion."

"I'm not really surprised. You know how I always felt about Arleo."

"Jane," he said sharply. "I refuse to go through this 'I told you so' nonsense again."

"But . . ."

"Forget it. I'm not condemning this man before I get the facts from him. He deserves the chance to tell his side of the story. If he's guilty, I'll take care of it."

"If he's guilty, it'll take care of you," she replied acidly.

Bill stared at her. She seemed a stranger. Why was she being so pig-headed about Arleo just because his name was Italian.

Jane stood her ground and looked at him cooly. Inside, she didn't feel cool. She felt fear and anger. Fear that he might have this career he worked so hard for go up in smoke. Anger because he didn't have the instinct to recognize a shady character when he saw one.

"I'll get to the bottom of it and that's all that's important. I'll have everyone on the carpet if I have to. I'm not going to have my administration smeared by innuendo."

"Your administration or your image? How public do you have to make this? What about us?"

"What do you mean?"

"How close will this come to us? You, me and the children? How far do you really want to go?"

"Look Jane, let's not talk about it anymore. I'm going to go for a walk. I want to do some thinking."

He left the room without another word and Jane felt the tears well up in her eyes.

Bill, his head down, hands clenched in the pockets of the tennis shorts he still wore, bumped into Simon and his big camera bag.

"Oh, I beg your pardon. Well, you look like you're off to take some pictures," Bill's automatic public smile creased his face.

"More than pictures. I think I'm on to something big. David and I are going into town to do a bit of sniffing around. There's some big undercover stuff going on, I think, with our handsome Prime Minister in the middle."

Bill looked at him sharply.

"Might be something to interest you. Would you

like to join us? You're probably an old hand at this sort of thing."

Perceval stiffened imperceptibly, the smile returned to a thin grim line. The only story he was interested in lay two thousand miles north. Had this young Englishman—after all he was a journalist of sorts—heard something concerning him or was it a mere coincidence that this island had troubles just as his island did? Better not chance it. He declined stiffly, pleading a previous date.

David rounded the corner just as Perceval cut into one of the stone stairways leading away from the hotel and towards the beach. David waved and was surprised when Perceval seemed to ignore him. "What's bugging him? He cut me dead." David observed.

Simon watched Perceval disappear. "He cut me dead, too, more or less. I invited him to join us, but he was barely civil in his refusal. Oh well," Simon remarked airily, "The affairs of state and all that . . ."

"O.K.," David smiled, "Let's get the show moving"

They drove quickly toward town, discussing possibilities on the way. Simon spotted a parking space and pulled the Rover into it. Even before they stepped out of the car, they were aware of the oppressive heat as soon as they stopped. They moved quickly under the portico which offered some slight protection from the blazing sun to anyone foolish enough to be out shopping in the heat of the day. The shops they passed were fairly typical of the little shops found in any tropical island town, a conglomeration of necessities and trinkets including the amulets and candle trappings of voodoo practice. The shops were singularly unappealing to the tourist trade, a far cry from the tempting treasures laid out for them in places such as Bermuda and Nassau. "Let's see what the local weed's like," Simon suggested indicating a small tobacco shop, devoid of any other customer.

The two of them entered and tried to strike up a conversation with the young black behind the counter. But their questions were answered with monosyllabic indifference.

"Laconic lad," Simon said as they found themselves out on the sidewalk once more.

"Probably seen too many American movies."

In another shop they picked up the island newspaper, and glancing down at the headlines while waiting for his change, David once more attempted to draw the native into a conversation. Here too the indifference he met with bordered on the rude.

After two more attempts at drawing out the tight-lipped shopkeepers had failed, Simon suggested sarcastically, "I could use a drink to wet my whistle after all this gay banter." David nodded his agreement and the two of them headed into a dark, almost deserted bar. The heat inside was even more oppressive than it was outdoors, and as the two of them stood uncomfortably in the determined silence of the bartender, Simon said, "I think we'd better split up. I want to get to Lalange. There's a better story there for my readership. You know, handsome black leader, takeover and all that sort of thing. And you might do better on your own."

David readily agreed. He had one good reason for not wanting to meet Lalange. And the novelist in him was more interested in the human side of the story. He also felt that the opportunity to discover what they wanted was best accomplished by operating alone. Together they were obvious intruders. No one could be more blandly indifferent than these soft, slurry, French-speaking natives, when they wanted to be.

"Why don't we meet back here in about two hours?

We can slip in for a tall cool one and compare notes, if you like," David suggested.

"Good thought," Simon agreed.

They synchronized watches and went off, each in different directions.

David ambled toward the center of town, not knowing what he was looking for or who might open up to him. He wasn't worried, knowing it would happen without his pushing. It always had in the past.

The town simmered under the hot sun. Women walked with undulating grace, huge baskets of laundry balanced on their heads, passing him with curiously lowered eyes.

He continued on to the native market place. It occupied one full square. Wares were displayed under colorful umbrellas and make-shift awnings. The fruits and vegetables tumbled out of boxes as sellers sprinkled them from time to time with cold water to prevent them from wilting in the broiling sun. Crates of live baby chicks chirped and defecated, adding another odor to the already redolent air. As he grew closer, voices grew louder. Arab merchants cried their wares from tiny stalls spilling bolts of colorful yard goods on to the street. Their harsh clicking voices mixed with the somnolent tones of the natives while car horns added more noise as they honked warnings to bicycles, motor scooters and pedestrians who got in the way.

The noisy, colorful market area was barely constrained by the cool pillars and columns of dignified white colonial residences, vestiges of the early colonization by the French, who tried to blend the elegance of the Boulevard Haussman with their provincial love of ostentation. The outcome of this strange architectural dichotomy was a group of simple Palladian-type structures, ornately plastered with stone flowers, lions couchant, medallions and fleur-de-lis.

David smiled in spite of himself. This mish-mash of style was an integral part of every out-colony he had ever visited from India to Australia.

The steady hum of noise took on a sharper, more strident note. David's ears picked out some angry sounds and he followed them. They led him to a cluster of natives surrounding what appeared to be an accident. Upon closer examination, David noticed a slim, dark man in white shirt, wide-brimmed hat and—of all things in this heat—a full Che Guevara beard. The man spoke loudly and clearly in crisp French to an audience that seemed totally spellbound.

Although David's French was of the adequate restaurant variety, he was able to pick up the gist of what the bearded man was saying. How many times had he heard just this kind of speech. The only thing different was the language. The point was all too clear. Get rid of the foreign exploiters. David felt quite at home with the subject matter and waited patiently for the speaker to finish.

The speech did not take long. This was not Cuba, after all. The people had other pressing things to do, like go to their jobs.

A scattering of applause mixed with a few boos, and the crowd dispersed, leaving the bearded young militant standing alone in the dense heat.

David approached him. "Parlez-vous Anglais?" He asked.

"Probably far better than you speak French" the young man let a humorless smile creep from behind his beard.

David ignored the sarcasm. "I'm curious about what you were saying."

The man looked at him with thinly-veiled suspicion.

"Interest or fear?"

David controlled his urge to smash him in the mouth, "Interest. I'm a writer."

"Ah, the fourth estate. I write a bit myself."

David thought to himself, I bet you do. Following the master's footsteps, for Che wrote also. "Well, then as one writer to another, perhaps you'd allow me to buy you a drink?"

"If you are paying, I will allow you."

"Is there a quiet place we can go?"

"Everything is quiet on our lovely island." The smile had no mirth in it and the sentence was like an expletive in the slash of his mouth. He took David by the elbow and with a strength that was not quite necessary steered him into the dark interior of a small bar. A fan whirred slowly overhead. Shades of the old Shepheard's Hotel in Cairo, thought David. Like its counterpart, it did little to cool the air inside, just moved it from place to place.

They settled themselves at a table. A handsome Creole in a native skirt approached them. Her walk was like the walk of all of the island natives David had seen thus far: an undulation, un unwinding, as if they moved to a never-ending piece of seductive music heard only by themselves.

The local beer was ordered and poured foamingly into two tall glasses.

"Perhaps we can begin by exchanging names," suggested David. "David Sampson's mine."

"Faisan Lalange." The other man said. When David extended his hand, Faisan hesitated, then allowed David to take his for an instant before he cooly drew it back.

"Lalange? Isn't that the name of your prime minister?"

"It is. We are cousins."

"Cousins? From what I heard earlier, I suppose it is safe to assume that politically you are unrelated."

Faisan lifted his eyebrows and smiled that mirthless smile again. "That is a fairly safe assumption."

"What's the problem down here? Your people seem quite contented."

Faisan parried the question. "You say you are a writer. What do you write? Fairy tales?"

"Hey, hold on. The sarcasm isn't necessary. At least, not yet."

"Pardon my bad manners. I've been out of the country awhile and one forgets the niceties of civilization when one fights for survival."

"Where were you? Cuba?"

"Cuba. Bolivia. Honduras." He reeled off the countries as laconically as a travel agent. "Unfortunately, you see our country as most tourists do. Instamatic paradise. All pastels and blue water and balmy breezes and siestas. Pineapples and coconuts growing within a finger's reach, fields bursting with cane, happy natives dancing and singing and swinging their hips, the harbor busy with boats. Eden on the rocks."

"I wouldn't go that far. Sure, it's a pretty island. So's Granada and Jamaica and Trinidad. But I've been in a few places in my day and I know how to read the signals. It's part of my trade."

"Perhaps this one is a little hard to read. We don't have the obvious exploitation you see in Central and South America. Or the cruel poverty of Bolivia and Peru. Our shanty towns have running water. They are no worse than your Levittowns."

David was surprised at the reference to Levittown but was more interested in other things. "So what's the problem? Your prime minister seems to be trying hard to make your island self-sufficient." David bit his tongue at this praise of Sebastian, but this was no time to let emotion obscure objectivity.

"Sebastian is empire building. As surely and as cleverly as the old French colonials."

"But he's one of you. A native of the island. Surely, that counts for something." David insisted.

"Exploitation is not the sole property of whites. Sebastian learned early here, perfecting his techniques in France and England. He has had a classical education. He is a black man. He is as much a foreigner here as you are."

"But why should that be? Who's better qualified? One of your own people with the advantage of education."

"Ideally that would be true. When we were boys we talked about it often as boys with dreams will do. We discussed for hours how we would change the island. We knew we were out of the mainstream here. Remote. Economically still victims of an old slave system. We hoped to change that one day."

"And haven't you? You're free of France."

"That's the irony. Politically we are not fully a part of France nor free of it. You think Sebastian was chosen by popular election? Hah! He was presented to the island in a travesty of an election."

"A little page borrowed from the Communists?" David suggested maliciously.

Faisan ignored the analogy. "He was hand-picked, trained from infancy for this moment. In school, who do you think was the serious scholar and who the charming dilettante?"

"That's rhetorical, I'm sure."

"So it was the charming dilettante who got the education I should have had."

So, David thought, it begins with jealousy. "Might I remind you of an ugly political truth. The best man doesn't always win. Often it's the man of great personal charm rather than the dedicated idealist." He gave the political career of Adlai Stevenson as an example.

"Yes, I know about him." Faisan said bitterly. His mind drifted away and with an effort he pulled it back. "Oh, Sebastian understands the problems here. But what does he do? Instead of instituting land reforms, he encourages tourism. He lets them build more and more hotels. He teaches the people to weave and make dolls and baskets and encourages the export of the native rum. And all this with the help of his white mistress."

David flushed, "I think if you knew the lady, you'd hardly call her that."

"My friend," Faisan slashed the word of all meaning, "I do know the lady. And you speak like a gallant white man. But let me tell you something. When Sebastian returned from England, it was with a black woman. Island born. English educated. She was an angel. Gifted, tireless, dedicated. How she worked here! I won't even tell you what she accomplished."

"Did they marry?"

"No, although many would have liked it to happen."

"What happened to her?"

"The usual human sacrifice."

"Whaa. ."

"No, no I speak metaphorically. Miss Guilford came on the scene. Sebastian set his sights a little higher and Miss Carmen Langford—that was her name—fell from favor. In our little island chess game, Sebastian chose to play white. Miss Guilford had connections. And Sebastian has always been impressed by connections. Especially white ones. From early youth he learned to suck up to the whites. He turned my stomach. Such gentle manners, such good behavior, such diligence. My God, if his skin weren't black, you would have thought he was Little Lord Fauntleroy. He knew which bread his butter would do on. White bread." Faisan spat out the words. "He would have sold his grandmother if it justified the ends."

David was fascinated by Faisan's hatred for his cousin. There had to be more to it than just Sebastian's success and Faisan's failure. The girl, Carmen? No, it had started before that. "Well, in my country, they call it political expediency. Still he seems to have managed to keep this island stable when you consider what's going on on some of the others."

"Well, we don't need basket weaving. We need our land and we need to work it ourselves, set our own prices for labor, educate our people, give them proper medical care, teach them about birth control, wean them away from witch doctors and voodoo, get them into the twentieth century. We can't do it with hotels and gambling casinos and the poor black man fetching and carrying."

"It's one way," David said to himself. Louder, "So you went to Cuba and learned how to make revolution."

"I learned many things. I learned how to handle exploiters. I learned you don't sit down at the peace table in Paris and talk like gentlemen for months and months, accomplishing nothing while you drink tea and behave pretty. You do it by scaring the shit out of the exploiters," he pounded the table, sending the beer glasses on the floor. "You make it ugly for them to be here and you get your land for your people and control your own destiny no matter what it takes."

"Even if you have to destroy the island to do it?" David asked softly.

"The fire burns everything clean—metaphorically speaking." Lalange combed his beard with his fingertips. David had a sudden urge to laugh. The gesture was so overdramatic, so Mephistophelean.

Lalange continued. "Like the phoenix who rises from his own ashes, so will come our new order."

"That's what Hitler thought. You know it never works like that. You'll have nothing. And in order to rebuild you'll have to make alliances, then you'll be at the mercy of other foreign interests who will be happy to offer you another kind of exploitation. And that's exactly what you don't want."

"The Hitler analogy doesn't work in this case. We are not barbarians and we have no master race, conquer the world theory."

"So better Red than dead?" David asked.

"Ah, so that's what you mean. You think in those ridiculous Cold War terms. That is not the issue here. Self-determination is the issue."

"But aren't you being racist in your own way?"

"No," Lalange spat out the word vehemently. I don't want to see this island go the way of your Virgins or the Granadines. We must develop our own resources, both human and economic. Our people must make their way."

"But does it have to be done violently?"

Faisan smiled with a surprised kind of innocence, "I did not mention the word violence in any part of our conversation."

"You have suggested it or implied it. And your speech earlier in the marketplace was not exactly pacific."

"If it is necessary, it is necessary. No revolution has ever been brought about peaceably. Your own is a perfect example." He leaned forward and locked David's eyes with his.

"Tell me, why do you Americans not understand today's revolutionary spirit?"

"We understand it. Our country was made up of different people then. We had an elite group of thinkers. And I don't mean to put you down. But most revolutionaries, the intellectuals of their society, are few and far between in today's emerging countries. You know that. Once violence gets out of hand, your few leaders will not be able to control it. One of the problems with revolutions is that intellectuals conceive them and violent men carry them out. Probably necessary that it works that way, but rational government cannot be responsibly run by irrational men."

"So you think I am irrational and Sebastian is responsible?" The statement was made without hostility.

"I didn't say that."

"You implied it."

"Think what you will, but I believe you must work with your cousin to bring about the changes you want. Besides your country isn't psychologically geared for revolution."

"Another mistake you make." David looked at him fearfully. Faisan—not wishing to give away his plans—switched to a softer dialectic. "Ah, it's the instamatic syndrome again. Happy natives, full of sun and rum, not caring about tomorrow. You are so wrong, M'sieur le writer."

"Well, I hope for your sake that your differences will be settled without violence."

Faisan leaned back in his chair and smiled a "we shall see" smile.

"For all our sakes," David breathed. A sudden loudness from the door caught Faisan's attention. His eyes narrowed and if a lip can indeed curl, his curled. David followed his gaze. His first thoughts were innocent. His second, when he saw who stood in the doorway, were not.

Duke Dexter, a dazzle of white against his Indian tan, was laughing in his ever-so-amused, high-pitched way. Standing next to him was an unusually handsome native boy. Slender with the high buttocks and arching back of many of the men, he wore faded denim pants cut off at the knee and a soft white planter's shirt. His eyes were slightly averted and there was something vulnerable, almost painful in his brilliant white smile. Duke was talking to him in

Creole French, a teasing, jibing tone of voice, suggestive even to David who could not understand a word he was saying. The boy, if it could be seen, was blushing.

"*Merde,*" Faisan spat out. "That's the kind of thing that makes me sick." Faisan turned to David, his eyes blazing. "There's your society and mine in microcosm. The exploiter . . . the exploited. That degenerate will have that poor dumb idiot running in circles and doing god-knows-what for a few promises."

David was taken aback by the virulence of Faisan's anger. The reason seemed deeper than just exploitation of one man by another.

Before David could answer, Duke had spotted him and moved to the table dragging the boy with him. His mocking eyes rested on Faisan. He felt a thrill of recognition, not for the man but for what lay beneath the angry tautness of his muscles. Duke felt a quickening as Faisan's eyes flicked over him like a stinging whip. "Well, Mr. Sampson, fancy seeing you here." The voice implied similar proclivities and David wanted to smash his too-pretty face with a broken beer bottle. Again that irrational feeling of violence. He was one to talk about non-violence.

"You know this scum?" Faisan said loudly enough for Duke to hear.

"Scum? You call me scum?" Duke was incensed. Little pools of perspiration stained the immaculateness of his white shirt. "Who the hell are you?"

"Never mind, Duke. Why don't you just get the hell out of here. What are you doing with that kid?"

"None of your business." Duke moved to turn.

David was up in a flash, a steel grip around Duke's arm. "Your timing is lousy. And so is your choice for an afternoon's fun. Now get rid of that guy."

Duke wrenched out of David's grasp with amazing strength. "Don't you tell me what to do. What are you up to . . . trying to make an impression on that one with the five-and-ten Guevera beard?"

"Look, I'm warning you. Get out of here. Or you'll be sorry. And I've never been more serious in my life. You're asking for big trouble. Take my word for it. I'll try to explain later."

Somehow David had managed to frighten Duke enough to make him believe him. He looked around uncertainly, then said a few brusque words to the boy who lowered his head and looked at his sandalled feet. His big toe moved up and down as if it were too much to shuffle from one foot to another. Duke turned and marched out.

Faisan stood and took the boy gently by the arm, bending his head close to the boy's ear. The boy whispered a few words back. Faisan listened attentively, patted his head and moved him easily to the door. He turned and stared at David for an instant. And without returning to the table, he called, "Our conversation is over, M'sieur le Writer."

"Hey, wait a minute. I have nothing to do with that man. He just happens to be a guest at the club. Do I get tarred with the same brush?"

"The conversation is over, I said." Faisan was adamant, but then he smiled. It brought a chill to David. "But don't worry, we'll meet again." And without another word, Faisan Lalange left.

David finished his beer and felt sick to his stomach. His instincts—hell, forget about instincts—his judgment said, trouble. But how to warn Shalimar's guests they were in for an unplanned piece of business this weekend? Something that might have dire consequences for them. Consequences? Christ, somebody might get killed.

David peered at his watch. He still had fifteen minutes before he was scheduled to meet Simon. He felt edgy as a fox about to be cornered by the hounds. He threw some money on the table and walked out into the afternoon. The light, blindingly brilliant, sent heat waves shimmering from the street. Deserted now, as people went home to lunch or in for siesta. David felt alone—and not so much lonely —as plain scared shitless.

When David headed for the native market, Simon had gone in the opposite direction toward the government buildings. They stood overlooking the town from the low hills that came down almost to the main street. The narrow area between the foot of the hills and the water's edge, not more than a city block or two wide, was cluttered with small shops and businesses as well as the marketplace. How perceptive nature had been, Simon thought to himself, thoughtfully providing the colonial governments in so many of these islands with the proper above-it-all setting for their government buildings. With just enough room left between harbor and the hills for the natives to cluster. Handy enough to service the government's needs, but at a discreetly and decidedly lower level. Simon thought to himself how those early colonists would feel about a man like Sebastian sitting up there on top of everything on top of that hill. He grinned to himself as he realized, you can take the English out of the colonies, but you sure couldn't take the colonist out of the English.

The day was warm and the sun beat down on him as he climbed to the large white central building which he assumed was where he'd find Sebastian's office. As he stepped inside, he blinked in a reflex manner at the sudden cool darkness. He could see no sign of air conditioning, and yet it must have been a good fifteen degrees cooler in here than on the street. You had to hand it to those colonial architects. Without twentieth century air conditioning to fall back on they had had to use ingenuity and the materials on hand to create a cool haven for the displaced ruling class which would inhabit these outposts of Empire. He looked up and noticed for the first time a large-bladed circular fan hanging from the ceiling, soundlessly stirring up an almost imperceptible breeze.

A black in a uniform that looked more like something that had escaped Covent Garden than the local battalion headquarters, sat at a large desk at the end of the long broad hallway. His eyes were on Simon as he walked the full length of the hall. At first his camera slung over his shoulder made the guard think it was just another tourist—probably looking for the men's room. But as Simon came closer, the size and complexity of the camera, coupled with the well-worn case made him change his mind. He looked up revealing no interest whatsoever in his bland black face as Simon stood across the desk from him.

"I wonder if you could tell me where Mr. Sebastian Lalange's office is?"

"Top of those stairs, third door on your left."

"Thank you," Simon said and turned toward the stairs. Before he reached the first step, he could hear the guard behind him dialing the phone—he'd be expected at least when he got up there. The second floor hall was a lot busier than the one he'd just left. You could tell, things were being run from here, downstairs was just the window dressing. Blacks, almost all in the conservative dress of Western businessmen moved easily from office to office and through open doorways, he could see black secretaries looking a lot like the ones he'd seen cropping up more and more in New York offices—the Afro hairdo sure, but the miniskirt was straight out of Carnaby Street by way of Seventh Avenue.

The door of the third office on the left stood closed and the gold letters seemed freshly applied: OFFICE OF THE PRIME MINISTER. He tapped lightly and when there was no answer tapped again.

This time the door was opened by another guard resplendent in the same uniform of the one downstairs. He stood blocking Simon's entrance, silently.

"I'd like to see Mr. Lalange." When the Black made no movement or in any way indicated he had heard Simon, he pulled out one of his cards and handed it to him. "I met Mr. Lalange at Shalimar last night."

Without glancing down at the card, the guard stepped aside and indicated with a motion of his hand that Simon was to be seated in one of the leather chairs lining the large well-proportioned room, Simon looked quickly around and saw that he was the only white man in the room, although most of the other chairs were occupied. He'd have plenty of time to wait, he was sure. He settled back, lighted a cigarette and cursed himself inwardly for not having had the sense to bring along something to read. He glanced around the room several times, but tried not to appear to be staring at or studying the others who were all waiting to see Lalange. On the panelled walls of the room he could see the faint outlines where massive portraits must have hung in years past. The only decorations in the room now were framed posters urging hard work, unity, and further education. The posters were done in a simple style but their vibrant colors made them seem both primitive and charming. He would like to have photographed them, but was afraid of upsetting the neutral balance in the room's atmosphere by bringing out his camera.

The guard had disappeared behind one of two doors that opened out of the room. A native dressed in a business suit came out of the other, crossed the room and left. Shortly afterwards, a tall slim girl came out of the other door, holding Simon's card in her fingers. She was dressed in the native costume, swirls of brightly colored cotton skirt reaching almost to her ankles over layers of ruffled petticoats, a fairly low cut blouse also of cotton, and a brightly patterned scarf tied around her head. She looked more like a native entertainer than a secretary, but that was evidently what she was. She came directly to Simon, who stood up as she approached. Then speaking in a voice that was just barely above a whisper said that Mr. Lalange would be delighted to see him if he would just wait a few minutes. Without waiting for a reply, she turned to one of the others seated there and indicated with a nod of her head that he follow her.

Simon glanced down at his watch, hoping that he would have time for a talk with Lalange before he was due back at the bar to meet David. The men waiting with Simon moved in and out of the two doors at fairly regular intervals, and when only one or two of the men who had been there before him were left, the girl returned and asked him to follow her. She led him directly into Lalange's inner office. The furnishings indicated either a catholicity of taste, or a complete lack of interest in such details. It was an eclectic mélange of colonial trappings, modern functional pieces and native handcrafts. Somehow Lalange himself managed to dominate it all as the tall handsome figure stood up to greet Simon.

"I'm sorry to have to keep you waiting," he said in that polished accent Simon found so disconcerting. "But to have let you in ahead of those who had been waiting, might have been misinterpreted and been politically unwise. I'm sure you understand," he added with a smile that was both ingratiating and sincere.

"Of course, I do. I should have called ahead for an appointment, but I was in town and thought you might possibly spare me a few minutes. I'm very grateful that you could see me.

"The press is always welcome here. Too many island leaders have run into unnecessary trouble by alienating newsmen. It's a mistake I'm trying to avoid." He offered Simon a cigarette from an ornately chased silver box, and took one himself. As they both seated themselves, he asked, "Now what can I do for you?"

"Just talk a bit about what you're doing here, what you hope to do, and let me take a few candids as you talk. My readers, for reasons I'm sure you're aware of, are vitally interested in these newly emerging countries. And it would be mutually helpful I'm sure if we could give them a little understanding as well as satisfying their curiosity."

Sebastian nodded his agreement, and as he spoke of the beginnings of St. Phillipe as a free country, Simon divided his attention between taking hurried notes, and adjusting his lenses. While Sebastian spoke, he moved softly around the desk, peering through his viewer, and clicking away for at least a dozen shots of the prime minister seated at his desk. By then Sebastian had finished the recap of his island's brief history as a separate country, and was talking of the current problems and future possibilities.

"I'm afraid the time has past when we can make it on our own strictly as an agricultural country. And without any natural resources other than our magnificent climate, we are hoping to attract a large tourist industry."

"I was going to ask you about that, as a matter of fact. The few dealings I've had so far with the islanders . . . they've seemed to resent the tourists. It's not just my thin skin either, David Sampson—you met him last night . . .

"Yes, I remember Mr. Sampson," Sebastian interrupted.

"Well, he noticed it too."

"I've been afraid of that."

"But why if they need the hotels for their economy do they seem to resent the tourists so?"

"Oddly enough it is all part of their emerging pride in themselves. In order to convince them they were ready and able to govern themselves, part of my job in the past has been to build up their own self-esteem."

"And now you feel you've done too good a job?"

"Not that really, self-esteem is good for a man and a nation—especially emerging men and nations. Unfortunately pride can also be a powerful weapon in the wrong hands. It can be twisted, made ugly, to serve unfortunate purposes."

"And that's what's happening now?"

"I'm afraid so. This newly found pride plus a certain amount of ignorance which we have yet to overcome is being used by self-seeking troublemakers to stir up emotions and cause dissension."

"You mean, to take over?"

"To take over—yes. And to replace what we hope to shape into a benign socialistic democracy with another communist satellite. Their propaganda and their methods are as unmistakable an export as their cigars. And the most dangerous practitioners of this philosophy are our own people who have been trained there."

"Has this been happening to many?"

"It needn't be many. Actually one or two of these well-trained, highly motivated men can do the job. Too many of them, in fact, and they are at each others throats. They've been careful about that. The man they have trained has come back and trained his own people in his own image. He is a powerful and dangerous man. For he knows the people—perhaps even better than I do—and he knows the way to reach and mold them. He has a very convincing story if you are young, aware of this new pride in yourself, and not too well educated."

"Are you so sure education would protect your people from such ideologies?" Simon asked.

"If not from such ideologies, at least from such obvious men. And I don't just mean the kind of education you get in the classroom. I mean a certain sophistication my people lack completely. They are far too unused to governing themselves to understand compromise and its uses. And you know that's something the French and the English have been getting by on for generations."

Simon wondered for a moment whether Sebastian was putting him on or down. But before he could decide, Sebastian continued.

"Unfortunately my people still see everything in terms that are quite literally black and white. They recognize no gray areas of compromise. They are childlike in their simplicity."

Simon noticed the slight edge in his voice, the definitely disparaging tone. He wondered if it was not the white blood surfacing in this proud black.

The man was far more complicated than he had originally thought. But he had neither the time nor the ability to get deep into Sebastian now. He'd have to keep to the safer shores of the present political situation here in St. Phillipe.

He put his camera down for a few minutes and for the first time, took a really hard look at Sebastian, wondering what actually motivated this complex man. What went on behind the handsome façade, the almost too-ready smile. He remembered having read the sparse little pre-packaged news service stories that reported the transfer of power from white to black hands. Certainly there had been nothing in those carefully worded communiques to indicate any dissension, or even any real competition for the post of the first black Prime Minister. To the world outside, the transfer of power from the French to the natives had appeared not only orderly and smooth, but welcomed on both sides. Simon could see why the French would choose such a man to succeed them. He would be far easier to handle than some untrained wild-eyed radical black. He was trained to their ways, and they most certainly knew his.

Long before the actual election, the break between Sebastian and Faisan had been complete. When Sebastian had returned from England, sporting a polished new accent and an even more polished Carmen Langford, Faisan had taken a perverse kind of pleasure in seeing the two of them as much as possible. At first there had been an easy give and take among the three of them. Their banter covered up for a good deal of the strain that grew as Sebastian moved steadily and surely toward the goal for which he'd been preparing his entire life.

Carmen became an integral part of his plan, through happenstance as well as design. She had from her first days on the island been deeply touched by the pitiful educational facilities alloted to the native children. And she began an untiring campaign to see that they were improved. Not only did she badger the French officials, but she worked closely with the children herself. She became a well-known and deeply revered visitor to their classrooms. There was hardly a child on the island who hadn't in some way been affected and benefitted by her presence and her efforts.

As Sebastian saw her popularity and influence on the people grow, he realized that she too could help him step into the Prime Minister's office. He made a point of having her at his side whenever he was seen or photographed in public. He even briefly considered marrying Carmen. But he rejected the idea. Not because he was necessarily a loner, but because something within him wanted the prize to be won strictly on his own, won not with the acknowledged help of anyone else.

As the political differences between Faisan and Sebastian grew, Carmen was drawn ideologically toward Faisan, although physically she was never anyone's but Sebastian's. He recognized the fact that an alliance—even a mere political one—between Carmen and Faisan might present a large stumbling block.

The transfer of power was still over a year away when Sebastian decided that the three of them were seeing entirely too much of each other . . . and being seen together too often. It was at this point that he came closest to marrying Carmen. But he decided to try one other means to his end first. And it worked.

Sebastian accused Carmen of being in love with Faison and meeting him behind his back. He carried on in jealous rages that were only partly feigned. For although he was cocksure that Carmen had never shared any bed on the island except his, he did resent and fear her growing attachment to Faisan's ideas.

Carmen was as surprised as she was delighted by these fits of jealous rage. And as they have since time began, they worked beautifully. She agreed never to see Faisan again, and Sebastian accepted her promise and appeared placated. He was even more pleased very shortly after this when Faisan left St. Phillipe for Cuba.

With Faisan out of the way, Sebastian had been sure his troubles were over. He had no way of knowing that Faisan would return with renewed determination and a bag of newly learned tricks that made him a far more serious threat than he'd have ever been had he stayed on the island. All Sebastian knew at the time of the election was that Faisan was away, Carmen was at his side, and the transfer of power went just as he had planned it would.

Of course there was no way for Simon to know any of this as he listened to the black man smoothly field all his questions while appearing to answer them openly. He had no wish to appear to downgrade the natives over whom Sebastian obviously felt he was in such complete control. But it was Sebastian himself who had first indicated some of their weaknesses.

"Even with their limited sophistication, I still don't see how this troublemaker could have turned your people against tourism," Simon went on, "surely even the least educated among them must see the kind of money that would bring to their island?"

"By using the pride we were speaking of a little while ago. That plus fear. He tells them that the hotels will be using them merely as servants, making 'Uncle Toms' of them. They are not sophisticated enough to realize they can take pride in any job or work if it is well done and provides them with a decent standard of living. They are eons removed from the kind of society you find, say in Denmark, where the garbage collector gets extra money because of the unpleasant nature of his work."

"Yes, I can see how pride could be used against tourism, but how could fear be part of it?"

"My people are being told that the hotels will be coming to the island with the idea of buying up all their land—right from under them. They cannot see that the half dozen or so waterfront spots that would be suitable for commercial development are not being farmed even now. Faisan—for that is his name—and his followers keep driving home the threat to the islanders that the developers will not stop until they have wrenched every tiny farm from its owner. The proposition is ludicrous in the extreme, but to an uneducated man who has just within the past few months wrested the control of his land from centuries of rule by outsiders, it is an easy story to sell." Sebastian glanced down at his watch, and Simon did too.

"I'm afraid I've taken too much of your time," he said, slipping the lens cap back on his camera and shuffling his notes together.

"Not at all—but I see it's time for lunch. Would you care to join me in one of our island restaurants—run by natives, of course," he said flashing Simon that dazzling smile again and winking broadly.

"I'd love to, actually, but I'm to meet David Sampson back at Mubar and I'm a little late for that now. But if you're going out, perhaps you'd let me take a few more shots of you in town."

Sebastian readily agreed, picked up his hat, a straw plantation overseer's hat with a broad, slightly curled brim, stuck his head into his secretary's office to announce his departure and preceded Simon through his outer office—deserted except for the guard—and out into the hall.

Simon took a few stock shots, with native child, with beaming mother, with gates of office, the stuff that tugs at the hearts of the gentle readers of the silent majority, regardless of country or national origin.

Simon spotted David pacing nervously back and forth in front of the bar. He saw him check his watch several times in the interval it took him to walk the block with Sebastian.

"David, ho! I'm sorry to be late." Simon called.

Sebastian approached, hand extended, "It's entirely my fault. Forgive me. I had a roomful of people."

David barely able to contain himself at the sight of Sebastian, managed to pull himself together and maintain a cool civility.

"Lalange, interesting coincidence. I just met a gentleman who has the same last name. Is it a common one down here?"

Sebastian gave David a hard look. "No, it's a rather uncommon one, as a matter of fact. So the man you mention must be my cousin."

"We had an interesting chat."

"Oh? He has some rather startling ideas, wouldn't you say?"

"Frightening, I'd say. Aren't you concerned?"

"Well, every government has its share of detractors and troublemakers."

Simon interjected, "Well, it wouldn't be a democracy without a vocal minority."

"If this vocal minority gets its way, it won't be a democracy much longer."

Sebastian took a large handkerchief from his pocket and patted his forehead with it. David watched him with some amusement. Was he sweating because of the temperature or the sudden palpable tension? Simon, unaware of the tensions around him, mentioned Sebastian's suggestion of lunch, but David, under the pretext of getting back to Karen, politely refused, asking to make it another time.

"Then gentlemen, let me say *à bientôt* and let you go on to your pleasures at Shalimar. I'll most likely see you both again Sunday to wish you bon voyage."

Sebastian shook hands with the two men, then crossed the street. They watched his receding back disappear around the corner.

"David, don't you think it would have been a good idea to lunch with him?"

"Yeh, under any other circumstances but these. I've got to talk to you and fast. I couldn't in front of him."

"Let's get in the car and we'll talk on the way back."

Simon got behind the wheel and they were off in the direction of Shalimar. As they drove, David described his conversation with Faisan Lalange. Simon's eyes left the road periodically to stare at David and his agitation.

"So, I think something is going to break on this island and damn soon."

Simon interrupted, "David, are you sure you're not just overreacting to some hothead? My conversation with Sebastian certainly convinced me that he is aware of what's going on and has the situation in control."

David remained unconvinced. "He's a smooth operator, I'll admit. But a politician's a politician and he sweats when he feels his power slipping. Besides Faisan is no ordinary hothead rabble rouser. He's cool, he's trained and he knows exactly what's up. And," he paused dramatically, "he is dangerous. I know. I've met his kind before."

Simon grew silent and remained so for the remainder of the drive, while David drew deep into thought. Maybe I'm overreacting like Simon said, David thought, after all this is a vacation. But the nagging premonition remained. He could put on his tourist face, but he couldn't throw that off.

Having fielded the invitation to join David and Simon on a trip to town, Perceval cut through the lush foliage and headed toward the beach on a little-used path, hoping to avoid the other guests. The beach stretched before him, unruffled by the presence of any living creature beyond a handful of beach birds, busily finding their dinners with each receding wave. It was just what he needed. A place where he could be alone with his wildly warring thoughts. A chance to release some of his pent-up tension with a little exercise. He didn't have the concentration for a hard fought set of singles, though the exercise would have done him good. Even yesterday—with a lot less bothering him, he'd been no match for Wilcox. He wasn't anxious for a rematch until his concentration was a lot better.

Maybe Jane was right, maybe he was overreacting to this first hint of scandal in his administration. But if the reporters were onto something, and it all came out while he was basking in the sun, it could cause irreparable harm to his image and his political future. He'd been elected mayor on promises to clean up the rampant corruption in City Hall. He'd been guilty of some bad blunders those first few months —those strikes one after another had tried everyone's patience. Now all that was behind, and the pollsters claimed his image was even better now than before the election. He'd never forgive himself, and neither would the voters, he knew. He hadn't come all this way to have his next moves blocked by some minor official's peccadillo. God, here he was himself already judging Arleo guilty. With nothing but a couple of rumors to go on! Maybe Jane was right about that, too, maybe politics had made deeper changes in him than he cared to admit.

And yet if she were so sensitive to inner changes in him he wasn't even aware of himself, how could she possibly have asked that question? Every political reporter in town had done at least one piece on his ambitions for and chances at the White House. Could she really be so naive as to believe that the height of his ambition was that pandora's box, City Hall? Unless you were one of the old-style political bosses, content to use the spot to curry favor and line your own pocket, who in God's name would want the job? In a city that size, the number and variety of problems were infinite, the number of solutions available pathetically few—and each solution seemed to bring on another problem or alienate another group. There couldn't even be personal satisfaction in a setup like that. Your hands were tied by the system which made you seem responsible for the city's ills, but kept you almost powerless to prevent or cure them. But difficult as the job was, it was still top spot in a city big enough to attract nationwide attention and headlines. City Hall—like so many other buildings in that city was a showplace. The city itself was both a great showcase and a training grounds, its ethnic mix, if anything even more irreconcilable than the national one. He was making no overt moves now—far too soon. And that plum on Pennsylvania Avenue always seemed to elude those who were too anxious for it. But he had to keep his skirts clean—his Captain Marvel image buttoned up.

Surely Jane must realize that. Any politician's wife would have to. And yet that was just the problem, Jane wasn't *any* politician's wife. And when he had married her, neither one of them had any inkling that she would ever become one.

Perceval had never regretted his choice, in fact he hardly ever thought about having made a choice. There always seemed to be such an inevitability about it all. Their families had had neighboring beach houses in Maine in one of those old towns where second generation summer people were still regarded as newcomers. It had always just been assumed that one day they would marry.

Those first few years in politics when he had been a young Congressman, the "show liberal" of his far-from-liberal party, Jane had been as enthusiastic about his work as he was. But something had happened lately. She seemed not only less committed, but actually anxious to get out of it all. Certainly her ambitions for him—at least in the political arena—had not grown as his had. She seemed to resent his work, more so with every passing day.

He was sure she was too young to be going through a change of life. But it was damned certain she was going through a change of heart. He wondered, but just fleetingly, if another child might be the answer. Now, just before it was too late. It would occupy her mind and her heart as well as all those hours she now spent alone. And into the back of his mind crept those irresistible baby pictures that would be such sure fire campaign material. Mentally he chastised himself for even entertaining such a thought. And, my God, if any member of the women's liberation group could see into his mind then, he'd lose that block of votes for all time.

For a brief moment, he wondered if she might perhaps suspect something about him and Suzanne. But she couldn't. He'd been far too discreet. Jane was sophisticated enough in the ways of politics to know that every candidate was surrounded by a magnetic field that proved irresistible to a certain type of well bred, long-legged, devoted young woman. Besides, she was straight arrow enough to have accused him openly if she suspected anything like that. Despite the fact that she heartily disliked what he was doing and where he was headed, he had to admit she was really the perfect politician's wife. She handled herself in public beautifully. And if she added no real glamour to his ticket, God knows she would never bring any shadow of disgrace to it either. He just wished all the people he'd gotten into bed with politically had worked out as well.

With all this and more on his mind, he wasn't sure how far from Shalimar he'd walked. Looking back, he could not see the club, but by then the beach had taken him into a cove surrounded by fairly high, lushly vegetated hills. Feeling as isolated as he had for so long, he was quite startled to find himself just a few feet away from Sandy Gramson, working at a portable easel. She was as engrossed as he was in her own private world, her back to him, facing the northern curve of the cove and with its towering hill above. He was actually quite close to her now, and afraid he might startle her if he spoke suddenly. He wished he had called out when he first spotted her.

To avoid this he turned his steps in the direction of the water, hoping she would catch sight of him out of the corner of her eye.

Sandy was, as always when she painted, deeply engrossed in her work, working quickly as the medium demanded. She had that enviable ability to find in her work complete detachment from her surroundings and whatever problems were bothering her. It was as though the concentration of the eye and the hand was all her mind could handle at the time. She was, of course, aware of her surroundings, but she had the self-discipline to limit her awareness to that area which she was trying to capture in her water colors. So it was not until Perceval was actually some way down the beach from her when his path crossed her view that she became aware of him. She called out immediately.

"Hi! I thought I was alone here."

He turned, oddly relieved that she had made the first gesture. "I did, too, as a matter of fact—until I almost stumbled into you and your easel a moment ago." By now he had retraced his steps and was within a few feet of her. Her easel stood between them, and he nodded toward it. "May I?"

"Of course," she said, stepping back from her work to allow him an unobstructed view.

"That's really lovely," he said, and meant it sincerely. He was quite right. Her work had a delicacy of line, which, combined with the soft almost muted colors she chose even here in this exotic background of florid colors, gave her work an undeniable charm.

"Do you like it?" she asked with the undisguised eagerness of a child.

"It would be impossible not to. It really is charming. Have you been painting long?"

"Just a little over a year. I find it wonderfully relaxing."

"You must find it enormously satisfying as well."

"I've never really thought of it that way, it's just something I do for relaxation and to amuse myself."

"May I see the other things you have in your portfolio?"

She bent eagerly and unsnapped the smart leather portfolio into which she had slipped the other two paintings she had done that morning. She held them up one at a time for his appraisal, and he found them equally as charming as the one on her easel.

"Have you ever had a showing of your work?"

"You must be teasing—of course not."

"But you really should—it's delightful and I know people would enjoy seeing them."

Now his praise truly embarrassed her. She thought what Marty would say to such a suggestion and the very thought of it brought a flush to her cheeks. He misread her blush and said, "There's no need to be overly modest, you know. Think of how you could help your favorite charity with such a show."

"I'll think about it, I promise," she said slipping her paintings back into their case. She straightened up and turned once more to the work on the easel.

"I won't interrupt you any longer, then," he said as he started back in the direction from which he'd come. "But do give serious thought to a showing, will you?" he called over his shoulder to her.

She smiled and nodded her agreement, waving him off with one of her brushes still in her hand.

He had been serious in his suggestion and he hoped she realized it. He would bring it up again in front of someone else before the weekend was over—that is if he had the chance, he thought to himself, once more letting his mind return to the problems that had driven him out on this walk in the first place.

Sandy had gone on painting after Bill ambled back down the beach toward Shalimar and another uncomfortable confrontation with Jane. It had been the first time anyone other than her instructor had ever encouraged her or admired her work. And Sandy never knew how much of his praise was really honest or just to insure her continued lessons. Perceval's praise had delighted her immensely. Perhaps he had been right, maybe she should arrange a showing. She might even try a small one here on the boat. It would give Marty a chance to show off the *Cassandra* without appearing obvious about it. And here there would be none of his New York friends and rivals whose opinions he seemed to value so, or the press who always considered him fair game.

Although Marty had never expressed himself about her painting, she knew he considered it just another whim and would never take it seriously. But then he never took anything seriously that didn't affect him personally—or his precious "share of the market." Yet he had never objected to her taking lessons. Then again how could he? Her instructor was one of those harmless effeminate types who covered up his basic problem with a rippling display of muscles and a gaggle of lady painters who always surrounded him. Marty had accurately sized him up the first time he had driven down to the Village to pick her up after one of her lessons.

After inspecting the studio and some of Ralph's work, he had said to her when they were barely out of earshot, "If that guy ever stopped flying around, he might make something of himself as a package designer." Grudging but definite praise from a man whose idea of a work of art was a package so well-designed, it upped the sales of a slow moving product.

Marty that afternoon was finding time hanging heavily on his hands. He was thousands of miles from his office where the bowing and scraping of underlings always acted as a tonic to his ego. He hadn't seen Joy in five days—though he'd spoken to her at least once a day on the ship to shore radio while they'd been at sea. Still he missed her presence and the stimulation of her ideas as they batted sales problems back and forth.

Sandy had said she was going to do a little painting today—and had been gone since lunch. He wasn't a drinker, or he'd have probably spent the afternoon in the bar. He found the changing atmosphere there fascinating, in the way a small boy finds any new toy engrossing. He had already told Joy about it and said he was thinking of installing it in their executive offices. They'd just moved into Manhattan's latest marble marvel and the bills for the original "do" by one of New York's poshest decorators were still coming in, but these picture walls really turned him on, the idea of a whole room being made to reflect something as transient as his moods appealed to him mightily. He had told Joy to start looking into finding someone in New York who could do the job. Knowing Joy, she probably had the whole thing buttoned up by now with at least two estimates for the work on his desk. It wasn't in her bailiwick—this sort of thing—she was really supposed to be in charge of sales promotions and advertising. But through the years, of working together, a closeness had developed between them. It was the marvel of an industry that doted on stories of the revolving door for executives at Gramson's. Now he shared everything with her. He was sure she wouldn't resent being asked to do this latest thing, and he was right.

Marty was no more of an athlete than he was a drinker, and so the afternoon hours were stretching ahead of him endlessly. After completing his third call that day to his office, he left his cottage and started to wander around the club. He thought vaguely of trying to put together a gin rummy game, but didn't really think he could with this bunch of sybarites. As he roamed restlessly about, his thoughts turned to Denise and his footsteps became purposeful rather than meandering. Married to that tennis pro turned international yo-yo, she must be almost as bored as he was, he reasoned. And every previous encounter he'd had with her had given him no hint that she would reject his advances. He knew his women well enough to have spotted her—she wasn't one of those damned teases who lead you on only to retreat behind a façade of assaulted virginity when you made your first move.

He crossed the cool white expanse of the lobby deserted in the mid-afternoon stillness and stepped out on to the terrace surrounding the pool. There she lay just as he had first seen her at breakfast. As close to nude as even today's loose morality allowed. She was lying on her back, the shells still covering her nipples and tiny plastic eye shades over her eyes. He walked quietly over to her, and stood staring down at her, and it was only after he had fed his lust with a long appraising look at every inch of her that she spoke, and he noticed for the first time the thin slits in the plastic eye shades she wore.

"See anything you like?" she asked.

"Ummm—I'll take one of each." He'd been startled to be caught in the act of sizing her up, but his recovery rate was fantastic.

"I thought you'd be off playing on your yacht this time of day," she said, still not moving a muscle.

"I would if I had someone to play with." He was not much for the niceties of this preliminary part of the game.

"Poor darling," she said with mock sympathy heavy in her voice. "What happened to your lovely wife?" And before he could answer, continued, "Too heavily burdened by all those jewels to be up and around?"

"Too busy playing with her paint box to care what happens to me. I'm deserted and depressed. And I need cheering up. It'll give the place a bad name if I'm seen wandering around in this depressed state."

"Then I suppose it's my duty to cheer you up." She let out a mock sigh as she sat bolt upright. Again the adherence of the two tiny shells made Marty marvel. "Do be a darling and toss me my top, would you?" she said indicating the upper half of her bikini on the arm of one of the nearby chaises.

"Don't feel you have to dress, just to cheer me up," he said, handing her the top. Then as she held it to her, he hooked it behind her, taking advantage again of the opportunity once more to stroke her skin, now glazed with a warm film of tanning oil.

"There's not much I can do to cheer you up here," she said with a sweeping gesture which included both the pool and the surrounding buildings. "I'm not good at word games."

"Then we'll keep the talk to a minimum," he assured her, helping her up, and pulling her toward him. "C'mon, I'll show you a few things that'll open those half-lidded French eyes."

She pulled back slightly from him, but still holding his hand and said, "I bet you will—I've never been on one quite so big." They could have been talking about the *Cassandra*, of course, for by now they were walking down the steps to the club's dock.

Hearing them coming, the crewman in the *Cassandra's* tender, had slipped the paperback he'd been reading under his seat. He stood up, saluted smartly, dropped down on the seat next to her, and as the boy turned and looked up the stairs to the club —Marty said, "Let's go—no one else is coming."

Once on board, he was more than ready for the main event, but she continued to tease, insisting on being shown all over the yacht. As he tried to hurry her from one lavish room to the next, she took a perverse pleasure in pausing here and there along the way asking where he'd found this lamp, or that objet d'art. She was driving him up the richly paneled wall. He had tried to show her the master bedroom first, but she had stood hesitantly in the doorway and said she wasn't "quite ready for that—there must be lots more to see in a boat this size." Now they had seen and been in every room on board except the master bedroom.

"Ready or not," he said, pushing open the door, "I'm running out of marbles to show you."

"Let's hope not," she whispered into his ear as she stepped in front of him and into the room.

"Make yourself at home" he said gesturing toward the huge circular bed. He unbuttoned his linen blazer and slid his ascot off with one gesture, revealing his bare almost barrellike chest underneath. Her back to him, she had slid off the top of her bikini and wiggled out of the bottom half. She was leaning over the bed, pulling down the heavy silk cover, revealing the eiderdown puff and the Porthault sheet turned back over it, when with a suddeness that shocked her, he was upon her. His weight carried her down onto the bed beneath him. There were no preliminaries. He turned her over, with one hand as he held his weight from her with the other. And in an instant he was down on her hard. Her eyes widened at his thrust, but she made no sound. He came fast and hard and there was no time for her to even simulate satisfaction if she had wanted to. It was only then that he spoke for the first time since they'd entered the room.

"We'll try some of your more sophisticated French ways next round. I don't like to be kept waiting."

"You should have brought your clippings."

"Jesus—that reminds me—I forgot to ask Joy how the press was in Houston on that designer tie-in show." Even as he spoke, he was pushing her aside. Her body, which only moments before had been the cause of his powerful drives, now was merely an obstacle between him and the phone. He glanced at his watch and realized he could still catch Joy at the office, if the operators would just get the lead out.

The sun was beginning to drop precipitously and the colors were deepening—losing their intensity. Sandy had done as much as the light would permit that day. She carefully wiped her brushes, rinsed off her palette in the surf and packed up her paints and brushes in the specially designed kit which Hermes had produced to Marty's specifications. She had been more pleased with this indication of some interest in what she was doing than with all the fabulous jewels which preceded and followed it. More pleased until a chance remark by Joy at one of their parties had made it obvious that it had been her idea and not Marty's. And not just her idea, but her design as well. The one gift from Marty that had meant so much to her because it seemed to involve a certain amount of personal feeling, became just another in the string of lavish but thoughtless presents with which he tried to make up for all that was really lacking in their marriage.

She walked slowly down the beach in the ever deepening twilight. The *Cassandra*'s tender was not at the dock, and she had forgotten her signal horn. As she stood there wondering how she would attract one of the crewmen's attention, Rod pulled up in the speedboat he'd been using for the water skiers.

"Anything I can do?" he volunteered.

"I wonder if you would take me out to the *Cassandra?*" she asked hesitantly as he involved himself with the routine of tying up the small powerboat. Without looking up, he quickly undid what he'd been doing, "Sure hop on," he said, helping her into the boat with her easel, paints and paintings.

"I'm sorry to put you to all this trouble," she said dropping down into the low seat next to him. "But the tender's out there, and I've no way to signal it. I didn't want to clutter up our cottage with all this," she said with a nod toward her painting equipment.

"No sweat—I've been hoping all day for an excuse to get a closer look at your yacht."

"Would you like to come aboard? I'll be glad to show you around, if you'd like to see her."

"I'd love it!" Rod said with an enthusiasm that was wholeheartedly felt.

By then they were alongside the *Cassandra.* Rod carefully maneuvered the boat up to the foot of the stairs. Sandy was surprised to find no one on the deck to help them secure their boat. But Rod was an expert and quickly had the boat securely tied up. He helped Sandy up the stairs, carrying her painting equipment for her. As she stepped onto the empty deck, she said, "Just leave those things there, someone will put them away later."

Rod's eyes were as large as saucers. He'd seen picture stories on the *Cassandra* in the flossier fashion magazines but somehow even the best photographs hadn't captured that ineffable something that said money down to the smallest detail. He followed her into the main saloon with its curved bay of glass looking out onto the rear promenade deck. She walked over to the built-in bar that revealed itself only when a great wall of books and paintings slid noiseless to one side.

"Would you like a drink—or a tour first?"

"The tour—if you don't mind."

"Of course not. I'll just ring for one of the crew to take you down to the engine room, I'm sure that will interest you most. Then you can meet me back here for a drink."

After she rang, a crewman appeared so quickly that Rod was convinced he must have been lurking in the passageway right outside the door. Sandy told him to show Rod around the boat. As they left, she dropped the ice she'd put into her glass back into the bucket. She'd clean up first she decided and wait till Rod got back to have a drink with him.

As she stepped out onto the deck she noticed that her painting equipment had already been picked up and put away. She knew Marty paid top dollar for his crew, but was still amazed at their efficiency and loyalty. Marty was right, money could buy anything you really wanted. After all it had bought her, she thought to herself.

She pushed open the door to their bedroom and was surprised to find him stretched out on the bed, the phone cradled in his shoulder. He was making some notes on a pad propped up on his knee. The door had opened so silently, that he was unaware of her presence. She was about to step into the room and head for the bathroom when she became aware of two things simultaneously: the splash of color on the beige rug where Denise's bikini lay, and the sound of the shower running. She stepped back into the passageway, closing the door silently behind her. Her head pounded with the effort she was making to control herself. She slumped for a moment against the passageway wall, then quickly pulled herself together afraid one of the ubiquitous crew would find her there. Of course they must know what had gone on there this afternoon—and yet there hadn't been a flicker in Tom's eyes when she had asked him to show Rod around. A cold chill ran through her and she headed back to the main saloon quickly. She poured herself a stiff drink—and swallowed it down straight up. This was no time for ice or her usual "splash." The liquor burned all the way down and momentarily took her mind off what she had just seen. She looked about the room quickly making sure she was leaving behind no trace that she had been there. Then rang for a crewman.

"Would you see if you can find Tom and Mr. Brigham, I'd like to go back to shore now. Tell him I'll be in his boat." She poured herself another drink—this one not quite so long—and swallowed it down.

Then quickly crossed the saloon, the deck, and started down the ship's stairs to the club's boat. Once in it she never looked up, afraid of what she might see, afraid of the confrontation it would mean. As she stared out over the water where the setting sun made a blinding path of psychedelic lights, she prayed that Rod wouldn't run into either of them. So deep was her concentration, that he quite startled her when he dropped down on the seat next to her. She hadn't even heard his steps on the stairs.

"I'm sorry if I kept you waiting—that's some boat!"

"I just changed my mind and decided to clean up and dress at the club." She searched his face for some indication that he was covering up or dissimulating, but there was none. He turned his head quickly, loosening the lines that held the boat, but not so quickly that he missed the heavy smell of whisky on her breath. He shrugged inwardly—funny she didn't seem like the kind who was a secret juicer. He wonder what the hell she had to drink about.

What *did* she have to drink about? To the women who read the women's pages and the gossip columns and the fashion magazines, Sandy Gramson was the luckiest woman in the world. Luckier than Princess Grace or Jackie or even Elizabeth Taylor. A jewel collection to make Harry Winston's mouth water, museum quality paintings and a town house, newly refurbished and decorated in the most authentic of authentic antiques, closets full of clothes, and a life of charity balls, opening nights and vacation junkets to all the four corners of the world. And she was pretty—to some even beautiful.

Sandy got to the door of their cottage, barely making it to the bathroom as the waves of nausea swept over her. She bent over the sink, dry retching sobs wracked her body. She turned on the cold water and dunked her feverish face into it.

How much longer could she face this kind of life with Marty? Not that she wondered about Marty's possible affairs. He was so busy, he barely had time for them—or did he? She didn't keep tabs on him. It was Denise. It was the choice that upset her. Denise had a cool, confident sexuality that she felt she lacked. But it was more than that. Why would Marty give her the most flamboyant luxuries of life, yet deny her the one thing she really wanted. Was it love/hate he felt for her? Was she just another possession? Or did she give his life a stability and a flow that he needed? He could just as easily have remained single after his first divorce.

Although Sandy was very skeptical about the psychological explanation for life, she thought now of Marty's background. The grinding poverty, the ugliness of the tenement he was raised in, the crime rate in the neighborhood, the determination and ruthlessness with which he raised himself out of his background and the dizzying speed with which he had achieved his success. Was this all over-reaction?

But even more important, why did she marry him? To show her ex-husband that she could attract one of the country's most eligible, successful entrepreneurs, because she wanted security and a father for her two children, because she was afraid, because she loved him? How could she not love him? When he courted her, he was the charming, thoughtful lover. What was there about her that attracted him? She had never asked, just had been willing to accept the fact that this dynamo had chosen her above the Joys and Ingas and Gretchens and Marias and how many other exotically named models and society females that had filled his life.

Somewhere under the veneer of success there was still the frightened, unsure needing man she had instinctively recognized when they first met. And perhaps that's what really kept her with him. Waiting for the day when Marty would again turn to her and say, "Sandy, I need you." That's what it was all about.

She wiped her tear-stained face with the Porthault towel and moved to the bed. Wearily she sunk down, the towel still in her hand and curled around it as a child does with a security blanket. The Porthault security blanket. It was ironically funny. She laughed and the laughter turned to tears. The security blanket became a crying towel.

Margaret Bradley stepped out of her shower and into the folds of her towel—Shalimar's, not Porthault's. It would never have occurred to her to bring her own linens. She moved around the room aimlessly as she dried herself. The mirrors threw back her image. She carefully avoided it. Margaret was not the kind of woman with a healthy curiosity or ego about her own body. She rarely looked at herself nude, avoided it actually, as if her body was some sinful receptacle she had to carry around with her. She never touched herself or examined herself as other women might have. As a child she had once been caught by her mother doing just that and the horrors of hell had been painted in such searing tones, she had never forgotten it. Even during her marriage, she cringed when her husband insisted on looking at her naked body. Sex for her in those days was a hideous necessity. After the girls were born, she used her body's discomfort as an excuse to avoid contact with Hal.

Margaret did not hide from the new morality. She had heard about the Masters and Johnson theory. She had even listened to the stories of affairs told by bored friends. She simply did not relate any of this to herself.

Then why did she suddenly find herself in such a disturbed state? She drew the towel away from her body and with a half-determined, half-fearful step walked to the full length mirror and gave her eyes permission to look.

The spare body reflected back long, slender legs, small rounded breasts, an almost flat stomach. Not a Playboy centerfold, she blushed, but nothing to be ashamed of. Then why was she?

It was Grov. He had triggered this whole appraisal. That accidental conversation a few hours ago.

Margaret had prowled around Shalimar that afternoon. Restless, irritated. Finally, she had wandered over to a small, secluded point overlooking the sea. There, from some mysterious source, the sound of good music wafting over the quiet beauty of the scene had drawn her. A hammock strung between two trees, swung in the light breeze, beckoning her. She had flung herself into it and as the breeze blew softly, the Debussy nocturnes had lulled her into a more restful mood. She made her mind a blank and rested in a state of non-thinking suspension until she sensed she was not alone.

Grov Wilcox had appeared around the corner giving a smile of such honest pleasure when he discovered her that she hadn't the heart to turn him away. With his innate kindness, sensing he was intruding, but loathe to leave, Grov had made himself as unobtrusive as possible and asked permission to share the music with her.

Margaret generally had a low curiosity level about other people's private lives, but somehow she had found it piqued by the Wilcoxes. They seemed so ill-suited. Grov, so crisply English, all manners and slick gloss. Denise wanton, sensuous, French, her appetite for living written in every line of her body. How do people so completely different find each other? Or better what do they find in each other to bring them together? As Margaret pondered, the sweet stillness was broken by the sound of a speedboat. Both she and Grov looked in the direction of the sound. The *Cassandra,* anchored in the cove, had just given up two passengers.

Margaret turned to Grov, "Isn't that your wife?"

Grov peered through the distance. "It seems to be." He didn't seem surprised and Margaret tried to hide the sudden nasty thought flashing across her mind.

"I guess she wanted to see what the *Cassandra* looked like. I know she's been curious."

Curious, that was a curious word for Grov to use. She would have expected him to show concern, seeing his wife leave that luxury liner in the middle of the afternoon. No, it was late afternoon already.

"Gramson seems to be coming back with her."

Margaret looked at Grov sharply. She wondered if he shared her suspicions.

Then Grov had done an odd thing. "You think I'm a little silly I bet. But I think a marriage is good when two people are getting what they want out of it. No other standards should be applied."

Margaret flushed and stammered. And Grov went on.

"Denise is a provocative woman. Most women would assume she was up to something. I know what people think of her. But they don't really know her or me, for that matter."

Grov had leaned back and launched slowly into a story of his first marriage to a wealthy, Englishwoman of the minor nobility. From what he left out, Margaret assumed she had been a coldly beautiful, austere woman who had given Grov very little warmth or love. Then he had met Denise and his life had taken a complete turn. She had been honest, direct, uncomplicated. She seemed to understand and fill his needs completely.

He had talked in general about first and second marriages, then asked her quite bluntly why she had never remarried. When Margaret blushed, Grov apologized.

Yet, she found herself warming to Grov and talking to him with an intimacy that astonished her. When she mentioned Phillip's name, Grov nodded in recognition, telling her he was sorry that Phillip had not come to the opening of the club.

As they talked about need, loneliness, and the marital state in general, Margaret thought of Phillip and it took quite a wrench to return her attention to Grov's conversation.

"You should marry again," he had said. "You're a lovely, well-bred, kind woman. And I think you need a man. But not an ordinary man."

She was touched by his sensitivity and her eyes filled with tears.

At that point, Denise and Marty had arrived at the top of the steps where Grov and Margaret were talking. Without a word, Gramson continued on to his cottage.

Denise's head moved back and forth between the two. Although Grov did not have a suspicious nature, Denise did. For a moment, she wondered, then dismissed the thought. That cold fish would never do anything out of place.

"Hullo, love," Grov called. "Come join us."

Denise blew a kiss in Grov's direction, "Later, *cheri*, I'm full of salt spray. I'll take a shower, then meet you in awhile. All right?"

A man like Grov. A man like Phillip. How alike they were really. Margaret thought back now to the little scene played earlier. And now the slender image of Phillip rose in her eyes. Gentle, patient Phillip.

Why should she keep holding him at arm's length? He had never done anything to cause suspicion or fear in her. How much longer would he wait? How unfair it was to him to tar him with the same brush as her ex-husband. How could one even compare them? Yet she was afraid.

Her head pounded. Maybe she should see a psychiatrist and get to the bottom of her problem. Yet Grov had seen through her. It must be easy. Of course, she didn't want to be alone. She was forty-three years old now and still attractive, but for how long?

Soon, she might be giving second thoughts to face-lifts and silicone injections and hormones. Most of her friends were already making plans to go to Switzerland in the restless search for youth.

Trivial as she thought they were, she found herself suddenly understanding their sad, desperate attempts to hold on, even to surrounding themselves with beautiful young men. And how they laughed, brittle, self-hating laughs, over the latest peccadillo of their paid companions. Yet under the brittle laughter, there were cries for help. Oh, dear Lord, not that for me. Margaret felt the tears rush to her eyes again. I'm going to call Phillip. I need him. It was the first time she had dared admit it to herself. The acceptance of it surprised her and finally, for the first time in years, she felt a calm.

Rod had watched Sandy disappear up the steps to her cottage, then finished securing the power boat to the dock. He thought to himself how differently money affected people. Sandy somehow seemed to have guilt-feelings—but those two gals this afternoon sure didn't. Maybe they didn't have as much of the ready as the Gramson's but he was sure there was plenty wherever Daddy kept it tucked away. You might envy them their money, but you sure couldn't resent them. They were far too likeable, too much fun, too ready to share. He wondered what they were up to now, and decided to clean up and see if he could run into them in the bar before the big hoedown tonight.

At that moment Pammy and Buffy were engaged in two of their favorite pasttimes: dressing and chatting. Their current topic: Karen Sampson. She had seemed so lonely and so ill at ease having breakfast by herself that morning that the girls had asked her to join them when they went waterskiing. She had been reluctant at first, but the girls were so persuasive she had given in and gone along. Although she seemed to be enjoying herself, she never lost her shyness, despite the open friendliness of Rod and the girls. Even Tiger had gone out of his way to be endearing, following Karen about all day, and flaunting his whole bag of look-how-adorable-I-am tricks.

Karen had been grateful for their interest. Despite it all, she had not really opened up to any of them, holding herself, not aloof, but withdrawn as though to have revealed herself would have left her open to criticism or ridicule. She was desperately unsure of herself and appeared to be even more so in contrast with the easy self-assurance of the girls and Rod. His was that lazy self-assurance of someone who has perceived the temper of the times and made it on his own, beholden to no one. Supporting himself with his own talents, his God-given body and its capabilities trained by him to be the instrument of his survival as well as his pleasure.

Pammy and Buffy, on the other hand, had natural self-assurance that only real security can produce. They had been born into the most sheltered of all possible worlds, and would undoubtedly never leave it except for the next. They had inherited their money and position as had their father and grandfather before them. And along with the old money had come the old sense of values. Marriage was for life, home is where the heart is and all that sort of thing.

Although they would never openly flout the establishment they were not prudes. Like their Victorian ancestor who had amassed the family fortune, they felt there was a place for experimentation, but it must be kept in its place. Today's hippie would consider them hypocrites, but their refreshing openness made that seem too harsh a judgment. If they were allowed one or two words to describe themselves, happy and normal would have to be the words they'd choose. Those who marched to a slightly different drum, were considered a little odd, more to be pitied than censured. Into that category fell Karen Sampson.

"Poor thing seems frightened to death. I wonder why," Pammy mused, stepping out of the shower.

"What would she have to be afraid of?"

"Maybe of him."

"Hardly seems likely—he acts more like a father to her than a demanding husband. Have you ever noticed how he kind of keeps an eye on her all the time?"

"I think it's her drinking he's watching—not her."

" 'Mmm that does seem to be a problem. Did you see how her hand was shaking this afternoon?"

"Maybe she's on something stronger!"

"Oh, honestly—I'm going to have to cut you off from the *Daily News* if you don't stop seeing addiction in every corner."

"But what would a girl like that have to drink about?"

"That we'll probably never know, but what I wonder about is what he sees in her."

"She's a pretty little thing."

"And half his age, too. But that's not what I mean. A literary lion like that used to prowling the better watering spots of the world must have had a pretty dazzling bunch to choose from."

"Maybe she told him she was pregnant."

"Oh, how working class can you get?"

"It happens in the best of families—ask our neighbor Mrs. Bradley."

"Oooh, that's right. I forgot about her carefully nurtured little flower. That had to be the most expensive shotgun affair ever."

"Maybe David just wanted somebody to worship at his feet."

"It's hardly flattering if your number-one fan is so plotzed she can't tell your golden prose from her laundry list."

"She probably didn't drink when he married her."

"Or maybe he thought he could save her from herself. There's a lot of that humanitarianism jazz in his books."

"If she keeps on drinking the way she is now, she'll need a keeper more than a humanitarian soon."

"Maybe she uses her drinking to hold onto him."

"I've never seen anyone that insecure. I'm sure she'd come apart completely if he did leave her. Do you think he ever would?"

"Why not? He left his last wife for her didn't he? That small thought probably creeps into her more sodden reflections often enough to make her damned insecure."

"He may be no chaser, but did you notice him with the little shopkeeper last night?"

"I saw they were dancing—I never did get close enough to hear what they were saying, but you don't act like that when you're discussing the weather."

"Well if he's keen on her, you have to admit his tastes are diverse at least."

"Don't think Karen missed it either. She never takes her eyes off him."

"Every girl should have a hobby."

"Honestly! She should get a therapist."

"And we should get a drink—don't you love that insane little bar?"

"Let's get Dad to do a room at the beach house like that."

"Super—but let's not let Dad pick the pictures! Wrap around Dow Jones averages!"

"Or the class of '40 at Yale!"

They giggled as they scooped up chiffon scarves and tiny bags. "What about our furry friend?" Pammy asked at the door. They turned and saw Tiger curled up on his flotation jacket, a custom-made curiosity from Abercrombie and Fitch.

"He looks too pooped to play."

"Let's just leave a light on and a couple of doggie doughnuts on the rug for him. In case he wakes up ravenous."

"Has he ever woken up any other way?"

"If overeating is a sign of insecurity, pound for pound he has to be the most insecure piece of fluff on earth!"

"Makes Karen look positively like the Rock of Gibraltar."

"Let's see how she's shoring herself up tonight."

When they got to the bar, it was comfortably crowded with other members of the club, all looking tanned and relaxed after two days. The conversation had reached a level that underscored the music cued to the changing pictures covering the walls. As the guests moved about, their tanned skins or the expanses of their dinner jackets momentarily caught and held changing pictures giving the entire room an existential look. As soon as you stepped into it you felt and became part of it. There was no awkward waiting for that first or second drink to take hold—for the person next to you to provide you with an opener. It was wraparound, wall to wall party, and you slipped into it as easily and completely as you did into your bath.

Pammy and Buffy were barely halfway across the

room when Rod caught sight of them and was at their side. "Where's the wild beast?"

"All tuckered out, poor darling," Pammy answered in mock seriousness.

"Obviously he's not in the same shape we're in," Buffy giggled.

"Obviously," Rod replied, "and too bad for him he isn't" he added, slipping an appreciative arm around each girl and heading them toward the bar. "How 'bout a blast before dinner and the native dancers?"

They joined Simon at the bar and Rod ordered a round.

"You're looking a bit down in the mouth, darling, did the empire just lose another colony today?" Pammy asked.

Simon smiled quickly, "If they have, word hasn't reached me as yet, but then the local courier system leaves much to be desired."

"We missed you today", Buffy said. "Rod took us water skiing out beyond a fascinating little island."

"Yes, it's adorable, all deserted and terribly Robinson Crusoe looking!"

"We're taking a picnic lunch out there tomorrow. Would you like to come?"

"I just might, as a matter of fact. Providing, of course, there's no big story to cover here."

"What big story could possibly happen here?"

"Duke's towel might clash with his bikini!" Pammy suggested.

"That might make eyes roll, but hardly heads," Simon smiled.

"Surely you weren't thinking of anything *that* violent?" Pammy said, the anticipation making her breathless.

"You never can tell—in these native uprisings" Simon said, half seriously.

"Native uprising! You can't be serious!"

"Well, actually *I'm* not, but our friend over there,"

Simon nodded in David's direction, "the one who manages to find a best seller in every change at court, seems to feel there's real trouble here in our little corner of paradise."

"Whatever makes him think that?"

"We were mucking about in town today, and he had quite a revealing chat with one of the local troublemakers—a native with just enough Cuban training under his belt to be dangerous, or so David thinks."

"Ooooh, maybe we should cancel our picnic tomorrow," Buffy suggested.

"Don't be silly—there isn't a single native on the island we're going to, and besides if any do come, we'll just throw coins into the water for them to dive for."

"You've a marvelously deep understanding of native politics, I can see," Simon teased her, "but if I were you, I wouldn't discuss your ideas with Mr. Sampson. He's a bit uptight about it all."

"He's not the only one—look at Marty Gramson over there. He looks like someone just slipped alum into his bath salts."

Rod was right, Marty did look agitated as he stepped into the bar, now reflecting giant jungle flowers from all sides. The guests appeared to be tiny magical figures in some exotic garden.

Marty had been surprised to find Sandy already dressed for dinner when he returned to the cottage from the *Cassandra*. She seemed strangely withdrawn, and he was sure it wasn't just his conscience making him imagine things. No sooner had he come in, than she stood up and said she was leaving and would meet him in the bar.

He was hoping they might have a drink together in the room, and suggested it instead but she was firm. She had said she felt cooped up and claustrophobic in the room, and would have a drink with him in the bar as soon as he was dressed. He was more disappointed than he cared to admit even to himself. It was a funny thing he realized, but everytime he did grab a piece away from home, it merely made his desire for Sandy stronger. Somehow his extra curricular activities made what he had at home seem all the more desirable to him. He would have liked to discuss this with Sandy, but knew that he never could. He'd even be afraid to bring it up with Joy, although he was sure she'd understand.

Marty had never felt the slightest need for a psychiatrist, though he felt one advantage of having one was being able to tell him anything that came into your mind. He wondered if under any circumstances he could ever bring himself to reveal his innermost thoughts and feelings to anyone. He doubted it very much. Even during those hard working early days when he and his brother had struggled together to launch their cosmetics line, when they seemed to be living out of each other's pockets, there was still some wall, some barrier that had kept Marty from revealing himself completely even to Harry.

In the end that had been a good thing—how else could he have so easily eased Harry out. For he knew a lot more about Harry than Harry had ever known or suspected about Marty. There was still a streak of the urchin street fighter deep inside Marty somewhere, and it made him a vicious competitor, a deadly enemy. It kept him, too, from being open even with Sandy. Although at times he desperately wanted to be.

He saw her now sitting in a corner table with Perceval and his wife. Whatever had been bothering her back in the cottage, certainly didn't seem to be bothering her anymore. She was all smiles and lively chatter. Seeing her that way, and knowing that his presence would undoubtedly change all that, he hesitated a moment before crossing the bar to join them. He stepped up to the bar and ordered a vodka and tonic—then changed the order to a double. While the bartender was meticulously following his orders, Marty looked around. Denise was not in evidence and he was oddly relieved by the fact. Duke was there with what looked like a miniature tape recorder, sitting at the small table with the Sampsons, evidentally taping an interview with the writer. What a tight incestuous little group they represented—each living off one another. He wondered how far Sampson's latest book would have gone if the manuscript had been mailed in cold from some little farm in Illinois, or some tenement in New York.

Marty swallowed the last of his drink and headed for Perceval's table. They did not see him coming in the play of color and light in the room, and when he placed his hand on Sandy's shoulder, she was startled and looked up suddenly. He could see the change of expression in her eyes and it saddened him further. That double hadn't helped at all.

"Is this a private party?" he asked the table in general.

"Do join us," Perceval said half rising in his seat. "We were just trying to talk your wife into having a little showing of her art work. But she's mighty hard to convince," Perceval added, looking directly now at Sandy, surprised to see the obvious change in her manner now that Marty had slipped into the seat next to her. He had his arm possessively around the back of her chair, and he gave her shoulder a little squeeze as he said,

"She's always seemed reasonable enough to me." And turning to her, his face just inches from hers, he added: "I think an exhibit of your work's a great idea. Why don't we have one here tomorrow—on board the *Cassandra*?" Before she could decide whether it was guilt or guile that had made him take this sudden and unexpected interest, he spoiled it all by going on, "that way if the pictures aren't popular, the guests'll have something else to look at."

Perceval would like to have smashed him in the face. He could see what it was doing to Sandy. "Your wife's paintings would stand on their own in any gallery. They've no need to rely on any background for borrowed interest." He could feel Jane's hand tightening on his arm. He had gone as far as he'd better. What had ever attracted a warm woman like Sandy to a beast like Gramson he wondered. He wasn't sure how long he would be able to remain civil to him.

Before Marty could attract the attention of one of the waiters to order another round, the chimes announcing dinner were heard over the music, and the walls of the bar reflected the same cool blue and white paisley of the dining room. Wilcox had had it photographed closeup so that the pattern in the bar became an exaggeration of that in the dining room. The guests quickly finished their drinks and began to drift in to dinner.

As Pammy, Buffy, Simon and Rod passed the table where Duke was gathering up his tape recording equipment, they overheard Karen's remark, "Just one more, please. You know how slow the service is in the dining room." Pammy and Buffy exchanged knowing looks, as David stood up determinedly and said, "Let's go—I'm starved."

That night's dinner was another glorious combination of French cooking and native food. Whether it was because the French had governed here so long it was impossible to say, but the foods which were indigenous to this island seemed to be at their very best when prepared in the French manner.

As the guests were finishing the main course, Grov stood to make the announcement that coffee and dessert would be served at the poolside where entertainers would perform. Almost all the guests drifted out to the pool and took their places at the prettily set tables. Sandy Gramson, pleading a sick headache, excused herself and went to her cottage where she took two sleeping pills and dropped into an obliterating sleep. After David had seated himself before her, Karen left saying she was going to their cottage for some aspirin and headed for the bar. She found it deserted except for Duke.

He was finding the time hanging heavily on his hands with no action in sight. He loathed these native entertainments. Considered them amateur night in black face. At least the bartender could fix a decent martini, and he was finding some solace in that as he toyed with the question of whether visiting the native haunts or having them perform in this exotic palace was the lesser of the two hypocrisies.

Making short work of their desserts, the girls waited for the rest to catch up with them. Pammy toyed with her coffee, but Buffy leaned back in her chair, happily sated and proclaimed just loudly enough for the rest of her table to hear, "On with the bongos and the fire eating!"

"Oooh," Pammy groaned in mock distress, "I couldn't even eat a match after all this."

Conversation around the pool had the pleasant steady hum of after-dinner satiety. An occasional clink of coffee cup meeting saucer, a burst of laughter, the sound of dishes being cleared away. The surface noises were suddenly hushed as a tattoo started on a pair of bongo drums. Several "shhhhhs" sounded as the guests of Shalimar settled into their chairs for the promised entertainment. A small breeze made the candles flicker and ruffled the palm trees. The only sound that could be heard was the rising crescendo of the drum.

Out of the darkness surrounding the tables, as if by some magic a form materialized. The theatricality of the lighting heightened the eerie silent effect of the man's appearance. He was well over six feet tall, so inky black that only the whites of his eyes could be seen. One spot, then another brought his body into sharp relief and now it was possible to see him. His loins were draped in leopard printed cloth, a leopard scarf tied around his forehead, and around his ankles, a bracelet of bones. He prowled around the small clearing as if in a trance and as he grew close to some of the tables, guests pulled back in fear, as if touching him inadvertantly would enchain them in some mysterious voodoo way. The native was sublimely unaware of them, as he prowled in cadence to the drums. Suddenly the drums stopped. He leaped in the air, descended in a crouched position, legs extended, knees flexed, hands on hips. A hand reached out, a torch flew through the air and was caught by his extended hand. The eyes remained in that fixed stare, the whites even more brilliant.

Slowly the native regained his full height, moving the torch in a slow mesmeric circle. In the light of the torch, his body gleamed as if it had been immersed in oil.

The bongos started again, now joined by a reed instrument.

He passed the torch over his body, the flames licking sensuously at the chalky blackness of his skin. Several gasps could be heard.

Buffy's voice rose over the silence, "He can't be terribly sensitive."

Rod put his hand over his mouth, "Don't worry about it. Just keep quiet and watch. It gets better."

The native started to move in frenzied pirouettes,

passing the flaming torch under his arms, between his legs and allowed it to lick at every exposed part of his body.

The bongos reached a crescendo as he passed the flame closer and closer to his face, then stopped suddenly. The torch was held extended in front of the native and slowly, almost with fear, he drew the torch towards him. His mouth opened, a yawning pink hole in his black face. He threw back his head and lowered the flaming torch into his mouth. As the crowd gasped, he whipped the torch out of his mouth and spit flame.

This sophisticated gathering had turned back in time to childhood. Not one face showed disdain or disbelief. It was like the circus, the center ring of Barnum & Bailey over again, where anything could happen and sometimes did.

Now, the native had picked up a jar of colorless liquid and rinsed his mouth with it. He brought the fire back to his mouth. For an instant he seemed to erupt in a burst of flame, then with a mighty expulsion of air, spat out the flame. In the ensuing darkness, the native disappeared as mysteriously as he had arrived.

There was a tentative scattering of applause which brought on the next group in a swirl of petticoats and the lilting beat of drums and guitars.

Buffy leaned back in her chair, "I sure could use a drink after an act like that."

Pammy suggested, "And why don't we send over a drink to that man who ate all the fire. He must have a powerful thirst by now. How does he do that?"

Buffy solved the problem neatly, "They must start playing with matches in their cradle."

The group leadenly turned their attention now to the not-very-good dancers, who went through their repertoire of native rhythms. Somehow, when they danced en masse, they did not display the grace and rhythm that marked their single approach to dancing.

Buffy looked at them, "Obviously, team sports leave them cold. I wonder who does the choreography?"

Most of the guests seemed bored by this presentation and there was an audible rise in the level of conversation for the duration of the act.

The group left to half-hearted applause.

A flute started a plaintive note and the crowd hushed again. One small spot illuminated a small circle around the pool and into it stepped a young boy. He wore a red and white sarong tied around his hips, so low, a few of the ladies blushed. His upper body was as smooth as a girl's, and each muscle stood out as if it had been carved in mahogany. His face was sweet, almost girlish, with a full lower lip and damp, dark, sensuous eyes that he veiled by lowering his lashes. He stood in the circle of light, swaying his hips.

Two young natives were setting up limbo poles as the young man continued swaying.

Duke stepped out of the bar as he heard the limbo music start. Now, he leaned against one of the marble columns, watching the slow undulation of the beautiful boy's hips.

A chill of pleasure touched Duke's spine as Toussain's eyes roved around the group of people, finally recognizing and resting on Duke's. It was almost an exchange of complicity and Duke bristled with pleasure.

The limbo poles had been set and Toussain started his approach to the high bar, skirting under it easily. He shuffled with the limbo dance step back across as the bar was lowered. Then with a dazzling smile at the audience, he commenced the dance again, slipping under the bar easily. Again and again, the bar was lowered until now it appeared to be only inches from the floor.

Duke skirted around the edge of the crowd, looking for an empty chair so that he could be closer to Toussain when he did this difficult maneuver.

He found one at a table with some French people he had not yet met and asked if he might join them. He spoke in English first, then realizing they might not understand, switched to French.

As Duke watched Toussain move his body lower and lower to pass under the bar, he fell into a wakeful dream. It was his body moving in those delicious undulations. The limbo pole became the gigantic penis of . . . Faisan! Duke could almost feel the black man tease him, touch him, whip him lightly with the pole. The bongo drums increased in intensity as Toussain bent lower and lower, his gleaming wet body almost parallel to the floor, the tight loin cloth seeming tighter as his body swelled with effort; then with a final surge Toussain/Duke had taken the limbo pole/Faisan with a burst of exquisite agony.

Simon who had been watching the limbo dance with faint attention suddenly felt David's hand grasp his arm. "Hey, you see that little creep doing the limbo? That's the one Duke brought into the bar when I was talking to Faisan. He's the one that started all the fuss."

Simon stared at the boy closely, "Are you sure?"

"Absolutely. I saw the kid looking for someone before he started his act and he found what he was looking for. If you have any doubts, look over there."

David indicated Duke with a nod, practically on the floor where he could be on top of the action.

Even Simon could see the expression and desire in Duke's face. His eyes were shining with a sense of possession. It made Simon feel a little sick.

Margaret, who was sharing the table with the Percevals was enchanted by the handsome young native's grace. Her own inability to relax and move freely made Margaret only too aware of others. How she would have liked to have that confidence in her body.

The boy prepared to assault the final and lowest level of the bar. As he repeated his swaying hip act, his hands moved to the knot of the sarong and slowly, like an experienced stripper, he untied the sarong, then whipped it away from himself, standing in a pair of bikini trunks, the same pattern as the sarong now in his hand. He inched around the limbo pole and when he got to Duke's side, he made a pirouette and danced away from him, then turned and threw the sarong into Duke's lap. Duke gathered the material to him and squeezed it. Faisan, standing in the darkness, saw the action. Toussain smiled and moved into position for the final assault. His body bent over in half as he approached the bar, his feet and legs fully extended as he inched his way slowly under, slowly, slowly until he was through, every muscle taut, strained until with a final thrust he was under and up, bowing to the applause, the wildest of which came from Duke.

As the boy accepted the applause, he was suddenly ringed by a group of men, who circled in rhythm around the floor, arriving front and center, then parting as a new man came into the spotlight.

In his hand he held a broken chain whose other end was attached to a shackle around his ankle. He dragged the shackled foot as if it were atrophied by long years of attachment. The crowd gasped at the sight, then tentatively applauded. He held his hands up for silence, then introduced his own act. "I am going to sing for you a group of slave songs which my people have sung for many hundreds of years working the cane fields. To many of you, this would be called folk music. Some of you from the States will recognize some of your own plantation melodies here."

Three guitars started to twang the minor key and the man shut his eyes. His voice was deep, angry, plaintive, sad, beautiful and he sang without interruption, the Creole language was not understood by all, but the meaning of the songs was very clear. The crowd was hushed.

As the man sang, Simon's eyes became fascinated by the way he used the chain. From time to time he seemed to bow under its weight, at other times he wielded it like a weapon. Slave or master, thought Simon. There was a little of each in the other.

David couldn't believe that that hoarse-voiced radical was capable of this beautiful bittersweet kind of singing. He touched Simon's arm again and whispered as softly as he could, "and that's the guy I was telling you about. Sebastian's cousin."

Simon stared with deepened interest, trying to bring the two images together. Not so difficult, once he thought about it. The same kind of passion that could give these songs such meaning could also find its expression in wanting freedom from the very condition that had created the music.

There was no question that this crowd was totally impressed with Faisan's presentation. Who but a group so far removed from the problems of slavery could feel so moved by the music that came out of it? A truck driver would not have been impressed.

Faisan finished his final song and stood in the spotlight, eyes squeezed shut, hands at his side, clenched in fists. The applause broke out and lasted a long time. Faisan opened his eyes and without smiling accepted their appreciation with a look of disdain, then bowed slightly and moved out of the light. The applause continued but Faisan would not return and finally it stopped.

Grov stepped into the spotlight vacated by Faisan and informed the guests that the band would play for dancing as they prepared for the final half of the show which would include a phenomenal acrobat, a group of Antillean folk songs, the famous glass dance and the zombie voodoo dance.

Realizing now for the first time that Karen had not returned during the entire show, David decided he'd better go look for her, and excused himself hastily. As he passed Duke's chair on his way to the bar, he noticed it was empty. Probably out in the bushes grabbing a piece of native entertainment, he thought to himself. He just hoped Faisan wouldn't catch them at it, or there'd be hell to pay for sure.

Simon, too, stood up and made his way to Rod's table. When he noticed Duke's empty chair, he assumed he was in the bar. And now that their number was an even one again, the girls rose at Simon's coming and the dancing began.

The second half of the show was a let-down after the intermission of dancing. By now pre-dinner drinks had worn off, and the crowd was both restless and bored. Only the voodoo dancer held their attention. And when the show was shortened by the sudden arrival of one of those brief but spectacular tropical storms, half the crowd took the opportunity to head for their cottages, while the rest made for the bar and a nightcap.

Grov thanked the entertainers and sent them on their way—even if the storm was to be a short one there would be no point in trying to regroup his guests for the show's finale. The storm while loud and wet for its duration was as brief as it was sudden. And Grov stood under one of the umbrella'd tables, surveying the sodden wreckage of the evening's entertainment. Pools of water had gathered on chairs, in ash trays and in unfinished drinks. He would have to rouse some of the staff which had already gone to bed if the place was to be put in proper order for the early risers. There would be no vestiges of tonight's storm when the first guests arrived at the pool for breakfast the following morning.

In the bar, the sound and light show had competed unsuccessfully with the even more spectacular one nature was playing just beyond the glass wall. But even before the storm had broken, David and Karen were in their cottage. He had found her where he had expected her to be: in the bar. There was no way of knowing just how much she had had to drink, but by the opaque film over her eyes, he suspected it was more than just a nightcap.

When Karen had made her way to the bar, she was determined to have only one small drink and let it go at that. The cockney bartender had peered at her so strangely she had nervously reached for her mirror before ordering the double. It went down so easily, she ordered another one to sip. The first drink had softened the edginess and she waited for the blurry warmth to take over. The second helped. Alcohol had become her surrogate lover, shutting off those parts of her brain that kept her feeling anxious and off-balance.

Her drinking had become serious and solitary, though she refused to think of herself as an alcoholic after Bert had thrown her over for the little studio stylist. Frigid cunt, he had called her. Dumb broad, he added. The alcohol helped to blot out the cruelty of those words.

Soon she was slipping a jigger of vodka into her juice to get her mornings started. And a year later, jobs seemed to be going to other, newer models. So her drinking accelerated as more and more things needed forgetting. No one had ever called her frigid again after Bert, for she had learned to simulate sexual heat with the subtlety of a method actress.

And she found that most men were so interested in their own responses, they were glad to accept her noises and writhings as proof of their virility. David had been the first man to make love to her, really make love and she had reached a climax with him that she knew was real. Now she believed he was the only man who could. With her belief came a dependency that weakened her even more. The alcohol, only the alcohol, could offer her the oblivion she needed to avoid facing herself and her life.

She leaned against him heavily as he put his arm around her shoulder and suggested that it was time for her to go to bed. She misinterpreted his meaning and agreed readily.

"Don't be angry with me, David," she pleaded thickly as he removed the clothes from her slack body.

"I'm not angry with you," he tried to hold the irritation in his voice back. "Give me your foot."

She lifted one and put it in his hand, then fell back against the bed. "I don't know why I do it?" She sniffed back some tears. "I'm so lonely." If only David would spend more time with her, in bed and out, she wouldn't be so haunted by those frightening doubts that flooded her mind. Alcohol seemed to be the only thing that dulled their pain.

As Karen felt her body freed from clothes, she sat upright and reached for David. He came to her, wanting to comfort her. There was no love or tenderness in the action, only a kind of patient futility. Her arms were like a vise around his neck and as she kissed him wetly and sloppily, he recoiled from the stale smell of alcohol on her breath. But Karen was not to be put off; she clung to him with arms suddenly hard and demanding.

David realized that she was only replacing one of her compulsions with another, equally self-destructive. Like a child denied gum, she took the candy bar.

Her hands tore at his clothes, "David, David," she moaned, "please love. That's all I want. I promise I'll never drink again, if you'll only love me."

He petted her like a puppy, as he undressed himself. A bit of his heart melted at her pain and he felt guilt, the reason for so much of it.

She was all over him, crazy with desire and when she reached for him and found him limp, with a little cry, she buried her face on his dead creature and tried to restore it to life with her mouth.

David responded to her ministrations as a part of himself stood aside and marveled at his own response.

As Karen felt him stiffen, she uttered a moan of triumph and pulled him on top of her. Now, David. She knew if she could only get him inside of her everything would be all right. She took his mechanical strokings for tenderness, his response to her mouth as love. She made all the mistakes of judgment a woman desperate for tenderness and love can make. All that counted was now. After, when his indifference was too much to bear, there was the bottle. But now, maybe the miracle would happen. David would love her again and say all those loving and beautiful things he had said once before.

She cried with a desperate joy when she reached climax, but would not let him go. And now David's stomach began to churn. He felt trapped, suffocated by her alcohol-relaxed body. He wished she would die on the spot and release him, then shook himself at the horror of his thoughts. She would suck him dry, leave nothing but his bare bones. He was saddled to a neurotic albatross and there was no out.

Her frenzied movements only turned him off and he lay on top of her passively as she writhed and called out words of love that beat against his tuned-out ears. Finally, he felt himself grow limp and slip away from her, felt her writhings stop as she fell into a deep sleep.

He rolled away and sat up, his head aching and dizzy. Karen lay like a discarded rag doll, breathing heavily; some secret pain had twisted her face into a frozen cry for help. Gently he rolled her to her side of the bed, then lighted a cigarette and paced the floor. Thoughts of Karen were pushed aside as he thought again of the day's events. With his writer's powers of observation, a book was slowly forming in his unconscious as he catalogued characters and diagrammed interractions.

He snubbed out his cigarette, then got into bed. Karen's hair was strung across his pillow and he buried his face in it for a moment. For some odd reason, he thought of Duke and wondered if he were still with that handsome native.

At that very moment, Duke's face was buried in the gay red and white print of Toussain's pareu, his eyes half-lidded in agony. The doors of the truck swung open and let in the harsh neon light of a native nightclub. But the light was blocked by the threatening bulk of Faisan. He reached into the foul smelling truck and dragged Duke out, pulling at his feet first, then at the red and white material with which he had bound and gagged the white man.

## *Sunday*

Bill Perceval gave a mighty yawn and stretched down to his toes. He tossed a mental coin in his head, get up now or give himself the luxury of a few more waking minutes to enjoy the comfort of the excellent Shalimar bed.

He rolled over on his side and looked at Jane's sleeping face. This woman he had lived with so many years never ceased to amaze him. Efficient, organized, practical, tireless, her character read like the Boy Scout code, yet in sleep, her face was unlined, almost child-like in its innocence. She slept deeply, in the same position, never had he heard her toss restlessly in sleep. She slept as she did everything, completely. He reached over and touched the springy short curls lightly with his fingertips and smiled. Slowly Jane's eyes opened and when she saw her husband smiling tenderly back at her, she felt an instant of confusion. When was the last time she had opened her eyes and found Bill staring at her with the mixture of love and respect?

She smiled and reached her arms to him. He moved to her and accepted a good-morning kiss.

"Is it another priceless day outside?" she asked softly.

"I'm sure it is. And it's just as priceless inside." He pressed against her and Jane had the grace to blush.

"Hey, you're blushing like a schoolgirl," he teased.

"Well, it isn't every morning I wake to see my husband bending over me like a lover." she smiled.

"What do you mean like a lover? I am a lover. Would you like some proof?"

"Can this be the honorable mayor of a great city I hear?"

"Even a mayor has his moments."

"And this is one of them?"

Bill found himself responding to Jane's lighthearted teasing and took her gently in his arms. As he bent to kiss her, the phone rang.

He pulled away almost guiltily. "Shall I answer it?" he asked.

"I'm afraid you have to, don't you?"

"Maybe it's a wrong number?" he asked hopefully.

She shook her head, "Wishful thinking."

The phone rang insistently. It was not going to allow itself to be ignored. Bill rolled over to his side and stretched his hand for the receiver, knocking it off the hook, then fumbling on the floor for it.

As soon as he answered it, he sprang to attention. Jane felt the bed shudder with his sudden movement and watched his face anxiously, looking for a sign. With sinking heart, she realized it was New York again.

She listened to his curt responses into the phone, no clue there. But she knew better than to interrupt him. Now Bill had risen from the bed and with the phone in his hand, he paced with the length of the cord, listening intently, answering in the same monosyllables. His face grew tense and whitened under his tan.

Jane got out of bed and threw on a robe, knotting it firmly around her waist, her eyes still on her husband's ever-tightening face. When he slammed the receiver on the hook, she went to him, "What now?"

Bill looked at her. Gone was the tender expression. In its place, a look of annoyance. For her? Or for the conversation just passed.

"I've got to get back to New York." And before she could protest or say a word, he reached for the phone and jiggled impatiently for the operator.

"Connect me with the airport, please." He tapped his foot and avoided Jane's questioning look.

Bill's annoyance grew with each moment as he discovered the only scheduled plane back would be late in the evening and he would have to charter one to take him to Martinique where he could pick up an earlier plane leaving from there.

He stripped out of his pajamas and walked to the bathroom. Jane followed him.

"Aren't you going to tell me what that was all about?"

"I warned you when we came down here that I might have to go back."

"Is it the Arleo thing again?"

Bill found it difficult to lie to his wife but at this point found it even more difficult to tell her the truth. "I only wish it were."

This phone call had not come from O'Hara, his press secretary, but from his Police Commissioner, Josephs. How could he explain to Jane that her dearly beloved son and his namesake had just spent the night in jail, picked up on a charge of illegal possession of marijuana. He wondered if the boy were guilty or being used. He had seen too many of his fellow politicos dragged into the white glare of publicity on just such pretexts. It was the newest ploy in casting shadows upon a liberal politician to make him go easy and it was the simplest thing to plant on an unsuspecting child, especially if his father happened to be in a high place.

And yet, hadn't he like all parents, wondered about his own children? Conversation about addiction was not hushed or glossed over in the Perceval household. He encouraged his children to air their problems, to discuss the ideas close to them and to enter into honest debate with honest disagreement.

He had never threatened them, nor warned them, only pointed out the problems, the excesses and the point of no return even as he tried to find ways to liberalize the harsh laws on possession of marijuana. It was not the pot that worried him as much as what happened afterwards with kids, looking for a new cheap thrill, who moved onto stronger stuff. And Bill knew that it was not only the ghetto kids or the disenfranchised minorities who looked for a way out with drugs, but the kids from good families who wanted to follow the pack.

He had even asked Bill, Jr. if he had ever smoked and the boy had answered him with an emphatic no. He believed him. The younger Perceval had no reason to lie to him because he knew he would receive no punishment, but only rhetoric. And Bill, Jr. had always teased his father about preferring not to do a forbidden thing if only to avoid the lectures he would be forced to listen to.

Had the boy changed his mind, or was he just an innocent, had the stuff been planted? At this point Arleo was terribly unimportant, it was his son who needed him now. And suddenly, he had an ironic thought, when the empire started to crumble, it went down with a bang. And all his dreams of an incorruptible administration, the clean sweep with him pushing the broom, the vision of taking his much-divided city and putting it together again paled as he thought of his inability to keep his own house clean.

"Jane," Bill's razor pulled across his beard with an intensity saved only by the dullness of the razor, "I'd like you to come back with me."

"Come back for what? More of the same?"

"I don't understand what that's supposed to mean." Bill replied acidly.

"More of a life where the only thing we share is your lofty office. The only problem is there's only room for one in that chair."

"There's room for two if we both make room."

"Meaning, that I haven't done my share?"

"Meaning that you have given me less than your whole-hearted support." Jane flushed. She held on to her hands with a ferocious strength because her inclination was to strike out.

"It is not easy to raise four children with an absentee father."

Now it was Bill's turn to feel anger. "That remark is beneath you. You know damn well I've tried to be with you and the children as much as I could. Even a businessman or a lawyer has responsibilities outside his home."

"Yes, but with you, the job of mayor is twenty-four hours a day, seven days a week with very little time off for good behavior."

"We've just had three days. And I was much against that. But I did it to please you."

"You make everything sound like a favor. I feel like one of your patronage jobs, you throw me a small reward in payment for my devotion to the cause."

"Jane, don't get that bitter, how-I-suffer sound in your voice. It's not becoming."

The tenderness of the early morning had gone down the drain along with Bill's shaving cream lather. The two stood exposed in their own anger and unwillingness to compromise.

"This is no discussion," Jane turned to leave the bathroom, "it's more like guerilla warfare. I'm not going back to New York to play dutiful mayor's wife while you try to show a united front to the press."

She turned in the door, "Even Rome didn't fall in one day. Your precious administration can wait another few days for its beloved leader."

"Jane," Bill warned, "don't talk like that anymore. I don't think you realize the damage you're doing to us."

"Then stay here and prove what you started to prove this morning." Jane took his arm and held it to her. He stiffened. She dropped it, tears welling in her eyes.

"You know I can't. For the last time, without asking questions and because I ask you to, please, for the love of God, come home with me now."

Jane was torn by her own ambivalence. She felt to leave now would be to acquiesce to how many more years of non-private life, his overwhelming ambition. And yet to stay without him was a hollow victory. She couldn't say the words he wanted. Instead, she said the first thing that came to her mind. It was thoughtless, dangerous and irrevocable.

"If you leave now, you may find yourself alone for good."

Bill gave her a long cold stare. "If that's what you really want . . ." his unfinished sentence hung in the air, threatening her with its implications.

She took a sharp intake of breath and was about to apologize but it was too late. Bill with a cold, "If you'll excuse me," had gently but firmly shut the bathroom door in her face.

Margaret Bradley, the needle-sharp shower dancing off her body, felt a strange elation this morning. The relaxation of mind and muscle once a decision has been made, seeped through her like warming sun. Suddenly she felt alive for the first time in years. And simply because she had made a decision. To allow Phillip into her life, freely. As she stepped from her shower, the phone rang. She ran to it, her naked body streaming water, and picked it up.

Margaret listened with unfeigned delight. Phillip's voice came across the long-distance wire with an unnatural hollowness.

In her new sense of freedom, she even felt the happy surprise in Phillip's voice as he listened to her breathlessly tell him how she missed him. When she asked how long it would take for him to get to the island, he promised her he could be there that evening in time to claim the first dance. He'd fly instead of sailing.

"And Phillip," she continued on like a child, "I'm ready, no more waiting I promise. No more silly, nonsensical holding-back. But we'll talk when you get here. Hurry, please. Promise you'll be here as soon as you can."

Margaret put her hands to her cheeks, they were flushed with heat and she caught her reflection in the mirror. The urge to stare at herself was unabashed and she looked at herself with a strange, new openness. The chrysallis had finally cracked and a butterfly was ready to emerge. She stared at herself as though she were looking at a stranger. In a way, she was.

And yet there was still enough of the old Margaret left in her to make her glance quickly at her small travel clock to make sure she had enough time for a cup of coffee before going into town for mass. She was not happy with the "new mass." She felt the church had lost a great deal more than it had gained when it had dropped the Latin and much of the pomp. She especially disliked touching total strangers at that point in the mass when the sign of peace was to be exchanged. And yet much as she dreaded the proximity with these sweating blacks who shared her religion, there was no question in her mind about attending mass. As she reached into her drawer and pulled out the small black lace mantilla, she wondered why the Madams of the Sacred Heart had had such a lasting influence on her, and almost none on her daughters.

Denise had had the pool to herself almost the entire morning. She wondered vaguely why that other sun worshipper, Duke, hadn't joined her, but didn't give it much thought. Except for last night's sudden storm, the weekend was going better than could be expected for an opening. Even Grov was beginning to relax a little. She silently thanked heaven for that. If things hadn't been going so well, she was sure he'd have made a fuss about seeing her yesterday afternoon coming off the *Cassandra* with Marty. She wished she could make him understand how little of herself had been involved. If only he could realize how disgusted she was with herself after yesterday afternoon's encounter.

There was a time when she would have been as faithful to Grov as to a lover. When they had first married and Grov had painted such glowing pictures of their future together. He had given up his vagabond tennis life and accepted the Wall Street job, rather than the hotel offer from Atlanta, filling her ears with how his clever investments for clients and himself would give them all the luxuries they craved. While on the tennis circuit, he had met numbers of wealthy men, who he thought, would be happy to turn over their portfolios to him. After a fruitless year, he discovered to his chagrin that his tennis circuit friends preferred non-tennis brokers to handle their accounts. Grov, with all his looks and charm, had goals and dreams that far exceeded his reach. Yet he continued to believe the promises he had made to Denise would one day be fulfilled.

Finally, when their bank balance was down to

pennies, Grov entered the field he had trained for. And the two of them with more than average good looks had finally joined the jet set crowd. The big difference being, of course, they were the hired help, not the privileged guests. Denise rankled under the difference and couldn't forget it. Grov had tried and succeeded.

Now their relationship had long since passed that point where self-revelation, and mutual understanding was expected or even accepted. Theirs, like so many of the marriages of the seventies had settled into a comfortable acceptance of each as a separate entity, free to come and go as he pleased within acceptable boundaries. In their particular strata, the boundaries were wide. It had not been an unsuccessful marriage, she felt, and was sure Grov would agree. If neither of them had brought to it, or gotten from it all that might be anticipated from the marriage of two such free and beautiful spirits, neither had ever openly expressed disenchantment or disappointment. Perhaps theirs was the best kind of marriage—touching but not feeling. And yet as she thought back to yesterday afternoon a sly smile crossed her lips and she really did wish she could share with Grov her discovery that Martin Gramson was as big a pig in bed as he was out.

Denise's enjoyment of her private little joke was interrupted by a sniffling cold nose in her ear and a tentative swipe of a little warm tongue along her heavily oiled cheek. She turned her head slightly, opened one eye, and found herself nose to nose with Tiger. Every inch of him vibrated to the happy tattoo of his tiny puff-topped tail. Denise was not ordinarily fond of animals—she and Grov had never even discussed having a pet—and yet there was something quite irresistible about this one.

"I know you", she said softly to him, "you're only interested in me because my suntan oil tastes good.

I know you sly Frenchmen." She patted him on his fluffy soft pom-pom and he threw himself down on his back, four tiny paws to the sky, in happy anticipation of the ecstasy of having his tummy rubbed.

"Oh, Tiger!" Pammy called to him in mock annoyance.

"I hope he hasn't been bothering you," Buffy added scooping him up and cradling him in the crook of her elbow. "He's really quite incorrigible." But her words were belied by the affectionate little squeeze she gave him, and the liver sliver she surreptitiously slipped him. "We're all just famished", she added, looking around for some sign of the usual breakfast buffet.

"We're planning a brunch out here, to be served in a few minutes." Denise said, then added when she saw the crestfallen expression on all three faces, "but you'll find fruit, coffee and sweet rolls in the dining room now."

"Thanks so much," Pammy was able to throw over her shoulder before the famished trio disappeared into the dining room.

With those three arriving for breakfast, the day at Shalimar had officially begun. But for one of the club's guests, the day had begun earlier. Duke Dexter had awakened, or more accurately come to, as the first rays of the morning sun found their way into the unbearably stuffy little storeroom where he had spent the night. Consciousness brought him an awareness of his body's aches and pains. Every muscle felt as though it had been stretched mercilessly, every joint throbbed with painful memories of last night's punishment. He lay perfectly still, hoping the stillness would quiet the pain. The sour smell of stale beer assaulted his nose. It was mixed with the rancid smell of sweaty bodies. He shuddered involuntarily and the reaction of his body brought back all the horror of the previous night. He'd have to get out of here before they came back. He knew himself well enough to realize that he was at the breaking point last night when a merciful unconsciousness offered him escape.

He struggled to his feet, looked down at his clothing and couldn't believe these filthy rags had once been a source of such pride of possession. Except for the single shaft of light that had found its way into the room through a crack in the blackened windows, the room lay in darkness. Scurrying sounds indicated that he had shared this room that night with a host of rats—or worse. The darkness which at first had seemed a blessing now threatened him further. He was sure now in his unconsciousness those same rats had probably scampered over his body. He brushed feverishly at his clothes in a futile attempt to remove traces of last night. Even that slight brushing with his hand awakened new agonies in his body. He looked around desperately for some avenue of escape. He clambered up onto a pile of crates to get away at least from those who shared the room with him. And so he was huddled like some hovering gargoyle when a door he'd not noticed was kicked open. The sudden oblong of brilliant light made him squint. But even through his half-opened eyes he could make out the shape of the dark giant almost filling the doorway. The silhouette moved into the room disappearing momentarily into the darkness. And at his elbow Duke heard the deep resonant laugh.

"Your morning coffee, sir". He thrust a fiercely hot tin mug into Duke's hand. "Can't have our guests complaining about the service—shouldn't want the place to get a bad name." He roared again at his own private little joke then appeared once more silhouetted in the door. "You take care of yourself—you have a big day ahead of you." He slammed the door shut behind him and Duke could hear the sound of his laughter disappear in the distance.

Denise had just settled down once more to take advantage of the powerful late morning rays of the tropical sun, when the crisp clear British accent of Simon called out across the pool, "Hello, there!"

She sat up and smiled a greeting. She couldn't afford to alienate such a powerful spokesman of the beautiful people and besides he was quite charming.

"I never thought I'd find you out here all by yourself at this hour," he said, now standing directly above her. "Where's the body beautiful?"

"I beg your pardon," she said looking disparagingly down at her scantily covered body.

"Oh, no," he said, blushing for the first time in years," I beg *your* pardon. It's just that you and Duke have been out here like beautiful bronzed bookends at either end of the pool every morning, and now you seem to be holding up your end all by yourself, so to speak." He fumbled again. "Actually I'm not much good at conversation until I've had my morning coffee."

"You'll find it in the dining room now, or here in just a few minutes."

"Then I'll wait, if you don't mind. And see if I can keep my foot out of my mouth." He waved a cheery greeting and announced, "And here comes the unflappable Mrs. Bradley. Her presence should be a steadying influence." He didn't mention it to Denise but he had to admit to himself that he had never seen Margaret Bradley looking quite as well as she did that morning. She wore a simple but well-cut shift from that little boutique in Mizener Alley. Those understated play clothes that had found their way out of Palm Beach and into the heart of every country club matron on the East Coast. Her hair was pulled back and tied with a silk scarf and she could have passed even in this uncompromising light for one of her daughters.

"Looks like we're the hungry ones in the crowd," Margaret said as the three of them turned their attention to the waiters who were even then wheeling in the brunch trolleys.

"Not really," Denise smiled, "the eager eaters took up advance positions in the dining room," and with a nod of her head she indicated, Pammy, Buffy, Tiger and Rod sheepishly looking out at the brunch.

Simon waved them forward and they fluttered to a table near him like exotic butterflies. No sooner had they taken their seats than one of the waiters brought over a small dish covered with an elaborate silver dome.

"Compliments of the chef, for mistuh Tigah" he said. Sweeping off the cover with an exaggerated gesture, he placed a dish of tiny tidbits on the table in front of Tiger who was in a fit of esctasy in Pammy's lap.

Margaret who had seated herself at a table, looked up delightedly as Grov asked if he might join her. "Of course, and your wife, too," she said smiling past Grov to Denise who by now had slipped into an opaque but scarcely concealing floor length caftan.

"Your club's opening seems to be going very well," Margaret said.

"Thank the good lord, yes," Grov said with feeling. "And Shalimar certainly seems to be agreeing with you. You look marvelous."

"I can't imagine anyone Shalimar wouldn't agree with, "Margaret replied.

"There's a possible exception at that table," Grov said, lowering his voice and nodding across the pool where Karen and David were sitting stiffly, as though to relax would crumple their carefully constructed façade. They had exchanged barely a dozen words that morning. Each had been preoccupied with his own special hell. And all they seemed to share that moment were the agonies of mutual hangovers.

Karen cowered like a frightened animal before his indifference. He in turn was being made equally uncomfortable by the guilt he was unable to ignore.

The tension between the Sampsons was matched by that between the Percevals who were then arriving. Stiff-backed, tight-lipped they hardly glanced to the left or right, but seated themselves quickly at a small table set up for two.

"I'm not hungry", Jane said and it was hard to tell whether the remark was meant for Bill or the waiter, who had by then wheeled up one of the lavishly laden trolleys.

"I'll have the pineapple and one of those little casseroles—whatever they are." Bill forced a smile for the waiter's benefit.

The waiter did not return his smile, but instead placed the fruit and casserole down in front of the mayor with a little more emphasis than was really called for. "Coffee now, or later?" he mumbled.

"Now, please, and for my wife." Leave some of the sweet rolls, too." Bill realized any further effort at civility with this waiter was undoubtedly doomed to fail, and he felt incapable of and unwilling to cope with any more hostility that morning. He snapped open the airmail edition of the *New York Times*. It was yesterday's but he was anxious to see for himself how the press was handling the mess at home. He scrutinized each story carefully looking for some hint that there was resentment or surprise at his absence during this time, but found none. Only in one of the editorials did he see what he thought was a hint of things to come.

"He's on to something, or thinks he is at any rate," Bill said more to himself than to Jane.

"Well, we can't have that, can we?" Jane said pushing her chair back awkwardly and leaving the table. Bill automatically rose and made a half-hearted attempt to help her, but she was unable to read the look in his eyes.

As Jane passed near the table where Margaret was brunching with Grov and Denise, Grov called out to her, "Was there nothing that appealed to you on the trolley?" And before she could answer, went on, "The chef will be glad to fix anything you'd rather have."

Jane murmured a flustered apology. She had forgotten what a tight little society she was living in this weekend. She quickly snapped on her public façade, all graciousness and eagerness to please. "Oh, no, everything looked absolutely marvelous, but I've a wicked little headache this morning and I thought a nap might help."

"I'm so sorry," Grov said. "Is there anything we could get you for it?"

"No, no. I'll be fine I'm sure after a little rest."

"You will be going to the art show this afternoon, won't you?" Margaret asked eagerly. She was as anxious as any one of the guests to get a good look at the *Cassandra*, but was loathe to admit it. She knew she would be much more at ease, and would enjoy the whole experience with the Percevals more than with any of the other guests, or even on her own. And Phillip couldn't possibly be here in time to join her.

"Oh, yes, of course. I'm sure I'll be fine by then." Jane assured her.

"Then I'll pick you up around 3:00 if that's all right."

"Fine, we'll see you then," Jane said moving on. The word "we" came so automatically to her lips, she could no more imagine a reply without it than she could a life without him. She was afraid now that she had gone too far this morning. Why under the sun, after all these years had she decided to take such an immovable stand on such a minor issue?

Could a marriage as long-standing and as seemingly solid as theirs possibly end on such a trivial note? She allowed herself the first smile she'd indulged in since this morning's discussion. Of course not, she reassured herself, a divorce would be as damaging to Bill's image as a scandal at City Hall. She was slightly embarrassed at how much the thought had pleased her. Then mentally patted her conscience, after all she'd endured the demands of her husband's political ambition long enough, why not now at least start enjoying some of its benefits. She let herself into their cottage, wrung out a face cloth under the cold water tap, then lay down on the bed with it folded over her forehead.

Pammy and Buffy having made short work of the "one of each" which they had jokingly asked the waiter for and then quite seriously eaten, now turned their attentions to Simon. Rod had finished his spartan meal quickly, and had gone to prepare the club speedboat for the afternoon's excursion.

"Can't we possibly talk you into coming?" Pammy pleaded.

" 'Fraid not, much as I'd love to. Duty calls, and the opportunity to catch on film every barbaric vulgarity on the *Cassandra*, for the titilation of the unwashed masses, may not present itself again."

"Simon, you really are a snob," Pammy giggled.

"High praise, indeed, considering the source," Simon teased her back.

"Well, if this dedicated member of the working press cannot be dissuaded, we'd better pull ourselves together. Rod must be ready now," Buffy said, dropping Tiger from her lap. "And there's no point in taking any chances on being caught up in the great cultural wave that's about to engulf

Shalimar." With Tiger dancing at their heels, the girls left for an afternoon of fun and games.

Although the forthcoming art show held some fascination for Emily, the prospect of mingling with the carefree guests of Shalimar did not. Knowing well that this Sunday would be a Sunday to remember, Emily had no real desire to mingle, instead she felt a strange urge to go to church.

It had been many years since Emily had set foot in a church. Like many young girls, she had become disenchanted. Not because the Bible conflicted with science and she was of the scientific age, but rather because religion no longer had answers for her. Blind faith was dead, God was dead, ritual was dead. There was no rationalization of a world in chaos and a benign God who promised if you were good you would find your rewards in heaven. Emily wanted her rewards now. Not in a selfish way, but in the way that promised a Negro, a Mexican or a Puerto Rican an equal chance to live a life of dignity with some hope.

But the childish feeling of loneliness, of no one to turn to, of another chapter in her life, albeit a strange one, about to close sent Emily back, back in time to the time when she went to church and prayed to God to help her, to comfort her and to sustain her.

She dressed in a sober navy linen, slipped on sandals, picked up a scarf for her head, climbed into her dusty little Volkswagen and headed for town. The Protestant church was on the outskirts of town, small, unobtrusive as befitting a minority church on a primarily Catholic island.

It was past the hour of official Sunday services for which Emily was grateful. She was not seeking the ritual, but only the solace of the cool white walls, the silent deserted pews, the emptiness. Her dialogue with God, if you could call it that, would be on a personal basis with no intermediary. As she knelt, it was not for prayer but rather in a silent confrontation with herself, a flashback of her life until now and the next step to take. She let—could she in fact stop?—the images of her Brahmin father and aristocratic mother pass by, her sister rose complete with her holier-than-thou attitude, the younger brother killed in Viet Nam passed fleetingly, then the harsh memory of David Sampson melted into the tender reality of Sebastian.

She bent her head in memory of the past evening with no shame at the thought of thinking of their love in this place. God surely could not frown on their feeling, it was real, true, unselfish. But still she had to leave. She had to give up this taste of happiness, the first real one she had known because the time and place were wrong. She knew it as certainly as Sebastian knew it.

To think it had been a black man who had taught her about love, who had helped her mature into the woman she was and would be. Their kind of relationship was better than Snick, than non-violence, than the Black Panthers, better than anything. It was what life was about. Two people helping each other, regardless of race, religion or creed. Could she ever return to life at home knowing what she knew now? Where would her place be in her own society? She was past student revolution. Where would she go now?

A sudden feeling of anxiety made her palms wet. The feeling in her stomach was one of hot coffee swallowed too quickly and she allowed the tears to fall now onto her tightly clenched hands. She did not pray. She had no right to ask God for anything, she knew that. All decisions were hers and all consequences, too.

She remained with hands clenched tightly together, staring ahead for many minutes, then got heavily to her feet and walked out of the church.

The blazing sun, after the semi-cool darkness of the church, blinded her and she leaned against the door for an instant to get her bearings.

Now, she felt a gnaw of hunger stirring. Being young and healthy, although distraught, meant an unimpaired appetite. She could still enjoy food. But Sunday in town did not allow much in the way of choice. Her favorite little coffee shop at least, might be open. It was the hub of the town, meeting place for all the islands's factions, and besides they made the best café filtre in town.

Emily headed for the café with shaky steps.

As she stepped through the beaded curtain across the doorway her eyes had to adjust again to the change of light. She stood uncertainly for a moment until the tables lost their ghostly shadows and took on shape, then spotting an empty one near the door, she lowered herself into a chair.

She looked around the café, uncrowded at this particular hour. Despite the emptiness, the few waiters standing around seemed in no hurry to take her order. She waited patiently for several moments and when there was no apparent change in the service, finally summoned one in an imperiously irritated voice.

The waiter shuffled to her with no haste, examining his fingernails carefully on the way. When he arrived at her table, he patently avoided looking at her directly. Emily felt the sting of his disdain and suddenly found herself behaving with an unctiousness that irritated her.

"A café filtre please and a sweet roll."

"No sweet rolls." he replied as laconically as possible.

"What have you?"

"Don't know."

"Could you check and see?"

"Chef gone off."

"There must be something left in the kitchen."

"Don't know," he replied.

"Could you find out?"

He shrugged and left. Emily tapped her foot impatiently until he returned. He set the little pot in front of her and made no attempt to pour for her. His hands were otherwise empty.

"I take it the kitchen is empty of any kind of roll or croissant."

"You take it right." the waiter said blandly and shuffled off again. By now, Emily's stomach was sending up a mighty howl. She couldn't understand the surliness of the waiter in the café in which she had spent much time and quite a few francs. Something palpable was in the air, but as yet, she couldn't place it. A sudden stab of fear caught her in her chest.

She poured the coffee with shaking hands, managing to get more in the saucer than in the cup.

"You seem a bit nervous today, Miss Emily." The smooth voice startled her and when she looked up and discovered Faisan standing in front of her, she didn't know whether to be annoyed or pleased.

"Faisan, what a start you gave me. Will you join me?"

"If you wish."

"No, only if you wish. If you have another appointment, please don't let me detain you." Emily replied icily. She did not have any strong feeling about Sebastian's cousin, only a guarded wariness.

"No as a matter of fact, it will give me great pleasure to sit and talk with you." The words were courteous, the meaning took on an ominousness that caused Emily's heart to beat much faster.

"Please, do, then. Perhaps you'll be able to get me

a croissant to have with my coffee. I seem to be doing quite badly."

"Oh, what a pity." Faisan's tone was so obviously exaggerated that Emily looked at him sharply.

As Faisan lowered himself to the chair, by magic Emily's waiter appeared at his elbow, the look on his face indicated that Faisan's most extravagant wish would be fulfilled in an instant.

Faisan gave his order and with a look at Emily, he asked for an extra croissant. He was feeling quite hungry. The waiter made a funny little bow and was off in a flash. And back in a flash with a pot of fragrant coffee, a tub of butter and quince jam and a basket full of sweet, steaming hot croissants and brioche. As the waiter set his tray down, he looked insolently at Emily.

She returned the look evenly, "I'm delighted to see that the chef has made a rapid recovery." Then turning to Faisan, "And equally delighted that you've arrived. Now, I can have a little something with my coffee. What does it take around here to get a bite to eat?"

Faisan looked at her smoothly and said, "You just have to be black, Miss Emily. It takes more than an intimate relationship with the Prime Minister to get fed here."

"Faisan, I would think a remark like that would be more appropriate to a man with half your education and certainly half your intelligence." Emily's New England background would never allow her to encourage virulent hostilities between the two. It was not the way to handle any situation, she was sure of that.

"You'd be right, Miss Emily, if I were half-white, but you forget I'm just a few years out of the trees. I mean I am pure black, unlike some other members of my family."

Emily drew back at the open hostility of the man,

it was no longer disguised by an ironic politeness. She felt oddly awkward with this man.

"Faisan, why are you treating me this way? I've been on your island all this time now and I thought I had a good relationship with your people. Why, now do I feel this sudden hostility from everyone? What's happening?"

He slapped the table with his hand. "You ask me a question like that. Don't you read your *New York Times*? What's happening is happening all over."

"But I'm not trying to exploit you. I'm trying to work with you. Why do you insist on ignoring that fact?"

"We don't need your kind of help."

"Don't be childish. You need all the help you can get. And I repeat, I'm not trying to exploit you. After all, I've worked very closely with Sebastian. He certainly understands what I'm trying to do.

"What does he know? He talks black and sleeps white."

"I ask you to repeat that remark." Emily and Faisan turned simultaneously at the new voice and reacted, each in his own way, to the towering presence of Sebastian Lalange. "Repeat that remark," Sebastian insisted.

"It hardly bears repeating, among us friends." He stressed friends. "I've no objection to what you do or where you take your pleasures. Forbidden flesh is always sweeter, I know that. But when it gets in the way of what's best for our people, then I object strenuously. And you'll see just how strenuously very soon," Faisan threatened.

"What exactly does that mean, cousin?" Sebastian inquired, not once having lost his cool superiority.

"You'll see, cousin."

"I insist you tell me, Faisan. If you're up to something, I want to know about it. I will not allow you to disrupt this island anymore."

"Do you honestly think you can stop me? Already our wheels are in motion."

"What does he mean, Sebastian?" Emily asked.

"I don't know. But Faisan has a predilection for the dramatic and like most of his type can't bear to keep the details to himself."

Faisan flushed, "Don't be so uppity, Sebastian. At this very moment, one of the guests of Shalimar is my guest."

"What do you mean?"

"Why don't you ask the person in question when he returns to Shalimar?"

"Who is it?" Emily asked fearfully. For some reason she was afraid it might be David.

"Just a minute, Emily. I want to know what Faisan is getting at." He turned to Faisan and gripped his arm in a steely vise. "Faisan, have you taken someone hostage from Shalimar? And if you have, what do you hope to gain?"

Faisan, wincing under Sebastian's grip, made a mighty endeavor to free himself. He was angry now, furious to have this small show of strength between himself and Sebastian be seen by his cousin's white mistress. He stood up suddenly and broke the grip, hissing at the two of them, "You'll see and damn soon, I promise you." Then rubbing his forearm, he stalked out of the cafe leaving a white-faced Emily staring in fear at Sebastian.

"What's happening, for God's sake, Sebastian?"

"I think Faisan is planning something. But I don't know where or how. I better get some intelligence on this situation before I do anything drastic."

"I've got to get back to Shalimar and see who's missing and warn Grov. We can't let all those people be jeopardized by a handful of rabble-rousers."

"Emily, please don't be an alarmist. Give me a chance to find out what's going on."

Now Emily was torn for the first time between her

trust in Sebastian and her fear for her own kind of people. It was the first confrontation between black and white to affect her so personally. She was confused, but her New England upbringing, all those generations of Puritans finally won the upper hand. "Sebastian, I must tell Grov. I can't do otherwise. Please understand."

Sebastian looked at her long and hard. "I understand Emily, I'm sorry you feel you must. But I won't stand in your way. Just don't make it seem more than it is until I know myself. I'll come to Shalimar as soon as I know, hopefully before the evening's festivities start. If I think there is to be trouble, I'll be the first one to let Grov know and help him take whatever steps we both feel are necessary for the safety of his guests. I'm sure though that all this talk of Faisan's is nothing more than talk."

"I hope you're right, Sebastian. But I have a feeling Faisan is out for blood." She hesitated for a moment and then looked steadily at him, "white blood."

Sebastian sighed. As close as he had come to Emily, he had not yet—nor had she—been able to bridge that vast difference between their colors. To love, to make love, to trust was one thing on a personal level, but to trust the fortunes of one race in the hands of a man whose color was different—that was a long way away yet. If Sebastian had had any doubts that last night with Emily, they were only increased now, he saw the fear in her eyes, the fear for herself and the people she shared her color with.

His way was clear now. As much as he felt for Emily, it was necessary for him to be first a leader and a black man. Everything else was unimportant.

The *Cassandra,* where the cultural wave was about to engulf Shalimar, looked more like a warship with every man at battle stations. The Gramson's had ordered coffee in their cottage and left long before the brunch was served to ready the *Cassandra* for Sandy's show. Van Goghs, Warhols and Dufys were carefully stowed and gave way to the delicate water colors of the *Cassandra*'s mistress.

In the yacht's sparkling stainless steel galley the real work of preparation was being done. The frigid depths of the *Cassandra*'s freezers had been filled with delicacies from all over the globe, but today's bill of fare would be a surprise for the jaded palates of Shalimar's guests. Sandy, having overseen the hanging of her paintings, made a brief visit to the galley. But everything was under such perfect control in the capable hands of Marty's chef, she returned quickly to the main saloon. There and on the rear deck, which would be the centers of the afternoon's show, the staff was working with precision. Setting up tables here and a bar there, they moved like men programmed for maximum efficiency. And because they had made these kinds of preparations before—in practically every fashionable harbor in the world, the work was done with an economy of motion.

Marty, finding Sandy standing helplessly in the midst of this operation, suggested an eye-opener for both of them, but she refused, with the inadequate excuse that she had to dress although the showing was not scheduled for another hour.

Shalimar's sleek inboard, with Rod at the helm, cut through the calm waters of Frenchman's Cove to the small deserted island which lay two miles to the south. As it drew out of the still cove waters into the swells of open sea, it dove and surfaced like a happy dolphin.

Tiger, a furry Captain Bligh, riding the prow barked happily at every wave, his ears streaming out behind him, pom poms bouncing in the breeze.

Pammy and Buffy sat close by in the cockpit

ready to grab a paw if Tiger should go flying into the water. But his little paws were as good as Top-siders and clung tenaciously to the fiberglass. Occasionally, he looked around to check the whereabouts of his two mistresses and assure himself that Rod was handling the boat with the proper deference for its precious cargo.

Rod handled the boat well, as well as he handled anything that had to do with equipment and sports. He treated the Shalimar boat as conscientiously as he treated himself. The results of care were obvious—on both of them. The *Shalimar II*'s brightwork was as glossy as Rod himself, its fiberglass immaculately clean, its interior tidy and ship-shape. Diving gear was stowed neatly away, lines curled and hanging off hooks, away from clumsy feet. The spray catcher was tightly rolled and battened down, tied with clever knots that would be easy to release as soon as needed.

The girls, who had spent many summers sailing on the sounds of several countries, were properly impressed with Rod's seaworthiness and kept respectfully silent during the trip, murmuring only to themselves.

Ile Dormir, the Sleeping Island, lay like a giant porcupine dozing in the sun, its bed a dazzle of white coral sand surrounded by a counterpane of brilliant blue. Stands of coconut palm huddled in the center with dense carpets of sword grass, trailing vines and otherwise impenetrable forestry. No one really cared, for the island's charm had to do only with its powdery sand and the fact that it set high on an underwater reef which broke steeply into a scuba diver's idea of paradise: some of the best coral scenery this side of the Great Barrier Reef.

Rod had dived here many times and in that vast underwater panorama had come as close to true peace as man can.

As he gunned the motor and shot the prow of the boat onto the sand, he squinted through the sun at the girls and Tiger.

"Now we have it made. It's just us, lunch, the sea and water sport. Boy, wait till you kids get zapped with that underwater scenery. You'll never go back to Locust Valley again."

Pammy sniffed with superiority, "We've been underwater before. And we've seen some pretty wild landscapes. Right out of Jules Verne."

"Screw Jules Verne. This is the end. You'll see."

"Are we going to have lunch before or after we dive?" Buffy asked anxiously. The needs of her stomach surpassed all other needs of her psyche. "Water sports are great, but baked chicken is better."

Rod gave a huge laugh. "I don't know how you do it. You eat like a truck driver and you're still skin and bones. Tiger, too."

Tiger hearing his name mentioned, stopped investigating the contents of the huge picnic basket just long enough to find out if he were needed. When no one acknowledged him, his inquisitive black nose returned to the snowy white folds of napkins that concealed all sorts of good things from his eyes. It didn't really matter for his educated nose conveyed messages of delight to his tail, now wagging in delicious anticipation.

Reassured that good things come to him who waits, Tiger walked off to investigate the sandy beach. He found a handsomely bleached piece of driftwood and planted his flag of ownership with a cock of his leg. Let any strange animal try to lay claim to that particular piece of property. Contented with a job well done, a sudden frenzy seized him and high spirits sent him running off in a burst of speed. He tore down the beach, skidded to a stop at the sight of a moving object, investigated the little crab, who, frightened out of its shell by this impetuous black menace, scrambled away and dug into the sand to escape. Tiger happily dug after it, but the crab had a head start. Tiring of this dull companion, he trotted back down the beach to the real action.

Rod, by this time, had unloaded the scuba gear from the boat and had it neatly arranged on the beach.

"Listen, it's early, we could make a dive and explore, then come back up and have some lunch. We'll have to wait at least an hour before we can go down again anyway, so what do you say?" Turning to Buffy, he inquired, "Think you could forget about your hungries for awhile?"

Buffy rolled her eyes, "We are all required to make sacrifices of a personal nature for the good of the group." she said pontifically.

"I love a girl with social conscience," Rod congratulated her.

"Besides I'm fascinated by the silent world down there."

Rod gave a laugh. "Boy, are you in for a surprise. That world's about as silent as 42nd Street on Saturday night. Wait until you hear it. It's a whole concert of electronic music."

"You're joking!" Pammy thrilled. "You mean all those Costeau films are a lie?"

"I don't know anything about Costeau, but if you'll gear up, you can listen to Brigham's Band."

With such an irresistible incentive, the girls got into their flippers, adjusted their tanks and waddled to the water's edge. Clumsily, they got in, listened for the reassuring bleep-bleep of the air regulator and drifted down. They flipped along behind Rod, following him like a school of exotic fish, hair streaming like seaweed. Holding their noses, they blew out to clear their Eustacian tubes and with the pop, commenced to breathe the cool air from the tanks, alternately breathing and releasing until they had developed a measured cadence.

Adapted to this new atmosphere, they moved along the sandy bottom. Before long they heard the first squeaks and whistles and buzzes. It was like having two stations fighting for control of the airwaves.

They watched a colony of eels with their tails buried in the sand sway like hula dancers in the bottom currents. A flight of angelfish scattered as they moved through the water and came to an eerie city of coral skyscrapers, pink and silvery blue in the clear water. Gaudy fish trafficked around the coral like ladies in bright summer dresses.

Rod pointed to a spiney creature and shook a warning finger. The girls detoured around the sea urchin with great care, remembering Buffy's swollen foot after a chance meeting with one in the Virgin Islands. Steady layers of air bubbles marked their passage through the depths of water and occasionally they would pause to listen to the strange underwater music they had never suspected existed.

Buffy, floating around a particularly beautiful piece of coral, tried to snap it from its foundation, but it clung with a tenacity to its life on the rock. She coveted the delicate fretwork. It looked a transparent leaf with all its veins showing, but decided not to risk scraped hands especially when she noticed a giant sand dollar not too far away. She went for it and tucked it carefully into the bottom of her bikini to protect the fragile thing from breaking.

Pammy meanwhile had found a magnificent conch shell, speckled like a thrush's breast and claimed it for her own.

Delighted with their unexpected finds, the girls were perfectly happy to follow Rod as he pointed up. Buffy had a roaring appetite now and surfaced as quickly as possible.

The three heads bobbed like corks on the water and Tiger, who had been resting on the beach with a small shell between his paws, rushed to the water's edge to meet them, barking with ecstasy to see them all together again. Maybe now they could get to a more serious consideration of the hamper's contents.

They shed their gear and the girls shook their hair free of water. Carefully arranging their treasures away from Tiger, they spread beach sheets out and reached into the hamper for lunch.

Grov had had the hamper packed for the threesome and stinted on nothing. There was cold chicken, cheese, fruit, salad and a chilled bottle of wine in a special thermal unit. Rod refused the wine when it was offered, going instead to the boat. When he returned it was with a six-pack of beer.

"Hey, where did that come from?" asked Pammy.

"Aha, you didn't notice me. It's an old sailor's trick. You just fasten the beer to the boat and it drags along, staying cool." He pulled one out, snapped the ring and took a mighty swig.

Meanwhile Buffy had arranged the food with one hand while fending off Tiger with the other. "Now, sit and wait," she commanded. Tiger, feelings hurt, crawled to the edge of the sheet and sat. "You behave now, or I won't give you anything." Tiger lowered his head to his paws, completely devastated by the threat and watched carefully.

The sounds of silence were broken only by three sets of perfect teeth crunching crisp lettuce, biting into juicy little tomatoes, gnawing on chicken and clinking on wine glasses.

The wine and the beer worked on all three and they settled into a comfortably sated laziness. Rod, giving a mighty sigh, crawled over to Buffy and laid his head on her lap. Buffy leaned against Pammy who leaned against the hamper. The sun at its highest point in the sky baked into their skins, sautéing them to a golden brown as their eyes lay at half mast, unwilling to remain open, unwilling to close. And so they reclined, three golden statues, soaking up sun and silence with the utter contentment of true primitives for whom the moment meant all.

Tiger watched them with some curiosity, having finally been treated to some chicken tidbits. He decided that these people were abnormal. Why lie in the broiling sun when with the tiniest effort they could walk up the beach and lie in the shade of a thick palm branch? He stretched and got up slowly, prowling up the beach, turning a few times to see if he was being followed. He was not. Crazy humans. What did they know?

It was Buffy who roused first. She fished for her watch to see the time. "Hey, it's been an hour. Let's go in swimming. C'mon! C'mon." She grabbed Pammy and tickled Rod sending both into disarray and then raced into the water, sending up a spray of wet jewels as she dove. The sea felt chilly warm and she gasped from its shock on her sun-warmed skin.

Rod and Pammy were practically on top of her. The three played like children, dunking and diving and splashing water amidst rollicks of giggles and gasps.

Pammy dove and stuck her head through Rod's legs, surfacing with him on her shoulders. He promptly fell over backwards and made a grab for Buffy. As she struggled out of his grasp, he reached for the elastic of her bikini bottom, stretching it away from her. She continued her struggle; and it was left behind in his hand. She was bare-assed and Rod proudly displayed his prize to Pammy.

Pammy laughed and made a lunge for the bottom, but Rod jerked them up and away as Pammy grabbed him by the trunks. As he turned to tickle her, he pulled the straps of her top down and yanked the ties in the back. Now he had Buffy's bottom and Pammy's top. Pammy's neat little breasts floated on the water like rubber balls, the nipples hardened from the touch of cool water on suddenly bared skin. Rod swam to her, tieing her top to his trunks, reached out his hands and cupped her breasts. They were warm to his touch and he bent his head to taste them in the seasoning of the salt water. Pammy wriggled to get free but he held her buttocks firmly as he worked on her. Then his hands explored her naked skin, skipping into her bikini bottom and feeling the rest of her. She turned in his hands, trying to escape half-heartedly, but she liked the feeling of Rod's hands on her and the unexpected novelty of love-play in the water.

Suddenly Buffy appeared behind Rod and grabbing his trunks gave a mighty yank, pulling them down over his knees and trapping his ankles. He struggled to free himself and with a yelp of triumph she held them over her head as a trophy, then flung them away. She floated back to Rod. He felt her smooth legs go around his waist and reacted like a shot. With one arm around him, she used the other to tickle him and when she inadvertantly tickled his backside, his stiffened penis jabbed her and she drew back in surprise, then on second thought encircled it with her hand. Rod released Pammy and turned to his new tormentor. But both girls came at him, one from the front and one from the back, teasing and taunting him with their nubile bodies. He allowed himself to sink, carrying both with him.

Buffy without her bottom, now released her straps while Pammy pulled off her own brief trunks. The little cove was now awash with gently bobbing pieces of swim suits, while the three stared at each other's splendid nudeness like children.

Rod hated to show favoritism so he reached for Buffy and treated her to the same delights Pammy had enjoyed.

He felt feverish even in the delicious coolness of the water. Aching to stick one of them, he didn't quite know how to handle it. Two girls at once was too much even for him. Buffy made up his mind by surfacing, so he turned to Pammy and caught her to him, lifting her on to him and plunging himself into her. They made love, treading water, even though the floating object was difficult to hold still.

As he released Pammy, he was suddenly seized by Buffy who had him erect again in seconds. Now it was her turn. Rod thanked the vitamins he took as a matter of course and his own powers of recuperation. Two girls in the space of a few minutes? Somehow he managed.

The three of them floated lazily, contentedly on their backs until the mini-tide washed them ashore and they lay in the sand, breathing heavily, half in delight, half with exhaustion from the intensity of their play.

"Hey, your knees are showing," he tickled Buffy.

"You should see what's showing on you," she teased back and bending over him gave it a rousing kiss.

"You're both in pretty interesting shape," Pammy breathed as she arched her back with a voluptuous yawn. "This is the best picnic I've ever been on."

"You going to tell the folks back in Locust Valley about it?" He smiled. "Hey, we better go salvage our swimming gear. Can you imagine arriving back at Shalimar, naked as jay birds?"

"So what? No one'll be there. They'll all be on the *Cassandra* getting bombed on champagne. We could probably walk through the whole place without a soul seeing us."

"Except for the kitchen boys. One look at you and you'll really have something on your hands." Rod winked broadly. "I understand they're really hot stuff in the sack."

Pammy sniffed, "That's a myth, everyone knows that."

"Prove it," dared Rod. "Why don't you just parade around in the buff and see what happens."

"No, thank you. I only strip for my most intimate friends and relatives."

"Besides we could always get it from the horse's mouth," said Buffy.

"Who dat?" Rod teased.

"Old fish face Emily. She probably could write a book on native hanky panky, don't you think? She's got the best piece on the island."

"Do you really think she's making it with good old Sebastian?" asked Rod.

"Oh, c'mon, Rod." Pammy was amazed. "Do you see the way they dance and look at each other? I think they'd do it right on the floor if they had the guts."

Rod was getting a little bored with the whole conversation. "What do you say we pack it in and get moving? There's a big night to look forward to."

And he gathered his charges together, launched the boat and headed back for Shalimar. Emily and Sebastian? That would be an interesting little bit to watch, thought Rod and he felt himself stiffen again just from the idea.

Grov was anxious to be the first aboard the *Cassandra*. Although Marty had assured him they would need nothing from the Shalimar kitchen or bar, he wanted to double check. If extra food or liquor were required, it would be far better to bring them on board before too many of the guests were there. For some reason Denise had seemed reluctant to join him.

He had decided not to wait for her, and calling over his shoulder that he'd meet her there, headed down to the dock and boarded the waiting tender. No matter what else you thought of the man, you had to admire his taste in yachts, Grov grudgingly admitted to himself as the tender pulled alongside the yacht's ladder. Yachting seemed to be one of the few areas, he thought, where he couldn't go far wrong with big money. There was something so determinedly traditional about all those European yards. They just wouldn't let you make a gaffe. Besides the owner's name, each yacht carried the yard's name, too, and there was a pride in those German yards, like Rassumussen's, Americans just didn't understand. He wondered as he climbed the stairs, how many god-awful scenes there must have been between Gramson and his designer before this jewel of the seas came down the ways.

A uniformed member of the crew saluted him smartly as he stepped on board, expressing his apologies that the captain wasn't there to greet him.

"I'm a bit early, I know," Grov admitted. "But I just wanted to be sure there was nothing needed from the club. Would you tell Mr. Gramson that Mr. Wilcox is here?"

As the crewman disappeared into one of the passageways, Grov allowed himself the indiscreet luxury of a careful investigation on his own. He noticed with ill-concealed curiosity, the buffet that had been set up.

One long, low, open grill, running almost the length of the table must have been specially designed for the yacht. Coals glowed almost to the white ash that would make them the perfect grilling temperature. He lifted the covers from several silver cannisters. Unless he was quite wrong, they were eighteenth century English. Inside one he found mustard, in another catsup and in a third, a common pickle relish. Uncovering one great silver bowl, he discovered hundreds of tiny Vienna sausages, and in another as many finger-sized rolls. Grov threw back his head and roared! How like Marty he thought, to serve this crowd—in these surroundings—hot dogs! He wondered for a minute whether he planned the ultimate affront, beer at an art show, but a quick glance at the bar reassured him. Pristine row upon row of crystal tulip champagne glasses reflected rainbows in the afternoon sun. Jeroboams of Möet et Chandon stood chilling in tubs of shaved ice. God, you had to hand it to the bastard, Grov thought, hog dogs and champagne. Who the hell else would have thought of that?

"Help yourself!" Marty boomed as he came up behind Grov, and with an off-hand gesture indicating it all, "This ought to help my wife's paintings slide down a little more easily."

"From what I hear of your wife's paintings, they stand quite well on their own." Grov couldn't restrain his antagonism toward this man. It wasn't like him either to give in to these feelings. After all, in his line of work, cosseting people like this was just part of the daily routine.

"No need to be polite with me, Wilcox. I know there are going to be more people here this afternoon interested in viewing the *Cassandra* than in seeing my wife's daubings."

"How fortunate that they can combine both." He'd have to watch himself, he was getting downright snappish. "I came a little early to see if there was anything you might need from Shalimar, but I can see how unnecessary that was."

"Yeah, well, you never know when you're gonna wanna ask a few people on board. Can't get the reputation for being stingy, now can I?" he asked slapping Grov too heartily on the back. "My reputation's bad enough as it is." He seemed almost proud of the fact. "Make yourself at home—relax—enjoy yourself. You're a guest now for a coupla hours, not the host. I'll get down and hustle up Sandy." Before he had gone three steps, he turned and asked, "Isn't Mrs. Wilcox going to be with us this afternoon?"

"She'll be along any minute. I know she wouldn't miss it for the world." Grov noticed the sneer on Gramson's face, but put it down to his natural unpleasantness. He wished Denise or some of the other guests would arrive. He never could understand this American obsession of never arriving at any social function at the specified time.

Margaret Bradley, still the product of her strict upbringing was one of the few exceptions to Grov's rule. Even as he paced nervously along the *Cassandra's* deck, she was tapping on the Perceval's door. She had heard no voices as she had approached their cottage and was hoping that she had not missed them, or misunderstood their arrangements for getting together that afternoon. But her first tentative taps were answered almost immediately by Bill, dressed for the occasion. He gave her a broad welcoming smile.

"Margaret, how nice. You're the only woman I know who's true to her word about time."

"Oh, I hope I'm not too early," she started to draw back from the open door.

"Not at all. We're both ready—Jane is just putting on her lipstick, I think. Do come in—she won't be a minute."

Margaret came in hesitantly, looking quickly about the room without wanting to appear to be staring. The room showed signs of recent attempts to quickly straighten out what must have been a hurricane of clothing and equipment. Suitcases stood open on the racks and on one of the double beds.

Margaret sat down on the edge of a chair as Bill quickly swept off his tennis sweater to make room for her. "Is Jane's headache any better?"

"Oh, yes, she's quite recovered now." He seemed oddly ill at ease here in the room. He walked to the door of their dressing room, tapped lightly and called softly through it, "Margaret's here, dear. Almost ready?"

"Be right out," Jane called back, and Margaret could hear the sound of running water in the basin.

"Would you like a drink before we go?" Bill asked gesturing to the set-ups on the coffee table.

"No, no, I'm sure Mr. Gramson will provide more than enough for my weak head. My capacity's strictly limited," she smiled.

"I've had to work on developing mine lately, but I still can't hold my own with some of those old time pols."

The door to the dressing room opened and Jane stepped out, in a crisply tailored piqué, a bright scarf tied at her neck, and large dark glasses covering half her face. Margaret was surprised by the glasses. She couldn't remember seeing Jane wearing them before. She had those deeply-lined squinty eyes that so many yachtswomen and tennis players develop, and Margaret assumed it was because she never protected her eyes from the sun. The glasses seemed even more out of place here in the cool semi-darkness of their room.

"Hi," Jane said as she touched the side of Margaret's cheek with her own. "Shall we be off to admire the paintings and play on Mr. Gramson's boat?"

"Let's!", Margaret answered, "I'm really eaten alive with curiosity."

"In the Sampson's cottage, Karen, too, was anxious to be on board the *Cassandra.* "David, for God's sake, get dressed."

"Relax, it's not like a movie you have to see from the beginning."

"I know that. I've been to art shows before, you're not my first brush with culture."

"You could have fooled me." He had decided after the agony of last night and the tensions of this morning that his best tack would be light banter. That way if her feelings should be further hurt, he could always claim he'd been teasing.

Fortunately she decided not to take him seriously, threw one of his brightly striped shirts at him and left. "I'll wait for you in the bar."

She couldn't have said anything that would have hurried him more. The thought of having to cover for her in the close and crowded confines of Marty's yacht when she'd had too much to drink drove his earlier guilt from his mind.

She was still on her first one when he got to the bar, and hanging on every word that came from the Limey photographer's lips. He liked Simon well enough, but found him terribly shallow and not at all as perceptive as his camera work had led him to expect. The charisma that had made him the favorite of the ladies around the world, escaped David completely. He put one hand lightly on Simon's shoulder, and the other on Karen's. "C'mon, all the great ones will be sold by the time we get there," he joked.

"We should be so lucky," Simon murmured, sliding back on his bar stool.

"But I haven't finished my drink," Karen protested.

"Don't worry. You have my word for it, there's more where we're going. And undoubtedly of better vintage, too." He put his arm firmly around her waist and eased her off the stool. To have resisted would have created a scene, and she wasn't far enough gone, he knew, to do that in front of Simon.

At the dock, the tender was just returning from delivering another group of guests to the yacht. On board the *Cassandra*, the show was in full swing. Guests, balancing drinks, wearing the casually understated clothes that looked so free and easy but were in reality a rigid uniform of their set, glowed in their recently renewed tans. It wasn't the kind of group that brought out the best in David, and he'd have to make a decided effort to remain civil, he knew.

The only thing that could make a gathering like this bearable at all, he thought, would be the presence of Emily. There was so much he wanted to tell her, so many things he wanted to ask. He quickly steered Karen away from the bar and toward the paintings then abandoned her saying, "Pick one out, honey. I've got to go to the head."

Karen began as serious an appraisal of the paintings as anyone could with absolutely no knowledge or understanding of the medium. David quickly lost himself in the crowd. His first scanning told him that Lalange at least wasn't there. That tall a man was easy to spot. Now David wanted more than ever to find Emily. He had to talk to her, and he didn't want that big black hovering around while he did. Christ—here he was, the anointed spokesman for liberalism and understanding, feeling the pinch of prejudice and bigotry toward this guy whose only crime seemed to be in treating Emily a lot better than he'd ever done. He hated himself for his feelings, but he could not help them, and he hated himself even more for this weakness of his intellect being unable to control them. He had been over every inch of the *Cassandra* that seemed open to the guests, always keeping a crowd of people between himself and Karen, and had seen no sign of Emily.

He'd better get back to Karen then before she found herself out of her depth or under the influence.

Simon was truly in his element. Even more so than at Shalimar. For here all the guests were compacted into one tight homogenous little mass on what had to be one of the favorite and most famous of this international set's toys. The show and the ship he was sure would supply ample material for his acid wit. And the guests he knew would be an eager and appreciative audience for his tidbits. He was right about the latter but completely wrong about the former. To have in any way ridiculed Sandy's work would have surely damaged his reputation far more than hers. She had a sure hand with color, he could see, and her slightly abstract land and seascapes and floral fantasies had an undeniable charm. They were the kind of pictures you'd find easy to live with, and hard to fault.

After one quick drink, Simon began to take his photographs. He had brought for this occasion his tiny lighter-sized camera, not so much because he admired the work it did, but because it was so fantastically inconspicuous that he could snap people even in these intimate surroundings without attracting undue attention. In his pocket was a slightly larger camera, he'd brought along if anything should go wrong with his Minox, but he hoped he'd not have to use it. He looked around, taking a quick inventory of the faces. He'd concentrate on the people now while they were all here and before they began to get sloppy drunk, and surely some of them would. The details of the *Cassandra* he could get later when the crowd began to thin out.

Seeing the Percevals now, all smiles and full of admiration for Sandy's work, it was hard to believe they had been so recently at each other's throats. This ability to put on a proper face had come not only from their years in politics. It was also the product of years of the proper schools, attending proper parties, and included making the proper marriage.

Today was actually the first time, except for their wedding day, he had seen her affected by what she was drinking. He doubted whether it was noticeable to anyone else, but he was aware of it. A slight slowing down of her speech pattern, that almost imperceptible sway to her walk you couldn't attribute to the movement of the boat which lay in a smooth-as-glass harbor. He realized she wanted to stay out on the deck rather than go into the saloon so that her dark glasses would not be conspicuous or seem unnatural. Only he really knew how unnatural they were for her. The flood of tears he had found her in when he returned to their cottage after brunch had left her eyes red and swollen. He had not noticed her taking more than one or two drinks, but then he realized she had had nothing to eat that day, just a half a cup of black coffee before she'd left him at the pool. She must really be feeling rotten, he thought, and yet she was keeping up the good front; together they smiled for the British photographer.

Karen wandered around the sumptuous yacht feeling like the girl from the other side of the tracks who had suddenly been allowed to cross over. Her relationship and subsequent marriage to David had put her in a blinding kind of limelight for which her simple country background had not prepared her.

Karen paused in front of a water-color and the tears came to her eyes. It was a sunset of such meltingly soft colors, a hidden part of Karen reached out and claimed it for her own. She turned to find David to ask him if she could buy it when she saw Sandy Gramson standing alone. She hurried over to her.

"Mrs. Gramson . . . Sandy . . . I want that water-color over there," she pointed. "I think it's so beautiful." Her voice caught.

Sandy stared at her curiously, "You're Karen Sampson, aren't you?"

"Yes, oh, excuse me, we haven't really met. But, of course, I know who you are. Who doesn't?"

Sandy smiled self-consciously.

Karen gave a quick look around, "I envy you so much. You have everything a woman could want and you have talent, too. At Sandy's protest, Karen smiled tightly, "I can't do anything very well. I can't even cook without burning the water."

"Why, Karen. You married one of the most successful writers in the world. That's something. A lot of women envy you. I do."

"You do?" Karen looked at Sandy incredulously.

"Oh, I can't tell you how much. Every time I read one of your husband's books, I think to myself, what would it be like to be married to a man who understands women so well. He's so sensitive to what makes us tick and his love scenes are so tender and passionate all at the same time."

Karen laughed. Her voice had a high keening edge and several people turned around at its sound. Sandy took Karen by the arm and steered her toward the bar. "Sit down and talk to me a moment."

"All right, but I don't know what to say. Except to tell you that I envied you. Married to such a successful businessman who gives you everything and probably can't bear to be separated from you for a moment."

Now it was Sandy's turn to laugh. It was not an attractive sound. She turned to stare into the tulip glass full of Möet & Chandon's best. "We always seem to want what we think the other has."

"What do you mean?" Karen asked.

"Oh, what you said before about my husband not being able to stand separation. Do you know the only time I see my husband is at the theatre or a charity ball?"

"Well, when David's writing, I don't see him for months on end."

"What about in the evening?"

"He comes in for dinner, that's true. But he goes back to his study almost immediately afterwards. Of course, when he's not writing, we have a pretty exciting life. Only," she turned and clutched Sandy's arm, "it always frightens me. I never know what to say. David's so glib and brilliant and has such positive ideas about everything. I don't have ideas on anything. I just listen. But I'm sure I embarrass him. He gets impatient with me." The more Karen sipped at her champagne, the looser her tongue became.

"Tell me, if your husband is always so busy, how do you stay sane, and how do you keep from being lonely?"

Sandy felt the tears rush to her eyes. Karen seemed so young and vulnerable. Sandy was perhaps a good ten years older than Karen but felt much more at this moment. This beautiful, long-legged creature, so confident looking, so immaculately groomed could have been wearing braces and pigtails, she was so unaware, so unsure of herself. They were sisters under the skin, only Sandy had years of experience in dealing with her problems.

Sandy smiled, "I have two children, I paint. I go to classes, exercise class and naturally, I'm always involved in some charity thing. So you see I don't have time to be lonely."

She bit her lip at the patent lie. At the plastic life she had constructed for herself because she was lonely. But she couldn't admit all to this girl. Karen obviously had already had too many little bubbles burst to accept the truth.

"We don't have any children yet. David has three

by his first marriage. His daughter," Karen blushed, "is almost as old as I am. It's a little embarrassing at times to think I'm her stepmother. David doesn't want us to have any yet. At least for awhile. But it is exciting to be married to a writer. We get invited to everything, parties, colleges, countries, even." The more champagne she drank, the more Karen babbled on, her conversation taking jagged turns up and down the mountainous roads of her thoughts. She skidded and slipped from one impasse to another until she finally stopped, lost in her own detours.

"David would kill me if he could hear me going on like this. He hates it when I drink too much. But I really admire you so much. I'd like to learn how to handle things as gracefully as you do. Really, I would." She finished lamely.

"You will, I'm sure. Just try to find something that really interests you and keeps you busy when he's writing. That way you won't be quite so dependent on him. It's good to feel you can do something yourself." Sandy, in trying to reassure Karen felt reassured herself. It *was* good to feel you could do something. The surprise showing today had convinced her to pursue her painting more seriously. Now, she might be able to create her own name, one that was free from Gramson awe and envy. Look how Karen Sampson viewed her. Strictly "Susie Says," not as a person but as an item in a column or a picture in a magazine. She hadn't the faintest conception of what it meant to be Mrs. Martin Gramson.

"Karen, I'm serious. Find something in yourself and do something about it. Otherwise you'll never be a person. You'll always live in his shadow."

"But I want to live in his shadow. I love him."

Sandy smiled sadly. And thought to herself. But how long will he love you after he finds out you can't breathe without his lungs? She had no idea how close she was to the truth of the Sampsons at this moment. How David was feeling the strain of Karen's cloying dependency. How all that sweet girlish charm and vulnerability was beginning to affect his work and make it banal.

David, who had been searching for Karen, spotted her at the bar with Sandy and with a clutch of irritation saw her drain the champagne glass. Christ, he hoped she hadn't been babbling in Sandy Gramson's ear like a love-sick puppy. After last night's maudlin scene, he was torn between guilt and anger, at himself, at Karen, at the whole bloody mess he had made of their lives. He should never have married Karen. She was going to drag him down to her level with all her insecurities and fears. Even now, with a new book about to start, he was worried about finishing it. Everytime he went to his studio, he'd be wondering if she was drinking and because of the drinking do something horrible to herself or to the house or to some poor unsuspecting stranger.

He had more than made up his mind to call his lawyer and have the marriage annulled. Better for both of them in the long run. Karen would take it badly, at first, but he was sure if he could get her to a good psychiatrist, she would straighten out. It was that or else give up writing and turn into a real hack if he wasn't that already. He just couldn't afford to spend his life catering to Karen. He needed someone to cater to him and someone who could be content to be alone for long periods of time. The life of a writer's wife was not an easy one, he knew, but there were women who could handle it. Emily, for example, she probably would have done it perfectly.

David brushed the thought of Emily from his mind and strolled casually to the bar. "Easy on the champagne, love, we still have a long day ahead of us." David bit his tongue at his hypocrisy.

"Oh, David," Karen's eyes were flushed and shining, "I saw a painting of Sandy's that I love. Could we buy it, please? I know just where to put it."

"Sure you can buy it. You didn't even have to ask." Then he turned to Sandy, "You have a lovely touch with your medium."

"Thank you, so much." Sandy said with graciousness. There was no malice or falseness in his compliment and she knew it. He was another surprise in a long list of surprises that had started with Bill Perceval. She wondered if an artist was ever sure of his talent until he heard it praised by other people. She blushed at calling herself an artist; that was a title she felt she hadn't quite earned yet. A talented dabbler, perhaps, but a long way from being called artist. Maybe not so long, not if she worked hard and really learned her craft. Now she was anxious to leave Shalimar and get back to New York and start classes in earnest and paint and paint. Maybe even more into some of the newer mediums, like acrylics and metallics.

"Hey, Mrs. G. you've got a long day ahead, too," David smiled mistaking Sandy's sudden shallow breathing for too much champagne rather than the excitement she felt about herself and her future.

"You're right," Sandy smiled, getting up from the stool. "I think I'd better circulate a little and see how I'm doing. Karen, it's been nice talking to you. Remember what I said, I'm sure you can do it. Just try." Sandy smiled and gave Karen's hand a squeeze, nodded to David and moved into the crowd.

"What were you talking about, you two?" David asked, prying Karen's hand away from the champagne goblet.

"Oh, nothing," Karen smiled airily. "You'll see. She's a nice girl and she makes a lot of sense. You'll see."

David shrugged. He really didn't care what they had been talking about. What could Karen say that would fascinate a woman like Sandy Gramson anyway?

He took Karen by the hand, and they found themselves staring into the lens of Simon's camera. An automatic smile creased their faces. Having captured those two uneasy smiles for posterity, Simon turned to his hostess. She was radiant this afternoon, Sandy couldn't believe it was actually happening to her. Here were all these people who had not only seen, but owned the finest art in the world, really enthusiastic about her work. So many of them had said such marvelous things! Jane Perceval had insisted on buying one of her paintings for their summer place. She could see Marty's uneasiness growing, but it didn't stop her from basking in this new found adulation. Being the center of attention because of her own work rather than because of the jewel collection she might be showcasing was a new experience for her, and she was enjoying it as much as Marty was obviously hating it. She had deliberately not worn any of her large jewels, but not out of any desire to irritate him. Marty had avoided her as long as he could. "And this must be the artist herself?"

"Oh, Marty, isn't it marvelous?"

"What's so marvelous?"

"The way people like my work . . . they really do!"

"A little fake admiration is a small price to pay for an invitation to spend the afternoon lapping up free food and booze on Marty Gramson's yacht."

"It's not that entirely, I'm sure. Jane Perceval insisted on buying one of the paintings."

"Just smart politics, that's all. He's expecting big things for his campaign chest."

"Don't be such a sorehead, Marty. Would it hurt

you to admit I might have some talents outside of bed?"

"Don't flatter yourself, you're no genius there either."

"That may be because I haven't had the experience you've had, but that can be arranged." She wheeled around away from him with a dazzling smile which Simon caught for posterity. There's nothing like a little open adoration to give a woman sparkle.

"Your paintings are really enchanting. I can't tell you how much I admire them", Margaret said as Sandy turned to her.

"You're a darling to say so," Sandy smiled back.

"Not at all, just truthful. I really feel as though I've made a discovery here this afternoon. But even if I hadn't seen the pictures, I'd have known what a marvelous feeling you have for color, just seeing that collection of needlepoint pillows over there. They are your doing aren't they?"

"Just something to pass the time," Sandy answered, smiling shyly.

"Don't be so modest—they're heaven—really. You've a wonderful touch. Have you ever shown in New York?"

"Good heavens, no! This is really the first time anyone outside the family's seen anything I've done."

"But you mustn't keep all this to yourself—that's selfish. When we get back to New York, I want you to have lunch with some friends of mine who have a small but busy gallery. I know they'd just adore your work. You really must share your paintings."

"I'd love to, I just never thought anyone would be interested in them."

"Then you're a much better artist than a judge. Your husband wouldn't object to your showing, would he?"

"He probably wouldn't object, but he'd certainly find it hard to believe." Sandy smiled to herself at the thought. What a kick in the head that surprise would be.

Marty was already surprised. Although to Sandy he had put down everyone's admiration as just politeness, he had to admit to himself, this crowd really did seem impressed with her work. For every compliment he'd had on the *Cassandra* that afternoon, he'd had at least a dozen on his wife's talent. Maybe he had underestimated her. What the hell, if she really was serious about all this painting, he'd buy her a gallery. He glanced around the main saloon and his eye caught Simon snapping a picture of the Sampsons standing next to one of Sandy's water-colors.

He wondered how straight that little photographer was. Straight or not, he obviously represented the market he was after with his new line of high priced men's cosmetics. A few minutes with him would probably give him more insight into what was wrong or right about the line than fifty interviews with Bronx housewives. As he made his way toward Simon, he wondered whether that research firm was taking him.

Simon noticed his host bearing down on him. "Your wife is an enormously talented young woman. You must be very proud of her."

"Oh, sure, but not for the reason you think."

"Oh?" One thing about these Limeys, Marty had to admit, they never lost their cool.

"Yeah, she makes a helluva chicken soup." As soon as he'd said it, he regretted it. If he was to get anything out of this trend setter, he'd have to watch his antagonism. What the hell did the English know about chicken soup! "I've got a little problem I thought you might be able to help me out with," Marty went on. "I'm bringing out a line of men's cosmetics soon—you know—not the usual pine and lime stuff aimed at the jock strap market, something with a lot more class. You know," he said elbowing Simon sharply. Simon dropped his camera quickly into his pocket, there was no telling when he'd need both his hands.

Marty indicated Simon's neatly trimmed but longish sideburns. "How long do you think this beard and sideburns thing is gonna last?"

"I've no idea, actually. But I would imagine it will last at least as long as all this unisex business. I'll be damned if I'll give up the one most visible indication of my maleness."

"Then do you think there's gonna be a market for moustache wax or some crazy beard dressing?"

"I'm afraid I wouldn't know. The beards I know are probably the last people on earth to consider buying male cosmetics. You'd be better off, actually, questioning Duke Dexter. By the way, I haven't seen him here today, have you?"

Marty felt an involuntary shudder go through him at the mention of Duke's name. He wondered if Joy would be able to come up with selling ideas that would appeal to a crowd like that. She'd made his cosmetics the hottest in the business and kept them on top for years. She was one goddamned talented broad all right. But she'd been well rewarded. Hell, he took better care of her kids than he did of Sandy's. She'd just have to learn to work the other side of the street. He was sure she wouldn't have any trouble figuring out what these freaks went for.

Over Simon's shoulder he noticed Denise and Sandy talking. He'd better get over there and cool that fast. Without another word, he turned and left Simon. As he moved quickly through the crowd toward them Marty thought to himself, that little French broad really had some chutzpah, making small talk with Sandy, and he grudgingly admitted that his wife had real style and unbeatable cool. But then he realized Sandy didn't know about yesterday afternoon's activity with Denise.

Marty like an arsonist returning to the scene of the crime strode up to the two women, and put his arm around Sandy's shoulders. He felt her shrink away from him and stiffen as he tried to pull her closer.

"Well, what do you think of my little Michelangelo?" he boomed.

Denise was amused, Sandy was not. "Don't you think your wife might more readily be compared with Monet?"

"What the hell—they're all the same. They all just splash a little paint on a canvas and call it art."

"Elizabeth Arden makes cosmetics, too," replied Denise. "You'd hardly want to be called another Arden, would you?"

But before he could answer, Sandy interrupted, "You'll have to excuse my husband, his knowledge of art is confined to the package designs of his cosmetics."

Marty was taken back by Sandy's remark. He looked at her with a grudging new respect. She had spunk. She talked back. Son of a bitch. She was feeling her oats. A little pat on the head for these splashes of paint had put some spine in her. Marty admired a woman who talked back, but he never wanted to marry one. Now it seemed as if he had.

His musings were interrupted by the arrival of Margaret who was breathless with excitement and admiration for Sandy's work. "I really must have one of your paintings—one I've just seen in the saloon. Come, you must set a price on it." As she took Sandy lightly by the elbow and began moving her off toward the crowded saloon, Marty turned to Denise and said, "Why don't you come with me, then. I'll show you around the *Cassandra*." The remark was one of those sulky little boy things he did so often, and it did not go unnoticed.

Turning and smiling sweetly at them both Sandy called out quite clearly as she moved away, "Oh, was there something you missed yesterday?"

A distinct chill could be felt in the early evening air. By now the crowds on board had begun to thin out. Having satisfied their curiosity, and finding little if anything to criticize, they had sated themselves on too much food and liquor at Gramson's expense. And now with that overstuffed, slightly headachey feeling that follows close on the heels of such over-indulgence, they were heading back to Shalimar, each to pursue his own remedy.

Grov was hoping for a re-match with Perceval on the courts, and was disappointed to learn that he was leaving that afternoon. He'd have to find someone else. It wouldn't be easy to find someone who could give him a good game.

The Percevals had been two of the first to leave the *Cassandra.* Bill had tried unsuccessfully to get Jane to have something to eat during the showing, but she insisted she wasn't hungry. He knew her well enough to know that by then she must have been ravenous. And so he had suggested they leave early. When Jane looked for Margaret to tell her, she saw her deeply engrossed in a conversation with David Sampson, and so the Percevals left by themselves.

At their cottage, Bill finished packing. It was the first time he could remember packing without Jane helping. She was always so good at remembering the little things he so often forgot. He had offered to order her a sandwich from room service, but she had refused, saying she thought she would just lie down for a while. He noticed uneasily that she fixed herself another drink before kicking off her shoes and throwing herself down on the bed. She really didn't need that drink. He knew what she really needed was a little solid food. But it seemed like such a petty point to be trying to make at such a time. He couldn't believe she was serious about this actually changing everything between them. She was far too sensible for that—they had too much going for them to break it up now. And yet he sensed a determination in her that he had only seen once or twice before—and each time it had been in someone who had gone to or beyond some personal breaking point. He longed to take her in his arms and try to straighten it all out now before he left. But he knew in her present state it would be futile. And besides he didn't trust himself to keep secret what he had heard about young Bill. Now that it had all come to this he regretted not having told her right away. Now when she learned about it, and he was sure that she eventually would, she would find it hard to forgive him, he knew. And yet if this was the point on which she was taking her stand, if this was to be her test of his feelings, telling her now was loading his side unfairly. Besides there was always the slim possibility that he would be able to get it all hushed up and she would never have to know. Funny, he thought to himself, here we are at the breaking point, and still my major concern is her peace of mind. Why was it so hard to make her understand that?

He had called for a cab and changed for the trip back, and now as he glanced down at his watch he knew it was time for him to leave. She was sleeping deeply now, the heavy sleep of someone who has had too much to drink. He decided against waking her, and instead, kissed her gently on the forehead before he left, closing the door silently behind him. He could see the *Cassandra* still lying at anchor in the harbor, the biggest jewel in Gramson's fabled collection. And he could just barely hear the music over the water.

Though the musicians were still valiantly repeating their limited repertoire of island songs, only one or two guests remained on board. Sandy had agreed to take Simon on a tour of the *Cassandra* so that he might get some pictures that would be exclusives for his magazine. Marty at first had been sullen about the idea, but with one of those mercurial changes that were so characteristic of him, he had decided to tag along. And now he was completely in charge. Like a small boy showing off his marble collection, Marty moved from one treasure to the next. Recalling with delight how he had out-bid or out-foxed some other collector for this piece of art, or that antique. His mind was as full of detail as to each piece's actual worth, what he had "stolen" it for and the circumstances surrounding its acquisition as a slick catalogue. Simon felt more like an insurance appraiser than a photographer getting the grand tour. He could see that Marty's braggadocio was embarrassing Sandy and he did his best to make light of it.

"We've nothing at all like this in England" he said, winking broadly at Sandy over Marty's shoulder. "Allowing me to photograph this for the enlightenment of my countrymen, is a damned decent gesture on your part."

"What the hell—we're allies—aren't we?" Marty boomed slapping Simon on the back with enough force to send him reeling. "And besides, England's been a good market for me, since you dropped your Yardley and old lace image and started to swing! Photograph as much as you want—one good turn deserves another—right?"

Simon smiled again at Sandy who now seemed to be enjoying the joke. "Yes, and you must feel free to drop in at the British Museum any time you're in London."

Marty wasn't sure just how to take the remark, but then much that had happened that afternoon had confused him. He never did understand that goddamned British understatement and he guessed he never would. And now it seems like he'd never really understand Sandy, either.

When the Gramsons and Simon returned to the main saloon after their tour, it was deserted except for the Sampsons and Margaret Bradley. Margaret and David were talking animatedly, and Sandy noticed as soon as she stepped into the room with them, Karen had once more withdrawn into that protective little shell of fear and apprehension she wore almost constantly whenever she appeared with David. That must drive a man like David wild, Sandy thought to herself. And she was quite right. But for the moment, at least, David was not thinking about Karen at all. For he had become deeply engrossed in his first real conversation with Margaret. He had always shared not only the natural resentment born into the poor or the really wealthy, but also a secret envy he'd have admitted to no one. His conversation that afternoon was an awakening for him. He found Margaret remarkably well informed, with a deep understanding, not just a surface knowledge, of many of his favorite causes. She was obviously one of the few who took her charities seriously and had become deeply involved. His opinion of her changed rapidly in the few minutes of conversation they had. For the first time he became aware of just how much a woman with Margaret's money and position could do when really involved.

As Simon approached them, he glanced down at his watch. "I'm afraid we're all going to have to leave this floating paradise and slip into our dancing shoes if we're to keep up with the rest of the members."

Margaret, too, glanced at her watch, surprised at how quickly time had passed, "I'd no idea it was so late," she said standing up quickly and offering her hand to Sandy. "It was a truly lovely show, Sandy.

And don't forget about our lunch when we're all back in town. Thank you for a delightful afternoon." She was anxious now to be back at Shalimar. If the weather were right, Phillip might even now be arriving.

David took Karen by the elbow, guiding her after Margaret. "We might as well all go together and save the tender an extra trip. He turned to Gramson who had followed them all out onto the deck. "It was quite an afternoon, thanks."

"I'll be expecting to read about it in one of your books soon," Marty boomed back and then laughed.

Simon, seeing the anger crawl across David's face tried to break the tension. "You're more apt to find what you're looking for in my magazine—complete with pictures in living color", he added, holding up his tiny camera before slipping it into his pocket.

As the tender moved across the short distance of water that lay between the *Cassandra* and the Shalimar dock, they could see the lights beginning to twinkle on in the cottages, in the club house and along the club's paths.

"It looks like a fairy-tale kingdom," Margaret said softly.

"I'm afraid it's in for a rude awakening," muttered David.

"I don't see how it could be," Margaret replied.

"Hopefully you won't see it," David said, letting his optimism overcome his apprehension as he thought of Faisan.

They parted on the path to their respective cottages.

As Margaret passed the Perceval's cottage, she paused for a moment, undecided as to whether or not to knock and invite them to join her and Phillip for dinner. But then, she realized, she wasn't sure just when Phillip would be arriving, so continued on up to the reception room of the club to see if there were any messages for her. Inside the Perceval's cottage, Jane was in a deep sleep, part exhaustion, part liquor, part escape.

By the time the last guests were leaving the *Cassandra,* Bill Perceval's cab was pulling into the island's primitive airport. He could see the small chartered plane being made ready on a deserted apron.

It had been an unsettling drive. His driver had recognized him immediately. But there was a hard edge to his banter that disturbed Bill.

"The island be-com-ing too hot for you, Mis-ter Ma-yor?" The lilt of his accent did not diminish the insolence behind the words.

"Not this island. My island."

"Trouble on your home front?"

"Nothing unusual for a city that size," Bill said defensively.

"Sure-ly noth-ing like what is about to hop-pen here, either." He said "either" the English way. "When *this* peaceful island blows, you will certainly hear it in the states."

"Why would this island "blow?"

"That is one reason right there. You prob'ly honestly do not know. You tourists are so accustomed to look-ing through us 'friendly natives' you never do see what we are. You think we are dumb, hap-py and la-zy."

"To tell you the honest truth, I haven't found the natives either friendly or happy here."

"That's even worse. You see our plight, but are indifferent."

Bill did not wish to pursue the conversation further, but he didn't know how to put a stop to it. He tried silence but that didn't work. He would rather be spending his time figuring some way out of the mess he was going home to than listening to this sullen black whose problems—real or imaginary—seemed remote, yet so personally threatening. He wished to hell he was on that plane already and out of here. And he wished Jane were with him.

"And you're leav-ing just before the real unfriendliness starts. Tsk. Tsk. This will be a night to remember on St. Phillipe. But you are one smart white man to get out this afternoon."

By now Bill's fears were overcoming his annoyance at this man. "You don't think there's any danger to the people at Shalimar, do you?" As soon as he asked the question he regretted it and despised himself for playing into this black's hands. The native, now that he had started, knowing he should keep quiet, could not resist showing off his privileged knowledge.

"You can believe it. They have had one of your playmates since last night. Has no one missed that pretty little girl-boy?"

Now Bill could feel the blood pounding in his temples. By God, he might be right. He hadn't noticed Duke today; surely he wouldn't have missed a chance like this afternoon's art show to make an exhibition of himself. He had to get to a phone. But just knowing Duke was gone wouldn't be of much help. "Where have they got him?"

"Don't really know if there's much left of him to worry about. And it would spoil the fun if you were to be let in on it, wouldn't it?"

The driver's insolence had grown with every mile. But now they were at the airport and Perceval allowed himself the tiny reciprocal nastiness of undertipping the driver. Instead of further surliness, he was rewarded with a hearty laugh.

"That's right, Mis-ter May-or—that's the way keep us in our place." Without waiting for Perceval's reaction, he slammed the door of the cab and was off in a roar, a squeal of tires and a great cloud of dust which engulfed, then settled down on Perceval and his luggage.

He picked up his own bags, there was no one else around who would do it, and headed into the small waiting room. An indolent young native, lazing behind the one ticket counter with his feet propped up on a box, was deeply engrossed in a well-thumbed, months' old issue of one of the more lurid American skin magazines. Perceval identified himself. After much paper shuffling, head scratching and fumbling, the young man pointed to the small plane on the runway waiting for him. With a nod of his head, the boy indicated a casually dressed man of about fifty, leaning against the wall and downing a beer. "That's the pilot—over there."

Perceval went to him, told him he had to make one phone call and then would be ready to go. The pilot nodded, glanced at his watch and said, "Anytime at all—it all goes on your tab."

Dealing with the local operator was even more of a challenge than usual, but he finally go through to Shalimar. He heard the signal indicating the phone in the cottage was ringing. After several rings, Jane's voice answered.

"Jane, it's me. I'm at the airport. I wish you'd reconsider and come back with me now. Frankly, I'm a little worried about what's going to be happening here."

"What could possibly happen here?"

"I don't want to go into it now on the phone—just take my word for it. You'd be a lot better off coming home with me now."

"Of course *you* would want me to. I can see it now: 'MAYOR AND HIS WIFE RETURN FROM ISLAND IDYLL.' It doesn't quite ring true when the Mayor returns alone, does it?"

"Jane, I'm thinking of you—not some half-assed newspaper picture."

"Such language from our spokesman of sweet reason."

"Jane, this is no time for games. Are you coming or not?"

"Have a nice flight Bill." The phone went dead in his ear.

The heat, his frustration and his inability to handle even his own wife infuriated Bill. He slammed the receiver down. He thought for a moment of what she'd said. She'd been wrong there, too. His coming home alone, interrupting his holiday actually made him look more concerned than if the two of them came home together. Thinking of homecoming brought Suzanne to mind. He lifted the phone again and started the frustrating process of putting through a long distance call. By the time he finally got through to her, he noticed his pilot downing another beer. How many did that make this afternoon—he wondered—and he wished it had been coffee he was drinking instead.

Despite the connection which gave every indication of being at best a tentative thing, he could hear the warm concern in Suzanne's voice. She was in the tiny apartment she kept in town for her use, when it was impossible to make the long commute to her family's place on the North Shore. In his mind's eye he could see it now. Small, but uncluttered, a perfect reflection of her. He told her he was on his way home, that Jane was staying, heard the sudden intake of her breath at those words. He suggested that she meet him at his place. He had no idea whether or not the press would be at the airport. But since Suzanne was a frequent visitor at the mayor's residence, her coming would attract no attention.

"Bring your brief case," he added. And with no further word, they both hung up.

Suzanne couldn't believe that Jane was not returning with Bill. There were a thousand questions she wanted to ask, but knew better than to air them over the phone. She wondered if Bill had kept the story from Jane—the one of young Bill's trouble. She'd have to wait—she looked at her watch—another four hours before she'd get the answers.

She pulled her neatly initialed brief case from under her desk, popped her cosmetic case and a nightgown into it. Then headed up town. She'd have just enough time to catch that new French movie she'd been reading about.

Emily had found Shalimar deserted by the time she returned from town. For the past several hours, she had been arranging and rearranging stock in the boutique in an attempt to make the time pass. She had even allowed herself the luxury of a quick swim in the deserted pool, but had felt too nervous to enjoy it.

Now she was prowling around the gardens of Shalimar, surprised to find that even the usual help was nowhere to be seen. Even though they had permission to go off for a few hours of relaxation, she felt that the hour was growing late.

She saw the Percevals come up from the dock and move towards their cottage. She waved but they apparently had not seen her. Assuming that the party aboard the *Cassandra* must be close to ending and Grov would be arriving shortly. She returned to the lobby of the club. It still seemed unusually quiet to her. She went to her boutique and sat wearily in a small wicker chair, realizing her heart had not stopped pounding since she had left Sebastian. Her eyes closed momentarily but she was on instant alert when she heard Sebastian's voice call her name. His level was quiet, his tone was not.

"Emily. I'm glad I found you alone."

"What is it?" She was up like a shot and her hand on his arm was strong with fear.

"Faisan was not making idle threats. He does have a hostage from the club."

"Who is it?" she breathed tensely.

"It's Duke Dexter."

"Thank God."

Sebastian looked at her sharply. "What do you mean? Who did you think it might be?"

"Never mind. It's terrible, no matter who it is. What have they done to him? Did you find out?"

"I don't know. But I know a little bit about the strange practices of my friendly brothers," he said ironically, "and it can't be too pleasant."

"They haven't killed him, have they?"

"I don't think that they would go that far. Besides that's not dramatic enough."

"How did you find out?"

"That's not important now. The important thing is that I didn't find out enough. I think we must tell Grov."

"Yes, we have to tell him about Duke. Everyone has probably noticed by now that he's missing. He's not the type that just disappears in a crowd."

"I couldn't discover if Faisan is up to anything else at this moment. But I think Grov should decide how he wants to handle tonight."

She turned from him and picked up a scarf, nervously pleating the edges.

"Naturally, I'll stay here and give Grov every possible support."

"Naturally." Emily said absently.

"Emily, I also want you to know that if anything happens here, whether tonight or next week, I still think it best if you plan to leave the island."

She turned to him, her face hurt and angry.

"Don't misunderstand. I'm thinking of your safety, not my feelings."

So, it was finally out. The feeling of Friday night, the feeling of separation was no longer unspoken. Sebastian had defined it; there was no mistaking it. The time was not now. It was the wrong time, the wrong place. Accepting it was the only sensible thing to do. Emily turned away, so Sebastian could not see her tears.

Sebastian didn't have to see them. He reached for her and held her close, kissing her eyes. "Emily, I did love you. You know that. Don't forget it, but don't remember it, either. It'll be better for both of us."

"Oh, there you are, Emily," Grov stumbled on the embrace but covered his embarrassment with his usual suavity. "And Sebastian. We missed you at the show this afternoon."

"Did you miss Duke Dexter by any chance?" asked Sebastian.

"Why, yes, as a matter of fact, quite a few people remarked on his absence. Not the sort of thing you'd expect Duke to miss."

"Grov, I'd like to talk to you for a moment."

Sebastian took Grov aside and in a few swift sentences outlined what had happened and what he feared might happen. Grov's face showed its first signs of age at Sebastian's tale. "The whole thing seems quite unbelievable," he breathed.

"Yes, it does, but not really, if you're an islander."

"What do you suppose they're after? Money?" Grov's naiveté was not hard to understand under the circumstances. Hotel managers managed hotels. They rarely became involved in native politics.

Sebastian replied, "Money? I wish it were that simple. I think somehow Duke offended them. And they are going to make some kind of object lesson of him. But I must warn you. It may not stop there."

"What on earth do you mean?"

"I'm not sure yet, Grov. Let's just keep things moving as if nothing had happened. I don't think you can let your guests in on this. There will be panic otherwise. And if worse comes to worse, I can always ask for help by calling out neighboring islands. There's quite a large fleet nearby."

"Well, I don't know," Grov rubbed his head. "Whatever you think Sebastian. We are in your hands."

"I'll try not to let this get out of those hands."

Slowly, the staff arrived back at the club and the sound of feverish activity could be heard as they scurried back and forth, setting up tables and chairs and flowers for the evening's formal ball.

The usual slow-paced sullenness had given away to high spirits and anticipation. Several of the boys could even be heard singing some of the slave songs of the other evening. But the tune was more triumphant than plaintive.

Emily and Grov moved about looking at each other, lines of worry creasing their faces. Sebastian was talking to one older waiter, the one who had been unusually surly at brunch. There were low sounds of heated words being exchanged. Sebastian moved around in a serious attempt to find out and forestall any happening and at the same time to cool any inflamed ideas the staff of Shalimar might harbor. He was not being successful in either. He could have been a stranger and this fact alone made him realize the imminent danger. These were the same people who only months before had seemed to be his strongest supporters. Now they seemed determined not only to disenfranchise him, but to disown any relationship to him. Sebastian did not look forward to this evening.

Neither did Grov. Without knowing one half of what Sebastian knew, his sixth sense told him that if he could get Shalimar and its guests through this evening, he would call it quits. Better to sell tennis balls in a pro shop than be responsible for the well-being of hundreds of people on an island ready to burst into flames. They did not teach this sort of thing at Cornell Hotel Management School. Perhaps if he got through this evening, he might teach Native Uprising 103 to anyone foolish enough to think running a luxury club in the Islands was a cushy job. He was surprised at his own levity. At a time like this!

Within an hour, Grov, in his most dazzling dinner jacket, was down in the ballroom making small talk with his guests. Denise, golden in white chiffon, held up her end as hostess, moving easily between the glitter of jewels and the opulence of beautiful people at their favorite indoor sport—dressing up.

The glitter and high spirits of the evening—now that the weekend was drawing to a close—was in strange contrast to the guarded wariness of Grov, Emily and Sebastian.

David and Karen, arriving a little later than the rest of the crowd, were swept up by the gaiety and momentum of the music. For the first time in the long weekend Karen's ordinarily pale cheeks were flushed with pink, as Simon, spotting her, swept her into his arms and whirled her off to dance. David watched her move off with a sigh of relief and immediately turned into the crowd, his eyes searching for the familiar figure of Emily. As he moved around the room, Margaret waved to him and he walked over to say hello. She, too, seemed unusually flushed and David was amused to see this mass madness seize the gathering. He must remember to work this into one of his books.

Candles flickering on the tables, the smell of fresh-picked gardenias filled the air and lent the night all the glamour of a junior prom. David hated candlelight. It disguised the banal and gave the real a blasé mystery. Women liked it because it was kind to their skin and gave them opportunities to go heavy on the make-up, like stage presences who had to be seen from afar. He disliked the artifice and knowing what he knew only served to heighten the unreality. He continued his search for Emily.

Simon caught David's eyes from the dance floor and walked over with Karen. She looked at David happily, "I've got to have a little drink. You don't mind, David, just a tiny one?" Simon signalled David behind Karen's shoulder that he wanted to talk to him.

David gave permission to Karen, "Go on, baby, just a little one. I want to talk to Simon for a moment." Karen swirled off with a rustle of skirts as David turned back to Simon, "What's up? Anything happening?"

Simon took him by the arm and they walked closely together to keep their voices out of earshot. "Have you noticed that Duke Dexter has been missing all day?" inquired Simon.

"Come to think of it, you're right. You think that means something?"

"I don't know. Don't you think it's rather odd?"

"Well, after that scene in town, nothing would surprise me with him. He's probably off in the arms of a native boy somewhere, showing how strongly he cares about integration."

Simon looked askance, "I hope it's no more than that."

"Why do you think it would be?" Asked David.

"I don't know," Simon said, "I have a strange feeling."

"Hey, by the way, did you say anything to Grov about our visit to town?"

"No, I didn't. I didn't know what to say. Did you?"

"No." replied David.

"Actually, I noticed Grov walking around while I was dancing with Karen. He seems a little distracted. Maybe he knows something already."

David replied, "I doubt it. He's probably just playing host. I know he left the *Cassandra* pretty late and I'm sure there were a lot of last minute arrangements to be made for tonight.

"I better go find Karen. Keep your eyes open and if you hear anything, give me a signal."

Simon nodded and hurried over to the table where Pammy, Buffy and Rod were holding a chair for him.

The noise level of the room increased with the high spirits and the amount of alcohol flowing.

"How was the art show?" Pammy attempted to raise her voice above the rest.

"Very good, surprisingly good. You should have come. You would have learned a great deal."

"We learned a lot too," Buffy said with significant looks at her partners in "water lore."

"Oh?" Simon raised a neatly arched eyebrow.

"Yes," Pammy explained, "we had an undersea adventure that Jacques Costeau never thought of."

Simon looked at their satisfied faces, "I think I have a vague idea of your afternoon activities."

Pammy giggled. Buffy blushed. Rod looked tired but smug.

Dancing continued through dinner as if the Shalimar guests determined to make their last evening a combination of New Year's and the Captain's Ball. The women were never more glittering. But it was Sandy Gramson on whom all eyes were turned. Her long brown hair was pulled back in a fat braid. Among the coils of the braid, the famous Gramson yard long rope of diamonds was interwined. Around her neck was the famous African Queen, ninety-eight carats in a single round stone, signalling like a traffic light from its platinum chain. Diamond pears swung from her ears and she wore the other famous Gramson stone, the one that had been removed from a fabled empress's crown. She was a glittering sight. And all the diamonds were set against the simplicity of her white crepe dress. She herself glowed with a brilliance that rivaled her own jewels.

Marty was following her around as if hypnotized, a moth constantly throwing himself against the light. It was the first time, in a long time that his wife had decided on her own to do him proud. He looked at her as though she were a strange, new woman and basked in the reflected glory of a creature for whose creation he took full credit.

With the security born of self-confidence, Sandy tonight could happily wear the Gramson jewels without feeling like Marty's Christmas tree. And there was something regal, indeed, about her carriage. She was breathtaking.

Margaret had waited as long as she could for Phillip to arrive and finally made a belated appearance in the crowded ballroom. She knew enough about the vagaries of flying, but not enough about the island situation to feel any concern for Phillip's tardiness. She looked around for Jane Perceval without seeing her, but she saw David, who had just retrieved Karen, at a table with room for one more. She walked towards them and was pleased when David insisted she join them.

As he stood to pull out her chair, he saw over her head the woman he'd been looking for all day and the man he had been hoping to avoid. He had never seen Emily looking as beautiful as she was tonight. There was something sad about her, maybe the pale celadon green of her simple chiffon dress, the innocent fall of her long blonde hair, the paleness of her skin under her tan. Her delicacy was in striking contrast to the rich strength and deep brown of Sebastian's skin.

Both were talking in hushed tones. Both had concerned looks on their faces. For a moment Emily's eye caught David's, she stared at him, and in the space of a blink knew that David was privy to the island's unrest. She wrenched her glance away and continued talking to Sebastian. David watched her glance away and continue walking with Sebastian. David watched her back, wanting very badly to speak to her. But he sat down with a nervousness he hoped was not noticeable to the two women.

As the busboys cleared away the last remains of dinner the music switched tempo and David pardoned himself and moved towards Emily and Sebastian's table. She now had a heightened flush on her face, not from alcohol he was sure.

"Emily," he presented himself formally, "I would be pleased if you would dance with me."

He had asked so graciously that Emily felt it would be rude to refuse, also difficult to explain to Sebastian if she had.

David swept Emily into his arms, "Ems," she shivered at his use of the pet name from the past, "are you privy to what's happening on the island?"

"What do you mean privy?"

"I mean has your island leader indicated to you that his paradise might be going up in smoke?"

"David, would you make yourself a little more clear?"

"Look, I have reason to believe that we are in for a very bad time and very soon. Maybe even tonight."

"What does that mean to me?"

Karen, who had watched David go to Emily's table and seen him move towards the dance floor with her, was finding it harder and harder to concentrate on Margaret's conversation. She wanted to know what "they" were talking about. It had to be more than idle talk from the expression on their two faces.

"Margaret," she put her hand on the other's arm to stop her in mid-sentence, "would you excuse me for a moment, I must go to the ladies' room." She rose and circled carefully to avoid being seen by David and Emily.

David, impressing upon her the seriousness of the situation, was trying to talk Emily into getting off the island as soon as possible.

"Your concern now seems very surprising. You didn't seem to have much when I really needed you."

"I didn't know that you were carrying my child."

Karen who had come abreast of David and Emily was just about to turn when she heard the last few words of David's sentence. Her stomach made a sick lurch. She felt her palms dampen. A tight pain flashed across her head. She stood rigidly, not more than two feet away from the dancing couple, so involved with each other, they were totally unaware of her presence. She swayed for an instant, then gathered herself together, knowing she had to get away before she fainted and made a spectacle of herself.

She was stumbling towards the ladies' room, when the flashing panorama in the bar pulled her in its direction. Shakily climbing onto the bar stool, she ordered a double and poured it down her throat. The liquor seared her throat but no more than the fear and anguish rising in her. She felt the tears brim in her eyes and asked for another. The second one calmed her somewhat, but it did not alleviate the sick anxiety, the hoplessness of her situation. She sat for a moment staring at the empty glass, then slid off the bar stool wavering unsteadily.

As she moved back into the ballroom, eyes glazed, steps uncertain, she paused for a moment. The music had stopped and several eyes turned to her as she regained the room. She seemed to be moving like a wind-up doll, mechanically, unsure of herself and her destination. As she bumped into chairs, apologizing woodenly, whispered comments swarmed around her. The usual tut-tuts, isn't it a shame, so young, such a problem with drinking.

Simon, noticing her agitation, went towards her. He felt very sympathetic toward this young lost creature. He had had much experience with her English counterparts. As he took her by the elbow, he was frightened by her distracted, glazed stare, her monotonous tone of voice.

"Karen, come and sit with me at my table."

She looked at him as if she had not understood a word he said, then smiled sadly and moved out of his grasp, looking around for an instant, finding Margaret, and walking crookedly towards her.

Simon watched her move away, shaking his head sadly. He had caught the strong fumes of Scotch on her breath and wondered what there was about her relationship with David that made her so frightfully insecure. Well, it wasn't his problem. As he turned to join Buffy and Pammy, he noticed a bright flash on the horizon.

He watched it curiously for a moment as he sat down at his table between Rod and Pammy. "Did you see that flash?" Simon asked, pointing to the tongue of flame, "It's not a flash anymore, it seems to be a fire."

"Oh," explained Rod, "don't worry, that's just a cane field. They burn it off after they cut it, it fertilizes the ground."

"Oh," said Pammy, "isn't it dangerous? Can't it spread or something?"

"No, they control it pretty well. It usually looks more dangerous than it is. Maybe because they do it at night."

"They certainly have a flair for the dramatic," Simon remarked drily.

"I should say so," Pammy observed, looking nervously out the window. "Look!"

The four of them stared intently. Other guests had

noticed the distant flames and were speculating in excited voices.

As they watched with jittery fascination, the first fire spead with the quickness of a match set to a gas ring, exploding in all directions at once. The orange flames licked at the black night, drawing closer and closer. Voices were raised. A frightened cry rang out. All attention was focused on the encroaching flames.

With a sudden flash, Simon realized that what he and David had feared was actually happening. Right here at Shalimar. Of the five people who had anticipated this—Simon, Sebastian, Emily, David and Grov—only Simon was to be unaffected by tonight's violence.

The guests surged forward to the vast glass window as if drawn by a giant magnet, watching the spectacle with the same concentration of children at a circus.

Suddenly all lights went off in the ballroom and with them the air conditioning. The darkness filled with a damp, fetid smell.

"We're being invaded!" a terrified woman screamed. The words triggered more screams, then sounds of broken glass; overturned chairs and crashing furniture sent the crowd into panic. Shuffling feet and clicking heels beat tattoos of hysteria as they scurried about in a search for escape. Many rushed to the window to look out and perhaps leave by the doors.

A mass of natives was now silhouetted against the flames. It was difficult to tell their number, they seemed to merge solidly as they moved with the flames.

Grov held his breath, waiting for Shalimar's auxiliary generators to go into operation, for he realized the main power line had been cut.

Simon felt a moment of panic. They were surrounded by a ring of flame and in its center, the bobbing puppetlike heads were coming closer and closer.

The screams of terror gave way to an eerie silence as if the crowd had been struck by a mass muteness. In the silence could be heard—like the wings of a mighty wind—the thunderous roar of the fire as it gained in intensity and followed close on the heels of the mob outside.

With a whirr and a flicker, the lights of the ballroom came on with a weak brightness. Simon turned to get his bearings and with a sense of real dread, noticed their encirclement was complete. Flames and mob on the outside and on the inside now, severe-faced natives blocking every exit from the ballroom. Only moments ago they had been serving dinner. Now they stood armed with kitchen knives and broken shards of beer bottles.

As the frightened guests retreated from doors and windows, Simon felt himself being pushed off his feet and struggled against the thrust of the crowd, now huddled in the center of the room like frightened sheep without a shepherd.

Grov materialized and moved quickly towards the sliding glass doors. Sebastian was right behind him.

With a tense motion, he slid open the doors and faced Faisan. Two men, one urbane, tall and elegantly groomed, the other black, dishevelled and garbed in the sweat-stained khakis of his trade, a 45 automatic holstered on his hip, an ammo belt across his chest.

"What are you doing here?" demanded Grov.

The smouldering eyes of Faisan moved not at all while his mouth slashed a cruel smile, "I brought you a little gift for your party." And without another word, he gestured to four men standing behind him, then stepped aside for them to enter.

They carried a crude pallet and as one woman let

out a scream, the crowd noticed a form wrapped in bloody rags. It was dumped unceremoniously on the floor. One of the natives with a gesture of contempt ripped back the sheet to display Duke Dexter.

The screams rolled around the room like a recoil of thunder. Men hurried to shield the faces of their wives from the bloody sight.

Sebastian caught his breath. It sounded like a sob. He recognized the handiwork of centuries, refined and brought to its lowest perfection on the bloody, bruised body of the man.

Sebastian walked forward in horror, slipping out of his jacket as he moved. He threw it over Duke half in protection, half in concealment. He knelt for a moment and picked up the limp wrist of Duke, feeling for a pulse. He held it gingerly, then rose and faced the crowd. "He's still alive, thank God."

A sob could be heard, then another, mixed with a few sharp intakes of breath as the guests noticed the holster under Sebastian's arm. The small calibre sidearm was menacing even in repose.

Grov was about to follow Faisan, when Sebastian arrested him with his hand. "Let me handle this, please Grov. I don't want you to be involved. This is my problem, not yours."

Grov interrupted, "It's mine, too, for God's sake, Sebastian."

"These are my people and this is my responsibility." And he gently urged Grov away, but not before Grov seized his arm, "Then for your own sake, get rid of that gun before you go out there."

Sebastian gave him a look that brooked no more interference. He turned to Faisan for the confrontation. Simon moved closer as if to cover his rear flank.

Faisan turned to the crowd and called out derisively, "Whose side are you on, black man? In here, you are waltzing with whitey. Out there are your black brothers."

Sebastian rose quickly to the bait, seizing Faisan's arm, "we'll settle this once and for all—in front of our black brothers."

He pushed Faisan ahead of them through the open door. The four natives who had brought in Duke closed in behind them. As they stepped out to face the agitated mob, Sebastian spoke under his breath, each word a slap, "When did you start talking like poor white trash? You know better than that."

"Oh, now he doesn't even like the way I talk." He called to the crowd again, then turned and said loudly so they and Sebastian could hear. "You're not going to like anything I have to say."

"I know what you have to say. I've heard it dozens of times and from others who have said it far better than you."

"Don't try me, Sebastian," Faisan menaced and reached for his belt. "You don't carry a big enough gun to be mouthing all that talk."

"I don't need any gun to talk to my people," said Sebastian, pulling his small pistol out of its holster, turning to the room behind him. Simon, who had forced his way through the blacks, was at his elbow. Sebastian handed the gun to him. Simon quickly placed it on a table nearby and turned back to the scene on the terrace.

Now the crowd inside the ballroom pushed forward to the doors, sensing the drama of the scene between the two black leaders. It was hypnotic and they held their breath.

From out of the black mob came the jeering voice, "We've heard enough talk from you, Sebastian, we want action."

Sebastian stepped forward and peered into the darkness, seeking to put a face to the voice. "Who speaks? Show yourself."

"I have no fear," the voice said and pushed through to the front of the crowd.

Sebastian recognized him. He was the son of a small farm owner on the other side of the island. "What action has Faisan promised you?"

The crowd answered for him, "Land! Land of our own! Our own property. Our own destiny. No more white man ruling." The words hurtled out from all directions, detached from sentences.

Sebastian put his hand up. The noise of the crowd reduced to an angry rumble. He turned to the young man who had stepped forward. "Pierre, your father is the owner of ten acres of good sugar field. How much does he make a year from this piece of land?"

Pierre looked sullen. "That has nothing to do with the question."

Now Sebastian seemed to grow in stature. His voice rose with confidence and knowledge. "It is the heart of the matter, and the proof that Faisan has made you hollow promises."

The crowd roared its disapproval.

"Silence!" Sebastian's voice thundered. "Listen to me. This island is small, our population is large. Simple division would show you that under Faisan's plan each man of you would end up with less than one acre of useable land. What one of you could live and provide for your families on this? Do you think it would be fair for Pierre's father then to lose nine acres of land just to give you each such a miserable piece?"

Seeing the danger real truth could have on his cause, Faisan shoved Sebastian aside and cried, "Don't listen. He lies."

The crowd seemed confused, confronted with the two clashing arguments.

The followers of Faisan cried for blood; the uncommitted insisted that Sebastian be allowed to speak.

Sebastian took his cue and shouldered Faisan aside, knowing the truth of his words had turned their original single-minded solidarity into a mass of uncertainty and confusion. He seized his opportunity. Now the Sebastian of London and Paris, the diplomat Sebastian, the magical leader used all the tools of his trade—not to seduce his followers—but to convince his detractors.

As Sebastian confronted the crowd, only he knew the trembling of his knees. This was his most important act. All his finesse, his superior education and knowledge would have to be used with an artlessness that was pure art. To convince, to bring them all into his camp; one false move would be his undoing. It must be a combination of sweet reasonableness combined with hard facts, the knowledge of which could change them from a raging mob to an amenable majority—on his side.

Faisan felt control slipping and cried out, "Get rid of the white oppressors."

Sebastian turned to him and asked with a calculating coolness, a deadly calm. "What white oppressor? Who has oppressed you?"

Then turning to the crowd, he asked, "What has the white man taken from this island? He broke in almost immediately on the crowd's mutterings.

"Let me tell you. He has a few miles of beachfront in which to place hotels that attract a tourist trade from around the world. This is land of no use to you, no value to you who farm." There was an outcry of disbelief. Sebastian realized he would have to move slowly and he raised his arm in a call for silence.

"The white man has no designs on your interior farmland. He asks only for the beach property and that's all he'll get."

A cheer rang out, strangely alone in the silence.

Sebastian now knew this first cheer marked a turning point.

He continued, "Now what does this small amount of beachfront property mean to you? Even now it produces eighty per cent of your revenue and we have not yet developed half of it. This is just the beginning."

The positive reaction that he had sensed earlier became stronger.

His voice strengthened, "Now, what does Pierre's father and the rest of the small farmers produce on triple the amount of land?" He paused, then provided the answer to the crowd. "Not even one tenth of one per cent of what we realize from the hotels." The staccato delivery had underlined the powerful truth of his words.

He allowed himself the luxury of questioning the crowd, "And what does this income mean to you?"

He did not allow the crowd the opportunity of an answer, he stepped in smoothly and said, "It means the expanded hospital which we have just broken the ground for. It means the schools which are being planned at this very moment for the far reaches of the island. It means roads and telephones and a market for your goods and services. And with this economic freedom it means total independence."

The crowd burst into his litany of promises with unbridled enthusiasm. One of Faisan's plants in the crowd, a skilled aide, trained in mob psychology heard truth work its way into the conscience of the crowd. He stepped forward to change the mood from cold fact to hot emotion.

"Easy for you to talk. You have the white woman in your bed and the white man's ideas in your head."

Sebastian felt his gorge rising. For a moment he felt they all deserved to go to hell with Faisan. But the years of careful training prevented him from stooping to the level of ugly passion. He drew himself up, a tall, dark avenging god and turned the question to his advantage, though he despised the words he heard come from his mouth. He remembered that night with Emily, their last night together. It burned with a fever of a knife in his groin. To use her this way, to sacrifice her; had she suspected he was capable of this that night? He was surprised at the levity of his own voice, "In a few short days, Miss Emily Guilford leaves for New York with many of our native handcrafts to seek outlets for them."

As Sebastian explained what they hoped to achieve, the word "compromise" flashed across Simon's mind. He remembered Sebastian's easy acceptance of it as being necessary and useful.

A low murmur of approval ran through the crowd at this new piece of intelligence, and then the sound of a shot shattered the night. There was first shock, then fear.

Its sound cleaved Emily and for a brief moment she felt rooted to the floor, unable to move or speak.

She cried in a voice of helpless terror, "Sebastian." And ran toward him.

Simon, hearing the shot first, then Emily's frightened scream, snapped to attention. He looked directly to Sebastian, but when the black man seemed unharmed and just as shocked as everyone else, his eyes flicked back to the table where he had placed Sebastian's gun only minutes before. Now it was gone.

Simon moved swiftly back into the room, instinctively feeling that the shot he had heard had not come from outside, but somewhere within the room. Then he knew. The low keening cry, the hysterical sound of surprise, the wracking sobs of a woman in shock. He looked for its source and saw in the riveted crowd, one woman kneeling over a prostrate form and crying.

"She shot herself. My God, she's shot herself."

And the wailing began again. It came from Sandy Gramson. The form on the floor was the crumpled body of Karen Sampson.

Sandy gently pulled Karen's lifeless body into her lap and cradled it, rocking back and forth, tears streaming. She crooned to her as if she were a child. Bright red spots appeared on Sandy's white dress as Karen's blood oozed from the bullet wound in her temple. "Oh, why did you do it? Why, why, why?"

Marty, hearing Sandy's voice, moved quickly to her side, gently trying to disengage her from her morbid burden.

The crowd by now had clustered around the two women, forgetting for the moment the danger that had threatened from the outside.

They were knit together in shared pain, yet their faces each showed their real thoughts: dismay, disgust, puzzlement, curiosity, horror, gratitude that it was not one of them lying on the floor.

"May I get through, please," the strained voice of David Sampson beat against their backs and they parted for him deferentially, all preparing themselves for the new role of mourning.

David knelt in front of Sandy. With an exchanged glance that was completely clear to both, he accepted into his arms his wife's limp body.

As he walked slowly towards a couch he looked at the peaceful face of Karen. Peaceful now. He had never seen his wife truly relaxed, quietly happy. There had always been a tension about her, a feeling of frustration. How many times had he imagined Karen a suicide, then brushed the thought angrily away as if it were some kind of inverted wish-fulfillment on his part? He certainly had never wanted to see her dead. Gone away, perhaps, but never like this. So young, so much yet to experience, not with him, perhaps, but with someone closer to her needs. David felt guilt, then sadness, then a sudden strangeness.

This was no longer a woman he had eaten and slept with, but a body with no life in it. He deposited it carefully on the couch and stared at her for a moment, then turned. His eyes met Simon's, then Grov's, both moved towards him as if summoned by a signal.

Grov's face was ashen. He was torn between his innate desire to comfort David and the necessity of getting Karen's body away from the stares of the other guests. And then with another shiver, he realized that Duke, too, was lying somewhere in this room. He felt his knees buckle and was relieved and grateful for the steadying arm of Simon.

"We must get her out of this room to someplace private," Simon said. He cast an anxious glance around the room. A distinguished looking man with a head of silvery hair, detached himself from one of the clusters of people and moved to the group by the couch.

"I'm Doctor Scali. Is there anything I can do?"

A whispered conference ensued and agreement was met. Grov summarily called two of the native waiters to his side and had them remove the body to a small private room away from the curious stares.

Doctor Scali offered, "It will be necessary, I'm sure to tell the authorities what has happened and sign papers before she can be sent home. I'm at your service."

"I'd appreciate it if you could do anything for that poor chap that was deposited on our doorstep tonight. He must be in serious condition. If you could . . ."

Dr. Scali nodded his great head and moved toward the bloody figure of Duke, ignored when the crowd's attention had turned to the more immediate danger.

Sebastian, stunned by the events of the evening, tried to offer assistance to David. "This must be very difficult for you now, but let me assure you I will do everything to make it as simple and painless as possible. Let me get my Minister of Police and an ambulance to prepare your wife for the journey home. I'm sure you'll want her to go back with you tomorrow."

David nodded and clasped his hand.

Sebastian returned to the terrace. The natives were still standing there, mumbling and conjecturing about the incident that had robbed them of their steam. Sebastian was ready with an explanation, "There's been a terrible accident. I beg you all to go back to your homes. Appoint spokesman for yourselves and I will meet with them tomorrow and we will continue tonight's dialogue."

Simon watched with the same shock as the other guests, as the two native boys removed Karen's body from the room. For the first time in his professional career, the desire to record the events around him gave way to the more human instinct of feeling another man's pain. He hadn't the heart at this point to raise his camera and record the scene.

Margaret Bradley, feeling desperately alone and friendless in this strange atmosphere, sobbed softly into her handkerchief as she watched Karen's body being removed.

Rod, flanked by Pammy and Buffy, had only curiosity on his face. The two girls exchanged meaningful looks, as if this held no surprise for them. Yet they felt touched and saddened by Karen's death. She might have been odd, but she was very close to them in age and they couldn't ever in a million years see themselves doing something like that.

Denise felt nothing, only a terrible tiredness. And for the first time in many years, her heart went out to Grov who surely was feeling everything that she was not.

The natives neither cared, nor showed curiosity.

Their concern now was to leave and regroup tomorrow for further conversation with Sebastian. Faisan's five aides remained at his side, watching bitterly as the force returned home. Faisan felt Sebastian's vise-like grip on his arm.

"Before you meet with your people again, there's something *we* must discuss." There was a significant pause before he added, "alone."

"There is nothing I can't discuss in front of my men," Faisan snapped back.

"There is—believe me." Then more softly, "Send them away. We can all meet later." There was something in Sebastian's eyes, something in his firm grip on Faisan's arm that drove home the importance of his words.

Faisan nodded to his men. "Tomorrow morning, then, in Sebastian's office."

As the group left, Sebastian took one last look around the ballroom. Dr. Scali was bent over Duke Dexter's moaning body giving him a shot of morphine to dull the brutal pain of his injuries. His slender hands ran quickly over Duke's body to check for broken bones and as he gingerly pulled away the greasy rags that covered his body, his eyes closed for an instant when he saw the mutilated, gaping hole that had once been his manhood. He called Grov to his side.

Dr. Scali spoke softly so no one could hear, "We must get this man to a hospital. He's been badly mutilated, and I'm afraid a great deal of dirt has gotten into his wounds. He'll need massive doses of penicillin to stop infection."

Grov looked horrified, but hastened to do the doctor's bidding. "There is an ambulance coming to pick up Mrs. Sampson. It can drop Mr. Dexter at the hospital."

"I'll go along with him," Dr. Scali said.

Grov thanked him with gratitude. Then with superhuman effort, he turned his attention to the remaining guests, suggesting they adjourn to a smaller dining room where they might have brandy and coffee. He stood for an instant, then turned back and saw a silent Margaret Bradley, wondering where her Phillip was. A suddenly solicitous Martin Gramson, his arm around his wife's shoulders, her blood-stained white dress an assault to the eyes. Simon, lost in his own private thoughts. And the sober faces of Rod, Pam and Buffy.

He shrugged as he looked at them. "We could all use some coffee and brandy, I'm sure." He turned and the remaining flock followed him out of the ballroom, grateful to be walking away from an evening that had started with such promise.

# *Monday*

THE BRIGHT ball of Caribbean sun rose this Monday morning as it had countless Monday mornings over St. Phillipe. It crept with relentless ferocity through the half-drawn blinds of the *Cassandra*'s master stateroom, slanting across Sandy Gramson's eyes with searing brightness. She woke with a start, tired beyond belief, as the night flashed through her mind. The horror of things recalled washed over her and she shivered.

Marty, feeling the sudden movement of the bed, opened one eye and looked at his wife, huddled with her arms around her knees. He saw her chills and quickly moved toward her.

"Okay, baby, it's all over now." She was strangely grateful for his heavy arm and the comfort it gave. She leaned against him.

"If I hadn't been there, and seen it I'd think I'd had a nightmare."

"Well, it was. Just that. But we're okay now. I'm glad we slept aboard last night."

"It didn't help. I must have tossed all night. I'm exhausted."

"You should be. After all, you lived through it

and you were the one who discovered Karen. The poor dumb kid."

"Not dumb, just desperate. I understand the feeling."

Marty had the grace not to probe. A feeling that had started at the art show had grown with amazing speed culminating last night at Sandy's spontaneously human gesture when she had rushed to Karen's side. Marty Gramson had finally accepted the fact that he had married a woman, not a showpiece. And part of his male pride made him want to be worthy of her.

"What do you say we call the launch and go to Shalimar for some breakfast?"

"Why on earth do you want to go back there?" Sandy asked incredulously.

"Maybe we can offer to take some of the people back with us. Like Margaret Bradley. Maybe she won't want to hang around waiting for a plane. We certainly have enough room." Marty seemed a little embarrassed by his own largessc. Or could you call it sensitivity?

Sandy tried to cover her amazement. Could this be tough Marty Gramson talking? First the sweetness and concern for her, now his generous offer of assistance. And he wouldn't even get so much as a lipstick sale out of either. What was happening to the great, hardened tycoon? Sandy was annoyed at her own cynicism. A man could change, couldn't he? After all they had lived through a rather extraordinary evening. And that was something. Don't question, she thought, accept and be grateful.

"Marty, that's a wonderfully thoughtful idea. But I just can't bring myself to go back there. I can't face it again."

"You stay here then," he said comfortingly. "I'll go and be right back." He dressed hurriedly and in moments was aboard the launch heading for the club.

The same sun that had wakened Sandy had brought the girls and their little dog out bright and early. The blasphemy of breakfast as usual had escaped them as well as Jane Perceval who had slept through the drama of last night.

When Jane opened the door of her cottage, she was struck by the sweet acrid smell in the air. Not the usual mingling of flower perfumes, this one made her dizzy and she felt herself gagging from its insistence.

A stab of fear struck her. It was a combination of waking up without Bill coupled with a strange stillness she couldn't quite understand in this brilliant morning. Everything seemed the same, yet nothing was. The sight of the two girls and their pet reassured her somewhat and she hastened over to them.

"Good morning, girls."

Pammy and Buffy were surprised to see Jane alone. "All by yourself this morning? Is His Honor off playing tennis already?"

Jane smiled, then flushed with embarrassment. "Oh, Mr. Perceval had to go back to the States. Something came up that needed his personal attention." She sniffed the air again. The smell seemed stronger. "What on earth is that strange smell?" she asked, not expecting the girls to be of much help.

Pammy looked knowingly at Buffy. Buffy nodded. "You mean you missed the native uprising last night?"

"I missed everything that happened last night. I took a nap before dinner and never woke up until this morning. You girls are joking, of course. Did I miss some native entertainment?"

"If you want to call it entertainment." Buffy held up her hand and ticked off on her fingers, "A blackout, a big scene between the two native leaders, a cast of thousands in the background—all black, poor Duke Dexter delivered on a silver platter and all carved up for the festivities, and the highpoint of the evening: David Sampson's wife decided to end it all."

"What are you girls saying?" Jane was taken aback by their careless litany of events. The girls might well be pulling her leg or making some horrible private joke which she could not share.

"It's true, Mrs. Perceval. Sebastian went out to talk to Faisan and on the way, he left the gun so they would know he wasn't armed . . ."

"What gun? What are you talking about?" Jane interruped.

Before Jane could question the girls further, the deep voice of a man interrupted.

Phillip Reed, casually dressed in immaculate khakis, blue shirt and linen blazer, cast a huge shadow over the table where Jane and the girls sat.

"What's all this talk about being armed?"

Buffy and Pammy stared at the tall, spare figure of the man, his silvery gray hair glinting in the sun. For a moment they thought it was Cary Grant, but then Jane turned and cried, "Phillip. Phillip Reed. How happy I am to see you."

"Jane. Good to see you. I'm surprised that you're still here."

"Well, apparently I slept through all the drama last night."

Phillip seemed confused. He was not referring to last night's happenings. But with a flash of insight realized that Jane might not be aware of why Bill had rushed back to the city. He wisely did not pursue the subject. "Where's Bill?"

Jane explained again about Bill. Then wishing to change the subject said, "Does Margaret know you're here?"

"No, I just arrived. Well, actually, I tried to arrive last night, but the tower very curtly told us the field was closed and we had to land in Guadeloupe.

I got clearance to leave early this morning and here I am finally. What's been going on here?"

"You'll have to ask someone else, my knowledge is scanty. I don't know what happened."

"Why don't I go find Margaret first and then maybe she can fill in with the details."

Jane told him the number of Margaret's cottage and he strode off in its direction.

As the night had turned to gray dawn, Margaret Bradley was still awake, mulling in her thoughts all possible reasons why Phillip had not arrived, going over every word she might have said that could have driven him away. They all seemed elusive and inconclusive.

Now, refusing to face the morning post mortems, she was nervously sipping coffee in her cottage when she heard the light tap on her door.

She opened it expecting, for some reason, to find Jane Perceval. When Phillip's tall, spare frame, stepped in, she let out one wail, burst into tears and threw herself into his arms. The tall man, slightly stunned by the outburst from the woman of icy calm, was mightily pleased. He scooped her into his arms and sat down in a chair with her in his lap, stroking her hair and whispering small words of comfort.

"Oh, Phillip," she mumbled through her tears. "I thought you'd never come. It's been horrible. You can't imagine." She tried to tell the story between sobs, but the memory refreshed made her incoherent. Now, she could abandon herself to her fears, her loneliness: Phillip's strong presence had opened the dams and she let all the pent-up emotions pour out.

He increased his efforts to calm her and finally she fell quiet under the gentle reassurance of his hands.

Suddenly, she pulled herself up, "But what happened to you? I expected you last night. Oh, how I wanted you to be here last night."

"Meg, dear," he used the tender nickname with

careful deliberation, "I tried to fly in last night but the airport was closed to traffic. I had to return to Guadeloupe and wait until this morning. But I'm here now. Everything will be fine."

"Everything's horrible. How soon can we leave this unhappy island?"

"As soon as you can get ready. But, don't call it unhappy. Whatever happened, it brought us together. And you know I've waited a long time for this."

"I know. I'm not worth all your patience. I've been such a ninny about us. But I won't be anymore. I promise." And shyly she reached down to kiss him. He held her tenderly and for the first time in years, she felt safe and comforted. How much time she had wasted. Now, she would make it up to him.

"Hey, hold on," he pulled her away from him as she rained kisses all over his face. "We have plenty of time for that now. No need to catch up. Get yourself together. And let me have some coffee. I haven't had a thing to eat in days it seems."

She sprung out of his lap and over to the table to pour him coffee and hand him a plate of croissants.

"Now," he said, "while I have some breakfast and you pack, tell me what in heaven's name has been going on here."

Margaret, feeling sanity return, tried calmly to outline the past evening for him. He interrupted several times to ask questions, to better fix the events in his mind.

"By the way, how did you know where to find me?" she asked.

"I ran into Jane Perceval at breakfast by the pool. She told me where you'd probably be. She didn't seem to know anything about last night's mess."

"She never arrived for dinner."

"Why is she still here?"

"What do you mean?"

"Well, Bill Perceval is back in New York."

"Yes, well . . ."

"Under the circumstances, I would have expected her to go back with him."

"I guess Bill felt she didn't have to be involved."

"I can't believe that. He's her son, too."

"Phillip, what on earth are you talking about? He went back because of something about the city."

"Is that what he told everyone?"

"What else happened? What's wrong?"

"Bill, Jr. was picked up on a narcotics charge. Good God, doesn't anyone get a paper here." And then he corrected himself. "Of course, it only happened. It wouldn't make the news here. But surely Bill told Jane."

"I don't think so. She didn't say anything. And if he had, I'm sure she would have gone with him." Margaret stood with a nightgown in her hands, then turned away from Phillip. "Do you suppose she hasn't an inkling?"

"It would appear that way. I don't understand Bill."

"I think they may have had some problems while they were here. Personal problems. Phillip, should we tell her?"

Phillip thought for a moment. "I don't think we should. It will only make her more miserable. Besides, knowing will not get her home any faster. When she's home, it'll be time enough. And perhaps by then, the whole thing will be smoothed over. He's a pretty straight kid. I think the whole affair might have been a frame."

"How could they do something like that to a child?" Margaret's naiveté amused Phillip.

"Meg, his father is the mayor. What better way to discredit a man than to attack him through his family? And today, even the nicest kids aren't safe from marijuana. Framing the boy is politically expedient, if you can look at it that way."

Margaret shuddered and returned to her packing.

"Is there anything you need help with, dear?" Phillip offered solicitously.

"No, I think not. If you'll just call for a boy to take my luggage, I'll be ready in a moment."

Margaret had moved back into her ordered life, yet there was a difference and Phillip recognized it with pleasure. She seemed more relaxed, more yielding, less afraid. He didn't know what had caused the amazing transformation and he didn't want to know. Suffice to say, the miracle had happened. The warmth he had felt lay under Margaret's carefully nurtured veneer had finally surfaced. She seemed ready to face life. And more importantly, to face it with him.

Margaret, who had gone into the dressing room while Phillip phoned for a boy, emerged now, dressed for travelling. She clicked shut her bag, gave a look around the room to see if she had forgotten anything, then turned to Phillip.

"I'm ready." And she never meant it more than she had now. "I'm happy to leave. I don't think I'll ever be able to read a society account of any event without wondering what really happened. Do you think the story will get back to the States? It could absolutely ruin Shalimar, you know?"

"I'm quite certain the powers that be here will move heaven and earth to make sure no one knows."

"But we know. Won't they be afraid of us talking?"

"I doubt it. These stories always seem to be fantastic exaggerations. To some, it will be reason enough to come down and see where it all happened. By next week, it will be old hat and there'll be new gossips and new scandals that will be more interesting."

"But we all could have been killed!"

"Well, Margaret, Caribbean and South American revolutions are almost commonplace these days. Just like hijacked planes and the war in Viet Nam. Everything is taken for granted. Even the horrors. It's a sad commentary but it's true."

She nodded. "I hope for Sebastian Lalange's sake, the island makes it. He's quite a man. Maybe you'll have a chance to meet him before we go. You could be a great help to him. Just as you were in Brownsville."

"Who told you about that?"

"Never mind. Why do you insist on keeping all your good works to yourself?"

"I don't. I just prefer not having a big splash of publicity everytime I do something."

"Do you feel guilty about all that money?"

"Not guilty, but responsible for putting it to work. At the risk of sounding like a fuzzy idealist, I think we have an obligation to society, at least to the really troubled members of society."

Margaret felt a swell of pride in this man. She thought back to her husband and the abuse of his wealth. The ridiculously expensive entertainments, the obscene cost of their daughters' coming-out parties, the waste of it all.

She took Phillip's hand and held it to her lips for a moment. Then smiled at him. Her eyes were wet. Phillip looked down at her and thought to himself we'll be all right. She understood now. The dynamo that ran Margaret Bradley had been wasted on fear and self-protection, now it was ready to move her into more important, useful things and he'd be there to see that the channels remained open. He felt good.

Emily Guilford did not feel well. The cold chill of last night's events still clung to her and even the brazen heat of the Caribbean sun could not warm her. A dull throbbing pain in head and stomach had followed her throughout the small hours of the morning. The aspirin was of no help, nor did the Alka Seltzer bring calm to the waves of nausea still sweeping through her.

Perhaps, an early morning swim would help, while the water still had the power to refresh. She quickly slipped into a swim suit, grabbed a beach towel and left her cottage.

The sun struck against her head with the sharpness of a whip and she stumbled momentarily, looking for a tree to steady herself against.

"Are you all right Ems?" The voice of David Sampson shattered her calm even more. He was the last person she wanted to see now. What to say to him? How to behave? Certainly not as if nothing had happened.

In explanation, David offered, "I've just come back from the hospital." The stubble on his face indicated that he had spent the night there. His eyes were reddened and weary from lack of sleep. "They're getting her ready for the trip home."

"I'm so sorry, David. Karen seemed to be a lovely girl." The platitude soured on her tongue.

"Thanks, but save it. Karen was born with suicide in her. I'm shocked but not really surprised. I just don't understand why she chose this time and this place for it."

"Do you think you might have said something or done anything that triggered it."

"I'm too tired to think about it right now. One day I'll probably understand, but this isn't the day."

David met Emily's long, hard stare without flinching. "You think I'm a cold-hearted bastard, don't you Ems?" When she was about to interrupt, he continued abruptly, "You're thinking back to our little affair, another time of cold-hearted bastardry. But you're wrong."

"I don't want to discuss that now. Besides it's all over."

"Is it?" he asked meaningfully. "Look, everyone's death diminishes everyone else. But believe me, Karen was better off than she realized. At least I understood her problems."

"Did you," Emily asked softly. "Did she know you understood?"

David started guiltily, remembering the night before the party, when Karen had come to him, pleading with him for love. She had been drunk, but that was no excuse to deny her. She must have sensed his revulsion.

Emily turned away from him and pulled the towel around her tightly as if to protect her from the insistent physical presence of David.

He seized her arm, not hurtfully, but with a gentle force that indicated he was not giving up so easily.

"Was Sebastian lying last night, when he said you were returning to the States?"

"No," the simple syllable was extended by pain, "I am leaving. We think it's better this way."

"For whom?"

"Oh, David, what does it matter?"

"Ems," he had loosened his grip on her arm and now he gently took her hand in his. "We're both going back empty-handed. A couple of dreams short. Maybe we can be of some comfort to each other." When she wrenched her hand away, he flushed.

"I don't mean like it used to be. I mean something new. A fresh start. Maybe nothing more than friends."

"You—be friends with a woman? Don't make me laugh." Her voice was raspy and David was startled by the sudden ugly look of her buried anger, surfacing now and suffusing the lovely features of her face.

"Okay, Emily. I'm sorry I suggested it. I guess

you're not ready for anything yet. You still have a lot to learn about people."

His criticism hurt her and for an instant she was the untried schoolgirl again, she wanted to turn to him and offer her hand, defend her maturity, prove it, by giving him some small reassurance of his value. But she couldn't. Not yet. He was still too much the reminder of a hurt not yet healed. And she was surprised to find that the wound still ached. Even Sebastian had obviously not been able to make up for all that.

"I'm sorry, David. Really I am. For everything."

"Forget it." he flung over his shoulder. "We'll probably have to see each other on the plane this afternoon, but I'll try to be as unobtrusive as possible."

Emily watched his stiff back move away from her, noticed the unsteadiness of his legs and felt an ache as the tears filled her eyes. All thoughts of a relaxing swim were gone now and angrily she returned to her cottage to pack and sort out the pieces of her life before facing the strange, new one in front of her.

She wondered where Sebastian was and if she would be able to have a few moments alone with him before she left.

The weariness that pervaded the guests of Shalimar was no less apparent in the face of Sebastian Lalange. His rich mahogany skin was tinged with an ashen gray, a dark stubble on his chin gave him a sinister look. He, too, had been up half the night. His normally neat desk was now littered with many cups, half-filled with the aromatic black coffee he loved. Notes and doodles cluttered the floor, waste baskets were filled to overflowing. He had been out of the office only an hour or two, and that time had been used to consolidate his position and re-establish his leadership with the influential members of his constituency.

Now as he returned, bone-weary to his office, his

only thought was to lie down on his leather couch and snatch an hour of sleep so he might be refreshed when the time came to bid farewell to the long-suffering guests of Shalimar. With irritation, he heard the insistent ring of his phone. For a moment, he debated about answering it; then realized he did not dare refuse any call at this time. Where was his damned secretary? When he needed her most, that was when she was scarce. With a deep sigh, he picked up the receiver and answered it. Grov Wilcox was on the other end.

"Sebastian, I hate to disturb you now. I know you must be exhausted but I'm very concerned."

He's very concerned, Sebastian thought.

"I'm concerned, too," Sebastian replied, "not just about your guests but about my whole island."

"I realize that. But you know, we are expecting a new planeload to arrive late this afternoon. I don't know whether to turn them back at Guadeloupe or allow them to come on in. Can you give me any guarantees for their safety?"

"Don't turn them back. You have my word."

"Are you sure there will be no repetition of last night's troubles?" Grov was over-anxious.

"I'm sure," Sebastian said firmly. And he was.

As he put the receiver back on its hook, he had a grim smile of satisfaction on his face.

He had used the power of sweet reason when talking to his people, but he had used a far more formidable power in dealing with Faisan, an hour later. It was the power that came from secret knowledge, the strength of your office that encouraged information to come to you at a price. It was that kind of information that had been his ace in the hole. Sebastian, although he preferred to use honesty, logic and truth in his dealings, understood the power and necessity of stooping below the table to deliver the coup de grace to an enemy.

Many months ago, a suddenly contrite member of Faisan's secret council had come to him with some astounding intelligence. It was almost too much for Sebastian to believe; after all, Faisan was so dedicated to his cause, it was unthinkable that he should permit himself such an indiscretion.

But he had been presented with a folder of such crude but damning photographs that Sebastian had to accept the stories as truth. The informer had been silenced with a generous payment and the evidence had been locked in a safe at Sebastian's home. Even though he swore to himself he would never use this information, it gave him confidence to know it was there and that he could deal from strength with Faisan. He felt a revulsion and a pity for him and resented the fact that it was Faisan, himself, who had forced him into using these underhanded tactics.

His meeting with Faisan after the abortive attempt to take over the island had led Sebastian, at first to reason with his brother. But Faisan's anger was so incendiary, his behavior so obdurate that Sebastian felt himself losing all control. And it was only after a harangue of several hours, when reason had failed, that Sebastian resorted to blackmail. At first, Faisan had denied any sexual relationship with the Cuban guerilla leader the informer had identified. He laughed at the possibility it could even happen. After all, they were involved in serious business. They were trying to free a down-trodden, exploited country. And Sebastian knew he was one-hundred per cent male. How could he believe his own cousin, friend or foe, would be capable of such perversions? Sebastian had been duped by a traitor to the cause, willing to swear to any lie to avenge himself for some imagined slight.

The more Sebastian pressed him, the more frenetic were Faisan's denials. When Sebastian suggested he had evidence, Faisan laughed in his face.

The sharp laugh brought back the memory of another confrontation. Sebastian and Faisan were in their early teens and inseparable, though they had little in common beyond their shared last name. Faisan's father was a tenant farmer, who, despite the fertility of the land, had struggled long hours to eke out a bare existence. He was a man hardened by the exigencies of the life he led. A life which left little time or love for his only son.

On the other hand Sebastian had grown up with as much security as a black man could have had at that time on the island. His father, secretary to the French Governor, had married a beautiful, convent-bred quadroon who had died giving birth to Sebastian, her first-born. Sebastian's father had tried to raise his son as he felt his gentle, cultivated wife would have wished. The boy lived at Government House with all the advantages of a white boy.

Although the two cousins had been close as brothers since early childhood, slowly Faisan had become aware of the differences between Sebastian and himself.

The incident that was to mark the end of innocence and closeness began simply enough.

The governor's speedboat had been a source of envy and longing for the two boys. Sebastian, running small errands and being naturally ingratiating, was certain that the Governor would repay him with a coveted ride on the boat. He was quick to brag about it to Faisan.

". . . and he promised to take me out real soon."

"Hah," Faisan laughed sceptically. "Real soon. I wouldn't want to hang by my thumbs, cousin."

"He promised." Sebastian insisted stubbornly.

"Yeh. It could be next Christmas or never."

"He wouldn't lie to me." Sebastian said.

Faisan couldn't know that gentlemen made promises to be kept. Promises had never been a part of his life. What Faisan wanted, Faisan took.

Here was his big change to show his cosseted cousin you don't have to be a white man's slavey to get a little reward.

One late afternoon while Sebastian was walking along the quay, he was surprised to hear his cousin's voice call to him from under the dock.

When Sebastian discovered its source and saw his cousin standing proudly at the helm of the Governor's speedboat, he was horrified.

"Real soon's today, cousin," he announced insolently. "Get in. You're gonna get your ride in the governor's boat today."

"You stole the boat? You're gonna get in big trouble."

Faisan displaying his convincing talents at this early age needed only a few minutes to convince Sebastian that they could have their ride and their fun and return the boat before anyone missed it.

Sebastian, torn between wanting and wrong-doing, felt himself weaken and allowed himself to be convinced by Faisan. The boat bobbing seductively at his feet was the final temptation. He could feel the wind behind him already. He scrambled in.

The boat sprang away from the dock like a spirited dolphin. The sense of power was heady and intoxicating. Faisan let it surge through him, loving every moment, aware for the first time of what it felt like to be in control.

But his triumph was short-lived. Faisan, accustomed to small outboard fishing boats, ran into difficulty almost immediately. The engine's power and speed were more than he could handle. The boat ran onto a reef and they were stranded. In horror, they watched the sea slowly drip in from a leak in the hull.

Forgotten was all pleasure. Now they only worried about survival. If they were rescued, they would surely have to pay the consequences, not to mention the injury to the boat. Sebastian was heartsick. Faisan was sullen.

It was dusk by the time the shore patrol had located them and returned them to Government House. Sebastian was prepared to take his punishment but he was not prepared to hear Faisan accuse him of stealing the boat. His weak protestations were not believed. Greater than the guilt was the realization of his father's hurt and the Governor's disappointment. It was at that point the ethics of two careers had been founded. The one based on the quick grab and the persuasive lie. The other, more convinced than ever, that true power came from working within the established patterns of give and take. As a punishment, Sebastian was sent away from his beloved island to school in France, eventually ending up at Cambridge and the Sorbonne. The punishment, insupportable at first, had eventually given him the education and sophistication to forge the mental tools which had led him to his present seat of power.

He had never again allowed himself to be tempted by a quick and easy out.

There was to be no quick and easy out last night. When Sebastian realized with sinking heart that no other avenue was left to him, he had turned to his wall safe and withdrew the incriminating photographs.

Faisan laughed in his face.

He recalled even now, the suspicion, the disbelief, yet the curiosity on Faisan's face. And as he dramatically withdrew photo after photo and placed them in front of Faisan's stunned eyes, he felt an empty feeling of victory. He would have preferred to win Faisan over with the righteousness of his conviction.

Faisan's defeated but defiant face told him the photos were authentic. And when Faisan demanded to know what Sebastian intended, Sebastian struggled with himself. It would have been easy to have Faisan executed as a traitor. But he was still his cousin. The complete and total collapse of Faisan as a threat to his people and his island had softened Sebastian's desire for revenge. All he wanted now was to have Faisan permanently removed from St. Phillipe—so that he could go about the enormous task of establishing the island as a self-supporting entity. Free of outside political or economic pressures.

Faisan, recognizing the power of the photographs that lay on the desk before him, feared more for his life than his cause. The enraged rabble, the emotionally volatile mass that made up his following would turn on him if Sebastian were to show them these photographs. There was an explicitness about them that required no captioning, that allowed for no apology. Whatever Sebastian had in mind for him as a proper payment for such excesses would be as nothing compared to the payment that his outraged followers would demand. The cat and mouse game was over. This was surrender, absolute and unconditional.

When Faisan asked for terms, Sebastian had replied: "Exile. That's all." No more punishment than that. The removal once and forever of his person from his island home. To Sebastian, this had to be worse than imprisonment, less merciful than death.

Now Sebastian recalled Faisan's words. "Do you think that by sending me away, my cause goes with me? The ideal is greater than one single man. To get rid of it, you would have to send half the island with me."

"No," Sebastian had replied. "You will speak to your followers. You will tell them that you and I have reached certain agreements. That the promise has been made that the foreign interests in the island will never exceed more than ten percent of the land. That you are satisfied and that I have given you permission to leave with four of your trusted lieutenants to go to other troubled islands like our own and offer them any assistance. But," he continued, "if you dare to disrupt any other island, remember, I still have these." He had pointed to the photographs, letting Faisan look at them one last time before he swept them into their envelope and returned it to the wall safe.

Faisan could do no more than agree. He left the room with as much dignity as he could muster. It was swagger pure and simple, but it did not cover the defeat visible in the slump of his shoulders.

Sebastian sighed with relief as the door slammed. Now, perhaps he could have an hour's rest before he returned to the office. There was still much to do.

It was still too early for visitors when an official-looking black car crept slowly up the gravelled driveway of St. Phillipe's hospital and pulled quietly into a reserved parking place. The colored driver leaped from his seat and opened the back door with a snappy flourish. A heavy man, profusely sweating, in white uniform and planter's hat, lumbered out, stood blinking in the sunlight. Then whipping out a huge white handkerchief he blotted his sweat-shiny face, ground a cigar under his heel and walked up the wide steps of the entrance.

The sudden coolness of the quiet reception area gave him a chill. Around him swished the long white skirts of the Sisters of Charity as they made their rounds. He approached the desk and asked the attendant a question, then hurried off behind one of the white-skirted nuns towards a room at the end of the corridor.

He knocked at the door and went in without waiting for an answer. A sister rose from her vigil at the bed and hurried to his side.

The man introduced himself, "Sister, I am the Chief of Police. Is Mr. Dexter able to speak?"

The nun cast a worried glance at her patient, torn between the two duties. She spoke softly, "He has lost so much blood. He is very serious. Must you speak to him now?"

"It's urgent that I do."

"Doctor does not want him to be disturbed."

"Let me speak to the doctor then."

The sister looked at him anxiously, then swept out of the room.

The Chief looked at the white face of Duke, deep purple smudges ringed his closed eyes. He seemed drained of all life. His head swathed in white bandages was in sharp contrast with an angry bruise yellowing under his hollow cheekbone. A frame hidden by a stiff white sheet indicated that the tiniest pressure could conceivably cause him great agony.

The Chief's eyes never left Duke's face. He felt no rush of sympathy for the battered man. Police Chiefs were not paid to be sympathetic, only to get the job done. In this case, Sebastian's orders were precise and laconic: "Get him to talk if you can. Faisan's the cause of this."

The sister entered again. Behind her, a young black doctor, very serious.

They exchanged words softly. "He's very sick. I wish you could wait until he has more strength. He's lost a great deal of blood."

Duke, although his eyes were closed, heard snatches of the conversation through the pain of his head. "Doctor," he called in a weak whisper.

The doctor moved to his side solicitously.

"What is it?" asked Duke.

"There's someone here who wishes to speak to you."

"I don't want to speak to anyone."

The Chief moved his lumbering body towards the bed, neatly cutting off the doctor. "Mr. Dexter, it is necessary to ask a few questions about your accident. We would like you to make an identification. Will you tell us who did this to you."

Duke's eyes fluttered. With fear or pain, no one knew. "It was just a mistake. An accident. No one is to blame."

"But Mr. Dexter," the Chief cajoled. "We can't let this terrible thing go unpunished. This week it is you. Next week it may be someone else. Don't you wish to save other innoçent people from your fate."

"Leave me alone," wailed Duke. "I will make no charges. Just forget it."

"But Mr. Dexter . . ."

"Please . . ." Duke's voice was getting shriller and his breathing shallow. The doctor stepped to the bedside and took the Chief's arm, "I must insist that you leave. You can see my patient is in no condition to talk."

"But the Prime Minister insists . . ."

"I will speak to him and explain. Now, please. I must insist that you leave."

The Chief threw a glance at Duke, whose eyes had closed again. His face now seemed drawn of all color, even the purple smudges under his eyes seemed gray. His breath came in shallow gasps.

The sister quickly wheeled a tent to his bedside, covered his face with it, turned a knob. The slow hiss of oxygen could be heard.

The Chief turned on his heel and left the room. He bumped into a sister coming in the opposite direction, sending a tray spinning out of her hands. And in his anger and frustration, he neither apologized nor offered to help.

His car sped off with the same anger, sending up a spray of gravel onto the carefully manicured lawn.

As he leaned back in the cushion, he took small comfort from the fact that although Duke Dexter would not reveal his assailant to him, he was equally sure he would reveal it to no one. At this point, one couldn't even be sure he would live. He lit his cigar. Sebastian would have to be satisfied with that small knowledge.

The steamy sullenness of the baked airport began to stir shortly after noon. It was to be the busiest day the place had known in its short life. Not only was the big charter plane due in to pick up the invited guests who had just launched Shalimar, but the Island Airways' scheduled afternoon flight from Guadalupe was expected with a full load, marking another first for the airline as well as the island.

Millions of dust motes hung suspended in the still air, for Sebastian had ordered a thorough cleaning of the airport that morning. He was determined after last night's disturbances to rectify the opinion of Shalimar's guests as best he could. Much damage had been done to the island's budding reputation as a suitable playground, he knew, but if reports were kept to word of mouth stories of returning tourists, and out of the press, perhaps too much damage had not been done. If Chief Bluet was right in his appraisal of the situation at the hospital this morning, at least that source of exposure was no longer a threat. The poor bastard, Sebastian thought, he'd carry the scars of this weekend's experience on his body and in his mind for the rest of his life. He'd seemed none too stable to begin with—would a thing like this drive him completely over the edge? There were too many other more pressing things on his mind now to waste any more time thinking about the fate of that one man.

The chartered plane which was to return Shalimar's guests to New York had not yet arrived, and the Island Airway plane was not due in until later that afternoon after the scheduled departure of the first guests. That at least was a blessing. There would be no chance for the first group to infect the second with any of their fears or stories. Sebastian intended to stay at the airport all that day if necessary to see that no untoward incidents occurred, and that the surliness of the cab drivers and baggage handlers that Simon had mentioned was kept to a minimum, or hopefully absent altogether.

He took a certain amount of pride in the recently spruced up terminal and as he looked out onto the runway, he noticed a plane being readied. It taxied up from the hangar to the terminal. One of the sleekest private planes Sebastian had ever seen, it shone like some highly polished jewel in the noon sun. The only identification on the twin engined turbo jet was a crest on the door. But it was so discreetly small, that Sebastian was unable to identify it before the door swung open and the crisply uniformed pilot of Phillip Reed's plane stepped out and down the steps.

The arrival of the island's only ambulance caused a stir in the airport's activity. Curious workers, anxious for any break in their routine, left their counters and desks to cluster around the back doors of the ambulance to see who was injured. But they were to be disappointed, for the two burly attendants, who had asked for help from the gathering group, had pulled a simple wooden box out of the doors. Inside it was the body of Karen Sampson. With their superstitious fear of death, they shrank back, away from the box as though in some way the evil which had struck at this young woman, might rub off on them as well. With an angry shrug of his shoulders, the larger of the two attendants, indicated that they would have to handle the transfer themselves. It was not too difficult, for the box was a simple pine one, and the woman had been quite small.

Sebastian crossed the cement floor of the terminal as the two men were maneuvering the box out onto the unshaded platform that served as the baggage area. No, that would not do, he told them. The curious eyes of the guests, anxious about their luggage might find it too depressing a reminder. Instead he directed them to place it behind one of the unused ticket counters. There it would be out of sight, as well as out of the beating sun. Sebastian barely had time to wonder where David Sampson might be, before a cab pulled up hurriedly to the terminal entrance, and the short stocky man, hurled himself out. Without seeing to his baggage, he rushed to the now empty ambulance, then entered the building, looking quickly around, and blinking in the sudden change of light from the brilliant outside, intensified as it reflected off the whitewashed building. Sebastian hurried to him, his hand outstretched.

"Mr. Sampson, allow me to express my deep sympathy for your loss."

Intending no rudeness, but preoccupied in his grief and distraction, David mumbled, "What have they done with her? I just missed her at the hospital." It seemed odd to be referring to Karen this way now, and yet he couldn't bring himself to call her the body. They really should do something about improving the vocabulary of death, he thought—the writer's mind wandering away from the bereaved husband's for a moment. Even the word Sebastian had used, "loss" was somehow inaccurate. It made Karen's death seem like some slight oversight. As though she had been carelessly left behind, like a lost umbrella. God, he'd have to pull himself together if he was going to get through this day.

"They've put the coffin over there," Sebastian indicated with a nod of his head. "Behind that counter."

The two men started in that direction, but before they were halfway there, David felt a tap on his shoulder. He turned and looked into the face of his cab driver, although he did not recognize the man.

"You want me to sit out there all day with your bags?"

"No, no—bring them in."

"That's porters' work—I'm a cab driver—and I haven't been paid yet."

David's hand twitched and moved slightly on its own. He was torn between reaching into his pocket and just handing this man anything he had there, and smashing the arrogant bastard in the face. Sebastian stepped in quickly.

"Let me take care of this, David. Go to her." And he turned his pent up fury toward the driver. This was the kind of attitude—the kind of treatment of tourists that could spell the end of all his bright hopes for the island's economy. Perhaps he had done too good a job in instilling self-pride in these people. If this man's arrogance was any indication of the attitude tourists would have to cope with, something would have to be done—and fast.

"Don't ever talk to a passenger like that again."

For the first time in the encounter, the driver recognized Sebastian. "You changed your mind about not knucklin' under to the white man, Mister Minister?"

"This has nothing to do with the color of that man's skin. He's a man who has just lost his wife in a tragic accident, and more important—as far as you're concerned—he's your passenger, and if you're to make any kind of living in the lofty profession of driving, you're going to have to keep a civil tongue in your head. Now how much does he owe you?"

"Twenty francs" he said sullenly and when he saw the surprised look on Sebastian's face added quickly. "We didn't come directly here from the hotel—we went by the hospital first—and I waited there for him."

Sebastian handed him the money then walked with him to the cab where he signalled to the airport's one porter to unload David's bags.

"That twenty francs was just the fare," the driver said managing to combine obsequiousness and arrogance at the same time. "That didn't include a tip."

Sebastian, barely able to control his anger turned to him, "You'll find the tip I gave you about minding your manners will be worth a lot more to you in the long run than the few coins you might have forced from that man." And he turned on his heel and went back into the terminal. He heard the driver muttering under his breath, and then the harsh slam of the door of the cab before it tore away, sending dust and small stones flying in its wake. All the sundrenched beaches in the world wouldn't be able to make amends to a tourist who had to deal with the likes of that one, Sebastian thought to himself. He started toward David hoping there was something he could say that might ease this man's pain, but he was interrupted by the clipped British accented voice of Simon Chadwick-Smith.

"You're just the chap who might help me," he said coming up to Sebastian's side. "I want to file a story on last night's business, but the cable office in town is closed. Is there any way we might get it open? I'm desperately anxious to get this out—it's quite a coup you know for a society photographer to have an exclusive on something as big as this!"

This was one source of unwanted publicity, Sebastian had not thought of. Simon had always seemed more photographer than reporter, but, of course, it would be a tremendous coup for him to break a story like this—and complete with pictures, he was sure. He made one desperate attempt to salvage the situation.

"I know how important releasing a story like this can be to you, Simon. But not releasing it is even more important to me, my people, and the work I've been doing here. I told you about it in my office that day."

"Of course, and I intend to give you all the credit for what you've done here, but this is a break I just can't let slip through my fingers. I may never have a chance at a story like this again. I'd like to help you out, but not that way. Suppose I let you take a look at the story I have roughed out here before I send it." He handed Sebastian a few sheets of Shalimar stationery with some handwritten notes on them.

A quick glance at the crabbed handwriting was all Sebastian needed. It was all there, the seething unrest Simon had noticed when he first arrived, the assurances that it could be handled by the well meaning, but (and this was only by implication) unaware Prime Minister that he could control his people, and then the holocaust on Sunday night. Even in these rough notes Sebastian could see that Simon had definite talent for capturing emotions and feelings with his pen as well as his camera. The terror of the guests stood out sharply against the background of the crowd descriptions. A story like this could cause irreparable damage to the Island's tourist economy.

"I'm not asking you to suppress this completely, but just wait until you have the full story to report. No one will beat you out with it—you have my word on that."

"What about that poor bastard, Dexter?"

"He wants only to forget the entire incident."

"As if he could, the poor devil."

"Just give me a few more weeks here, then come back and cover the whole story—at St. Philippe's expense, of course."

"I don't think I can—I'd look a perfect fool if the story did break and I hadn't said boo about it to my editors."

The heat of the day and the logic of Simon's arguments reached Sebastian at the same time. He could see the danger this man was to his country's infant tourist trade. Of the 100 guests at Shalimar this weekend, only three had real access to the mass media. Duke who only wanted to forget, David whose next book could not possibly appear for at least a year and Simon.

There would be no way of stopping the word of mouth stories. But other islands had lived with plenty of those. St. Phillipe could, too. One thing Sebastian had learned from the other islands, these horror stories had to be kept from the press. He had not wanted to bully this Englishman, but there seemed no other way.

"You'd look an even bigger fool, you'll admit, if you returned to England with no pictures at all. I know as well as you do that if I should tear up this story," he continued, holding out the few pages of scribbled notes, "it would take you no more than an hour or two to rewrite it. But how much importancc would your editors give a word picture from Simon Chadwick-Smith not accompanied by your incisive photographs? And as Primc Minister here, I do have control over my customs officials—on my orders they would search your baggage and confiscate your films—all of your films—as endangering the Island's government."

"I'm afraid you've got me, Sebastian. Suppose you keep my story here, and my word that I won't release any word or pictures about last night's confrontation until I have your O.K.?"

Sebastian smiled broadly, hoping to take the cutting edge off his next words as he slipped Simon's notes into his pocket. "It is not, you must understand, that I do not trust you to honor your word as a gentleman, but merely as a precaution that by some accident last night's pictures should be developed and circulated—I believe 'leaked' is the proper term—that I must ask you to leave the undeveloped films you took last night."

"I am to take *your* word that news of last night's affair will be kept under wraps, and even more important, there will be no repetition of the events? And yet you won't take mine?"

"But I am taking your word that the films you leave with me are the damning ones. Without developing them, and there's no time for that—or exposing them all—which would leave you without any coverage of the Shalimar opening for your editor, I've only your word that you are leaving the films I want. I am to take your word—and you are to take mine."

"Fair enough—I suppose. I'm a bit better off with half a story than with no story at all."

"I was hoping you'd see it that way." Simon began shuffling through his film case, sorting out the various rolls—cryptically marked so that only he really knew what each contained. He handed some to Sebastian. The prime minister slipped them into his jacket pocket. "They'll go right from here to my safe—to await your return to the island to finish up your story on the successful putting down of an abortive coup, and the burgeoning tourist economy of this secure little island."

"You sound very sure of yourself—I hope you're not just whistling in the dark."

"I've good cause to whistle, Simon" Sebastian said, looking beyond him to the arrival of Faisan and his lieutenants. "Perhaps you might like a brief impromptu interview with the former leader of my government's 'loyal opposition'? It might set some of your doubts to rest."

Simon turned and followed Sebastian's glance. He recognized Faisan immediately in his rumpled army battle jacket, his ever present ammo belt slung over one shoulder, and it was not until Simon was practically upon him that he noticed the holster at his side hung empty. The men with him, too, looked familiar, he was sure he had seen them last night at Shalimar —and Saturday when he and David had been nosing around town. Two uniformed members of the island's small army stood discreetly a few steps behind the group, but obviously keeping them under surveillance. They moved a step closer to the group as Simon spoke to Faisan. But on a signal from Sebastian, made no attempt to interfere.

"I'm a British journalist, sir, and I wondered if you might have a statement to make about last night's events?"

"No, none at all," Faison said, ducking his head as though to avoid being photographed, although Simon had not taken his camera from its case.

"Well, do you plan another such uprising?"

"I've nothing to say." He insisted and started toward the exit facing the field.

"Perhaps you might bring yourself to make just one brief statement for the press." It was Sebastian who spoke and he was right at Simon's elbow. "It would be reassuring to your followers, if nothing else." The insistence and the authority could both be heard in Sebastian's low voice. By now, seeing their prime minister and the rebel leader talking together, the airport hangers-on and employees had drifted toward them and formed a loose circle. They were quiet, but obviously expecting a show of some kind.

Faisan looked quickly around the crowd, then at Sebastian whose eyes never left his cousin's. Simon thought he detected some kind of plea in the look that went from Faisan to Sebastian, but it was so fleeting he couldn't be sure. Avoiding the inquiring looks of his lieutenants, Faisan spoke directly to the tiny group surrounding them. He straightened his back and Simon saw some of the arrogance he had seen in this man return.

"My lieutenants and I are leaving St. Phillipe today" he paused dramatically, and was rewarded for his effort by a questioning murmur that ran through the crowd. "We are leaving because—with your help—we have accomplished all we had set out to accomplish here. We have obtained assurances from your Prime Minister that the invasion of the white man on St. Phillipe will be limited and under your government's control. The white man will be limited to the shore areas, and your farms will be in no danger." Scattered applause and encouraging sounds now came from the crowd.

Almost inaudibly Sebastian spoke to Faisan, "Isn't there some last word of advice you might give your followers?"

Faisan stared back at him for a moment, and then realizing the hopelessness of his position made the final capitulation. "For your own sakes, and for the growing prosperity of St. Phillipe I urge you all to stand behind your government, and to welcome the white people to your island, knowing they present no threat to you now—but rather a golden opportunity." He looked sideways at Sebastian who nodded slightly. Sebastian turned, and standing shoulder to shoulder with Faisan addressed the crowd. "I'm sure we are all grateful to Faisan for the work he has done in obtaining so much for his followers and for now uniting us all."

The crowd broke out in a well-meant but disorganized kind of cheer. Despite the apparent feeling of camaraderie, there was just a touch of the bum's rush, Simon felt in the way Faisan and his men were hurried through the terminal, out into the blazing sun and onto a waiting plane. It was a small two engine plane, carrying the government's insignia, and represented the full strength of the island's air force. It's cruising range was sufficient to take it island hopping, but that was all.

"And when I return for the rest of my story, do you intend to tell me what that was all about?" Simon asked Sebastian.

"I think Faisan spoke well and clearly of his intentions not to stir up any more trouble here—". Sebastian spoke convincingly, but beneath his words lurked a nagging doubt: Faisan might return.

"The clearest thing about what he said was he's knuckled under to you—for reasons unknown. I'd just like to know those reasons."

"Hopefully you will never need to, for Faisan has my word and I have his."

Sebastian walked to the exit gate to watch the departing plane, shielding his eyes from the sun. As Simon moved toward the small refreshment stand, he noticed David for the first time, standing alone at one of the empty counters.

"There you are, David. I looked for you at Shalimar before I left to see if there was anything I could do. Are you all right?"

"Sure, thanks. I left early to make sure Karen would be going back with us." No sooner were the words out of his mouth than he regretted them. Again he had failed to find the proper words to express himself. He saw Simon's eyes widen. "I went to the hospital to pick up the casket, but it had already left and I just caught up with it here," he said nodding his head, and indicating the coffin which Simon could see now just behind the counter. "They've tucked her away here, out of sight of the revelers," David added with that trace of bitterness that Simon had noted marked so many of his statements. But for this once, Simon could not blame him.

"Well, no one will disturb her there," and realizing how ill-chosen his words were, continued hurriedly. "Let's see if we can't find someone to pour us a couple." He put his arm around David's shoulder. Somehow the stocky little author seemed to have shrunk overnight. His jacket hung loosely from his shoulders. David took one last look behind the counter and then walked with Simon to the makeshift bar that had been set up to offer native drinks to the afternoon's arriving guests.

The main party of departing guests were even then being served their farewell drinks in the pristine coolness of Shalimar's entrance loggia.

Try as he might, Grov was unable to recapture the holiday feeling that had been so much a part of Shalimar until last night's events. Instead he found himself reassuring guests who time and again asked if he thought they were safe in going to the airport. Or did he feel safe staying on at Shalimar? To all of them he repeated Sebastian's assurances that the trouble had passed and there would be no reoccurrences. He wished he could be as sure as he made himself sound. It was too late now to do anything about his incoming guests, or to do more than appease the worries of his departing ones. As he looked around the room he noticed that the crowd was not only more subdued than it had been, but considerably shrunken in size. David Sampson was not there, and Simon was missing as well as Jane Perceval, Margaret Bradley and the Gramsons.

Had Grov looked out across the small bay in front of Shalimar, he'd have seen the *Cassandra*, the Gramsons on board, heading toward the British Islands. After a quick reconnaisance tour of the club that morning, Marty had returned to report to Sandy that Grov seemed to have everything under control and there was no need for them to stay on. A hurried consultation with his captain indicated that given favoring seas, they'd just be able to make Race Week at the nearest British Island.

Jane Perceval had found the girls' tales of last

night's events so thoroughly confusing that after breakfast, she had gone to Margaret Bradley's cottage and found her packed to leave.

"I was just coming to find you," Phillip had said as she entered. "Margaret and I are leaving right away for the mainland, and we hoped we might be able to talk you into joining us."

"Is there really a danger here?"

"There certainly was last night, and it seems foolish to take any chances on anything happening later today. My plane is at the airport, and we can leave as soon as you pack. You will come with us, won't you?"

"Whatever you think best. It won't take me long to pack, I'll meet you in the lobby in fifteen minutes."

And so as the remaining guests were having their farewell drinks at Shalimar, Phillip's Lear Jet was streaking through the Caribbean sky toward New York. Far out over the water it passed the charter plane bound for St. Phillipe to pick up the other guests.

Pammy and Buffy had stretched out their leave-taking to include a hearty breakfast, a last swim and frolic with Rod and an hour or more of Caribbean sun. At least they'd have marvelous tans to show off when they regaled their friends with the goings-on of Shalimar.

Now they stood on the cool marble steps with their Vuitton luggage about them. Tiger, in his special travel collar and Vuitton leash was giving the resort's foliage a final sniff and watering and he shook with excitement at the prospect of a new adventure with his trusty companions.

They were the last of the Shalimar's guests to take the waiting cab to the airport.

By the time their cab arrived, luggage had been loaded onto the waiting aircraft. In the middle of the

Vuittons and Bill Blass's and custom-made Gucci and Hermès luggage, a simple pine box rested, a strange contrast to the flamboyantly expensive canvas, leather and tapestry.

In a few minutes, the last call rang out and the beautiful people of Shalimar filled the cabin of the plane. They were the living counterparts of the luggage that had been stowed.

Sebastian allowed himself a final breath of relaxation as he watched the plane bank sharply after its climb and turn into the horizon.

On the plane went two people who had his concern. One, David Sampson, with his tragic cargo. The other, Emily Guilford, his moment of happiness. His instincts told him there was a connection and he wondered if Emily, knowing David's loss, would be drawn to him in the same way that she had been drawn to other sad, lost people. Himself, for example. There had been a kind of hopelessness about him when he met Emily. And she had done so much to reinforce his own image of himself and his dreams for his people. Emily was drawn to causes and star-crossed figures. Why not David? He had all the prerequisites.

He thought of her now with a great sense of loss. Even though he knew she was returning to the States to further the cause of the islands and its handicrafts, he knew he would not see Emily again. He had watched her carefully at the airport as they had made awkward last minute conversation before the plane. Her face had been etched in his mind during those minutes. The real farewell—and they had both known it—had taken place that Friday. Everything that needed to be said had been said then. They were both walking through roles they had written that night.

Sebastian turned to survey the waiting scene. Rows of taxicabs waited the arrival of the new planeload of guests. He moved down the line of cabs, greeting most of the drivers by name.

He sensed the changes in their attitude since last night. Could it be possible that it could happen so soon? They had all been present during Faisan's leave-taking. He hoped the attitude would spread and that finally he could start his real work with their cooperation and support. The next opportunity had just landed on the air strip.

Sebastian now turned his full attention to the new planeload of island security arriving. He stood at the gate, watching the debarking passengers and wondered if there would be another David Sampson, Simon Chadwick-Smith or Margaret Bradley among them.

A sudden noise captured his attention and he turned to watch a huge man come down the steps. He had a Hasselblad slung over his shoulders, but Sebastian was sure the owner was no professional, his look was one of sheer money. He watched with utter fascination as the man elbowed his way ahead of the other passengers with an imperious air. This was a man who not only was first in line but refused to line up.

The man snapped his fingers at a porter, who ran to his side and accepted the baggage tickets from the carefully manicured but pudgy fingers. He strode through the gate, and brushed past Sebastian, almost knocking him down. About to apologize, he noticed that Sebastian was black and said peremptorily, "Why don't you watch where you're going, boy?" The voice was Texan, the snap of his fingers universal as he hailed the first cab. "Keep your meter running, boy, the baggage will be here shortly." He settled his massive bulk into the back seat and wondered why it took so damn long for these islands to discover the air-conditioned car. He lit a large Havana and fanned himself with his Panama hat.

Sebastian watched him with a little curiosity, a little anger, and some amusement. It had started. He caught the eye of the cab driver who shrugged, then flashed a wide grin.

Sebastian returned the gesture. As he turned away, he heard the Texan say, "Take me to Shalimar, that *new* resort."